Chapter

I HAD TO WORK hard to stop my right leg from jiggling. My nerves wanted to show themselves and I wasn't going to allow that. Mercifully, the people around me all know my history with the Bruce Denton case, how the very mention of it can act as a trigger and that I have been avoiding it for years on doctor's orders. They all knew about it, but that wasn't enough to stop the furore that exploded when the camcorder showed up out of the blue.

Murdered in his own home thirty years ago, Bruce Denton became the scab I just couldn't stop picking. In the sleepy seaside town of Herne Bay on the southeast coast of England, my superintendent took the role of senior investigating officer but deferred to me to do the legwork. Mostly this was due to laziness on his part, but also because I begged him to let me. I was desperate to prove myself, or so he believed.

The truth of the matter is very simply that I already knew who beat Bruce Denton to death. I even knew what weapon was used, how the killer got into and out of his house, why the police would find so little evidence, and how it was that Bruce attracted such a grisly fate. I knew all these things because I spent more than a week planning his death before I perpetrated the crime.

In the days, weeks, months, and even years that followed, I stayed doggedly on the case so that I could ensure I was the one who intercepted any new evidence. Not that there was any, but when it is your life and liberty on the line, going the extra mile seems like the smart thing to do.

However, my belief that the crime would never be solved or even looked at again went out the window a week ago when a university professor's research assistant wandered into the nick in Canterbury. In his possession was a sealed evidence bag with my name on it. Inside the evidence bag ... well, let's just say the contents had me on edge.

On edge? I couldn't sleep, I was off my food, and my heart rate wouldn't slow down to a normal level until I put a worthwhile amount of alcohol into my body.

My boss told me about the evidence bag the day after it was found and that was three days ago now. The tech guys opened it, extracted the old video camcorder, and got it working. When

The Lies We Tell Ourselves

DS Tony Heaton's Cold Cases - Book 2

Steve Higgs

Contents

I heard that, it took all my acting power to pretend I was thrilled and excited.

New evidence? Yay!

I threw the damned camcorder into a bog at the edge of Monkton Nature Reserve thirty years ago. It was at the edge of a road in the middle of nowhere, yet I recall how many times I looked over my shoulder to see who might be watching as I waited for the bag to sink. Looking back, I guess I should have tossed it into the sea or burned it down to a charred nothing. At the time the bog seemed like the perfect choice and I just happened to be passing it.

The section of the tape in question was shot nine days before Bruce Denton was killed. Taken by Jamie Porter, an eighteen-year-old kid who lived three doors up from Bruce with his mum, dad, and little sister, it shows the victim walking into his house with a woman on his arm.

"Tony?" My partner, Ashley, touched my arm to get my attention and passed me a steaming cup of coffee. "You doing okay?"

Though we are the same rank, Ashley Long is more than twenty years my junior. He got assigned to work with me when he was picked to be part of a taskforce investigating a glut of unsolved murders. According to a recent survey, the county of Kent was second worst in the whole of England for that particular statistic. Consequently, the county's chief constable was in a bit of a tizzy. I wouldn't exactly label us as friends ... honestly the term partners is pushing it, but we have come to respect each other, and Ashley is not the worst person I have ever worked with.

He asked how I was doing because he'd been treated to one of my very best fake panic attacks. When we first met, he was all over the Bruce Denton case, desperate to reopen it, especially with me in tow, and I had to work hard to dissuade him. It worked, or it appeared to, but the sudden and totally unexpected reappearance of the camcorder footage changed everything.

"Almost there," reported Aidan, the geeky tech guy fiddling with his laptop. "We had to do a lot of work to scrub up the footage." He was six foot eight inches tall and skinny as a beanpole. He wore glasses with a designer label, a cardigan as though he got dressed from his grandfather's wardrobe, and running shoes beneath trousers that had to be the bottom half of a pinstripe suit. Add a little dirt and few holes and he could pass for homeless in a heartbeat.

Frowning, my boss, Superintendent Charters, said, "I thought the evidence bag protected the device inside." Clearly that was what he'd been told, and it was the same report that had me so on edge.

Aidan looked up at my boss when he replied, "Yes, sir, that's correct, but the old magnetic tape inside was never great quality even when it was new. Thirty years in a bog and I'm surprised we managed to get anything from it."

My eyes flared though I tried hard not to show the surge of excitement I felt. It died no sooner than it bloomed, my paranoia convinced the tape would show something. It had to show enough or they wouldn't have bothered gathering an audience to watch.

The swirling in my gut made me want to vomit. I gulped at the coffee hoping it might quell the rising bile. This had to be what the condemned felt like on their way to the gallows. Any second now Aidan was going to start the footage and life as I knew it would end.

He held up a lead, stared at the end, bent to check the port he wanted to stick it in, and a heartbeat later the ceiling-mounted projector beamed a picture onto the wall we all faced.

Chapter 2

SUPERINTENDENT CHARTERS LOWERED HIMSELF into the chair next to mine, his eyes facing firmly forward. He was just one of a dozen of us in the briefing room located on the lower floor of Herne Bay nick.

"Is this what you saw, Tony?" he asked without turning his head. He didn't often address me by my first name, not that I cared, but it was usually DS Heaton, or just plain Heaton when he wanted me. The first name thing probably indicated he hoped I was going to land another big arrest and make him look good.

I mumbled, "Maybe," and continued to stare at the wall. There was no sound to accompany the picture, a bit like my marriage when I push Mary too far or refuse to tackle the mounting garden tasks. The picture itself was grainy and discoloured.

Frowning again, the superintendent raised his voice to ask, "Is this what we are supposed to be seeing?" He posed the question because he already knew the answer. When Jamie's parents were made to watch their son's amateur video footage, they were shocked to see their recently murdered neighbour in the background. They also realised the significance of the woman he was with because my team and I had been canvassing the neighbourhood hoping to identify her.

We found long, blonde hair on Bruce's pillows along with other evidence to show a woman had been in it. However, while my boss at the time thought I was trying to find her, my questions were designed to make sure no one knew who she was. Finding her would have led straight to me and I couldn't have that.

Mr Porter called our hotline and had me on his doorstep less than thirty minutes later. I had him playback the footage there and then and arrived back at the station looking ruined and guilty. I told everyone the camcorder with the tape inside was stolen from the front seat of my car along with the evidence bag I put it in. The part about stopping to refill the tank of my car was true. I simply omitted the part about driving to the bog.

It would have been shown on the local news, and someone would have come forward to identify the woman. Of that I had no doubt whatsoever. Not that I needed them to. I knew who the woman was even before I saw the footage at Jamie's house.

"It's just coming, sir," reported Aidan, oblivious to the super-intendent's tone which would have made most men hurry the tape forward to the right spot.

We were watching eighteen-year-old Jamie Porter messing about with his motorbike. He had the camcorder set on a wall or a post or something so he could be hands free. In the street, he was messing about on a rallycross bike, showing off his skills by performing bunny hops over a piece of wood and popping wheelies. It lasted for less than a minute before it cut out completely. A second of nothing but fuzzy static was replaced by Jamie filming with the camcorder on his shoulder. I knew this because I asked him about it thirty years ago.

He was filming his bike which was now parked on its stand. He was talking, and though there was no sound now, that part of the recording having corrupted completely, I could recall his voice from the first time I watched it.

Standing in his living room, watching it play on his parents' TV screen with his whole family around me, I needed less than a second to realise how incendiary the footage would be if anyone else ever saw it.

And that's precisely what was happening now.

In the background beyond the bike as the camera aimed down the street, Bruce Denton's car came into view. He drove a nearly new Vauxhall Astra. Exactly the sort of car a teacher might drive - affordable, dependable …

The car passed by, the sunlight striking the windscreen making it impossible to see the occupants. It filled the background before it exited the shot to the right. In my head Jamie continued to drone on about his bike and the upcoming kickstart championship he was due to compete in.

The Astra reappeared less than a minute later coming the other way. I never found out why Bruce wanted to park facing the way he did, but I suddenly saw it was going to play into my hands.

Jamie's filming was a long way from TV quality, his hands shaky and the point of focus shifting constantly as he moved his head. Despite that, I found it impossible to breathe when the driver's door opened and Bruce Denton came around to get his passenger out.

"See that, gentlemen?" asked Doris, craning her head around to look back at the men in the room from her position near the front. "Chivalry."

Superintendent Charters said, "Shhh." The rest of us would have been barked at and told to "Shut up." Probably with an expletive added. Doris was multiple years past retirement age though and likely to put laxatives in his coffee if he dared to try the same on her.

I half expected someone to point out that the 'gentleman' in question was dead a little more than a week after the video was shot and that the blonde woman now seen exiting his car was a suspect. They didn't though, everyone opting to stay silent lest they incur the boss's wrath.

Bruce helped the lady from the car, scooping an arm around her waist and kicking the door shut.

"Is she drunk?" asked Gavin Dobbs.

I had only watched the footage once, but seeing it again, I could see why he would question her sobriety. Bruce did appear to be aiding her to walk. It correlated with what I knew.

I held my breath, watching the couple walk to his gate. So far we had only seen the woman from behind but they were about to turn to go down the path to his house. No one had shouted to say they recognised her, which came as a huge shock. I had been certain she would be identified in a heartbeat.

At the gate we got to see them side on, but the woman was the other side of Bruce, his head and body blocking ninety plus percent of our view. Then they vanished behind the hedge and were gone. We might have got another look at them as they reached his door and went inside – a slight upward slope meant their heads would probably appear above the line of the hedge, but Jamie wasn't looking that way.

"That's it?" asked my boss, aiming an accusatory glare my way. "I read your original statement from 1993. You said the woman could be identified from the video."

He was right, I had said those exact words, but thinking back to it now, I guess I was still in a state of panic when I made the report. To me it was easy to identify who the woman was. After all, I was married to her.

Chapter 3

We watched the same piece of footage, all fifty-seven seconds of it from Bruce's car appearing to Bruce and the woman disappearing behind his hedge another five times. People got up to get closer to the projected image. They tilted their heads, they squinted, we had Aidan pause it multiple times ... there just wasn't a point where the woman's face was visible.

The tech guy said he would be able to sharpen the image some. It involved digitising it and something about pixel remapping. I didn't bother to listen. My heart was slowing, returning to something close to its normal pace. Not that I was relaxing, far from it, but the video footage, which I still couldn't believe had survived, wasn't nearly so damning as I thought.

Regardless, it would be scrubbed up by the techies and shown on the local news. Heck, given how big the case was in 1993 I wouldn't be shocked if it made the national news. The hope, of course, was that someone out there would recognise the woman. In fact, the chatter in the briefing room questioned whether the blonde woman might come forward if she was innocent of his murder.

I listened to it all, knowing full well that Mary wasn't about to expose herself to the world, but that didn't mean there wouldn't be someone out there who might remember the dress she had on or the way she wore her hair that summer. The possibility terrified me, and a fresh wave of cold sweat crept up my spine.

Disgruntled, which was standard stock for Superintendent Charters, he left the room without bothering to wrap up the meeting or make a final point. Seeing him go, Ashley wandered over.

"You doing okay?"

It was the second time he'd asked in the last fifteen minutes. He was showing concern for my mental wellbeing, a subject that would never have raised its head a decade ago. Now it was a daily subject as though we were all supposed to get in touch with our feelings and share them with everyone around us. Nevertheless, he demonstrated genuine concern and I had to thank him for it.

I grumbled, "Nothing a stiff drink wouldn't fix," and left it at that. My emotional turmoil regarding the Bruce Denton case has always been fake and I have learned that less is more and easier to disguise. If I embellish too much, or expose my PTSD in too great a detail, I risk deeper questions. So I make sure they can see it bubbling beneath the surface and leave them admiring how I put such a brave face on it.

"You really ought to see someone, you know," Ashley chided gently. "It might help you to move on and focus on it less."

I shook my head. "Distracting myself has always worked well enough. Let's get to work."

He raised one eyebrow. "You don't want to talk about the video?"

My face pulled into a frown. "What is there to talk about? I was wrong. It shows nothing. The footage is thirty years old and the woman won't look anything like that now. We're going to show it on the news and all we'll get is a thousand hours' worth of duff leads to sift through before we finally accept it was a bad idea."

Ashley kept his eyes on me, assessing, questioning without speaking. I could see his tongue moving about in his mouth while he considered what he wanted to say. He was experienced enough to know I was probably right about the thousand hours. Any time the police show a piece of CCTV footage or a video reconstruction intended to jog people's memories, they get idiots coming out of the woodwork. Granted, occasionally someone has a genuine lead and some of those have led to a conviction. Those instances are few and far between though.

After what was becoming an increasingly uncomfortable period of silence, he asked, "What made you think she would be identified from the video back in 1993?"

And therein lies the problem with Ashley Long. Coming from a long line of senior police officers, many of whom are still serving, Ashley possesses the kind of mind that knows what questions to ask.

I turned away to hide my expression and threw a dismissive arm in the air.

"I don't remember."

"I also read the statement you gave when you lost the camcorder. You provided a very accurate description of the woman and her clothing."

"I was trying to salvage a bad situation. Losing the video killed the investigation, not that we were getting anywhere, but the whole team believed someone would have identified her and it could have been the big break we needed. The fact that Bruce's girlfriend never came forward despite appeals made us all question why she chose to hide. What was she guilty of?"

I wanted Ashley to stop talking, but he wouldn't. "I ask because the forensic report suggested the killer was almost certainly male given the power behind some of the blows inflicted."

Yes, I recall only too well how the rage I felt fuelled my body that night.

"It could have been a woman," I muttered. "But probably not that one." It would have been folly to suggest otherwise. Ashley had read the reports and had seen the video. The blonde woman was too short, too petite to have beaten Bruce Denton to death, even with a bat in her hands.

Ashley opened his mouth to speak again and suspecting he was going to press me on the subject once more I held up a hand, palm out to stop him.

"Can we not?" I asked, pressing a hand to my gut as though I was suffering discomfort. "They are going to enhance the video and show it on the news, and I am about to be thrust back into the nightmare of Bruce Denton's case no matter how I feel about it."

Ashley offered a sympathetic expression. "You know I don't think it would take much to get you removed from the case. You have medical history citing mental ill health triggered by this very case. All it would take ..."

I held up my hand again. Now was the time to tread very carefully. I had to maintain the air of someone injured by the stress of the investigation in 1993, but I couldn't distance myself from what was going to happen now. More than ever, I had to be at the spearhead when they reopened the case. Only there could I hope to intercept and control any information that might point a finger my way.

Bruce Denton had to die and thirty years on I was yet to feel one jot of remorse. Yet I also knew no one would agree with my thoughts on how he deserved what he got, at least not out loud. If caught I would face a life sentence that would see me in jail until my final days.

So I was staying on the case, but that didn't mean I couldn't divert Ashley's attention away from it.

Picking up my coat, I said, "Come on, let's get back to Whitstable and a case we at least stand a chance of solving, however slim it might be."

Chapter 4

A Frenchman called Michelle Canet was found stabbed to death from a single knife wound three years and a bunch of days ago at the end of summer. The knife entered his chest at an upward angle suggesting it had been thrust from waist height to enter beneath his rib cage. The blade carved a path through his lung before the tip penetrated his left ventricle. He would have died quickly.

But who killed him?

Superintendent James Prince, acting in the role of senior investigating officer, performed a fine job with his team, but failed to identify Michelle's attacker. Now it was down to us to see if we could do better. Frankly, I thought that was not only insulting to the original team, but laughably optimistic.

Unfortunately, optimistic is a word easily associated with my young partner. Not least because we just closed a case that defied everyone's expectations. Including my own.

Assigned to a taskforce reopening what the world calls cold cases, we have a list of failed investigations and carte blanche to poke our noses into any or all of them, such is the power of a county's chief constable.

Superintendent Prince retired more than a year ago and the detective chief inspector running Whitstable nick had been replaced just a few months back. The new guy, DCI Jacob Tanner seemed fine with having us on his turf, but he had no connection to the Canet murder. Some of his subordinates did, but even they weren't overtly hostile. I would have been if it was one of my old cases being scrutinised.

We started looking into Michelle Canet, his movements and his murder, two days ago, but that was just on paper. Ashley would have plunged straight into it, and argued that we should until I reminded him that I was not only very old now (for a cop), but was officially supposed to be on sick leave following a rather nasty bump on the head. Besides, I felt a break was not only well-earned, but necessary considering I almost died in the process of closing our previous case.

It involved a missing teenage boy who we always believed to be dead. Finding his body and the people who put it there caused a press frenzy that ate up a bunch of our time, so I never really got the time off I'd hoped for. It was unavoidable, entirely due to the same Chief Constable of Kent who wanted to show his boss how seriously he took the bad report on unsolved murders. There was rumour of a commendation, not that I gave a stuff, not this close to retirement. It wasn't like I could exchange it for cash, but Ashley was thrilled. Not that he admitted it, but it was easy to see and understandable. His family expected him to climb to the upper echelons and who knows, maybe he would.

So, two days into our investigation we were precisely where we were when we started. Precisely nowhere.

Getting to Whitstable from Herne Bay, the next town along the coast and where I have lived all my life, takes anything from ten minutes to more than forty depending on the time of day. Ashley drove, as was our habit, taking Whitstable Road through the smaller villages of Swalecliffe and Tankerton. To our right, the coast was hidden by buildings, many of which had been standing for centuries. The scent of the sea was ever present, waves beating against pebble shores held in place by ancient breakers that reduced the longshore drift and made a home for molluscs. I could remember being sent to collect them as a kid which was insult enough in the bracing cold sea air, but worse when I was then fed them for my dinner.

Mussels are an expensive delicacy, but you can keep them if it's all the same.

Parking in Whitstable can be a challenge in the summer or at the weekend when people come to the coast for any number of reasons, but on a lazy Tuesday in late October, the Keam's Yard car park right on the seafront was less than twenty percent full.

Unlike the previous case, I'd managed to do the pre-reading for this one which was how I knew the details of the autopsy report for the victim. I also knew he'd had sex not long before he was murdered and was known to be gay and promiscuous. That could be a factor in his murder but could just as easily be a red herring. The investigating team from three years ago were unable to identify his lover though there was a long list of suspects who all denied their involvement.

Several men were questioned in connection with the murder, but all were released without charge when either alibis came forward to place them elsewhere or there simply wasn't enough evidence to approach the crown prosecution service for a conviction.

One thing that stuck out to me was the presence of a large quantity of ketamine. It was found in the back pocket of his jeans, just waiting there to be discovered. Did it have any bearing on his murder? It seemed like that should be an obvious 'yes' but Michelle Canet passed through customs where sniffer dogs would have sensed it, so we could be confident he didn't have it with him when he entered the country. In which case he bought it in England, but Michelle was out of work, bumming around Europe by finding bar work and other jobs. He could have arrived with a wedge of cash and a plan to make more buying and selling illegal narcotics, but there was nothing to indicate he'd ever done that before.

The drugs felt incongruous. However, noted in the case file was an unexplained assault on a known member of a local drug ring. Oliver Humphries, a teenage boy at the time, was nothing more than a street pusher, a small cog in a much bigger machine, but he was found unconscious in a back street less than half a mile from Michelle Canet's body, and it happened on the same night.

Superintendent Prince's team were unable to establish a correlation, but they believed the drugs found on Michelle Canet were those Oliver Humphries would have been selling. The gang behind him were known for pushing Ketamine though the people manufacturing and distributing it had never been tied to those caught in possession.

And that's the big challenge for the cops investigating the narcotics trade. There's almost no point catching the little fish because they know better than to admit anything. That's how it went with Humphries, the eighteen-year-old showing wisdom beyond his years when he claimed to know nothing about what happened to him and denied any involvement with the drug trade despite the residue they found on his skin and clothing.

We would look at Humphries again, but first we were going to the spot where Michelle's body was found.

Chapter 5

THERE WAS A LITTLE moisture in the air coming in off the sea. The tide was in, hiding the oyster beds beneath murky water turned grey by the sea water washing over the mud flats. Were it not for the mud, one could walk out across the seabed for miles once the tide went out.

One of my first ever bodies was on the same stretch of beach, just a few miles west. The man, whose name escapes me now, had drowned while taking his morning swim. His widow told me he'd been doing the same thing each morning for years but on that occasion he had a heart attack. On shore or at home with his wife, it might have been survivable. Out in the cool water of the Swale Estuary, it was fatal.

Keeping to the path, we skirted along the beach. On a busy day it wasn't wide enough to accommodate the amount of foot traffic wanting to use it. Today we were the only people on it. It took us west from Keam's Yard car park to a cut through that led past an historic boat preserved as an item of heritage, to the next street, Island Wall. I had passed the boat dozens of times in my life without ever stopping to read the plaque to know what significance it held.

Just beyond it, we came to the spot where Michelle Canet died. We were not there to discover anything, just to familiarise ourselves with the spot. The forensics team had collected all the dirt and dust, fibres and hairs from the area in the hours following the body's discovery. Their analysis was in the case file and the physical evidence was in general storage. They also took a stack of photographs which we had both looked over.

From memory I could orientate where the body had was found. Ashley walked on, reaching the end of the cut through where it met Island Wall. It was a residential area with houses facing out to sea and more backing onto them on Island Wall and all the streets leading from it.

Most of them would not be occupied at this time of the year, the owners astute enough to rent them out for the tourist trade that flocked to the coast in the summer. We had the same thing in Herne Bay except Whitstable was more popular and therefore commanded significantly higher prices.

Ashley waited for me to catch up, his eyes trained to the east where the town centre could be found. Michelle had worked there, serving drinks in a busy pub where he must have proven popular. Above all else Michelle Canet was attractive. He looked like a Ken doll who went to the gym except he had flowing blonde hair like Thor.

"It's not far to the bar," Ashley observed. "I'm going to walk the route and see what I find."

I could have elected to do something else, but I was just as curious. The murder occurred when he should have been working, suggesting he ducked out and planned to return. We know he had sex shortly before his death, but was that why he was at the cut through by the boat?

We walked past small terraced houses that opened directly onto the street. The front doors were inches shorter than they make them now, and from experience I knew the ceilings were low inside. They always felt imposing to me, like I was being crowded and crushed at the same time.

We passed a couple of alleyways, pausing at each to note its position. Why Michelle went to the cut through was just one mystery we needed to solve. There had to be a reason and I didn't like the drug angle.

At the corner of Sea Lane where it met Middle Wall just past Squeeze Gut Alley, we came to the Old Shipwright. That the alleys had names was unusual and made me curious about the town's history. No doubt the locals gave them names as points of reference and they became accepted to the point that someone on the local council chose to erect name signs.

The floorboards in the Old Shipwright would have some tales to tell. How many centuries the building had occupied the same corner plot, or how long it had been a public house, I did not know. Yet there was a boot scraper set into the wall, a device fitted to many houses back when the roads were made of dirt and horses left their offerings in the street. Horses still do that today, of course, but they are few and far between now but would have been regular transport when the pub first opened for business.

It was too early in the day for the pub to be open, but we found a side door with a bell. Shortly after pressing it, a shadow fell behind the small, frosted pane.

Ashley flicked his warrant card out as the door opened to reveal a short, stocky man in his early fifties.

"Good morning, I'm Detective Sergeant Long. This is Detective Sergeant Heaton. We are looking for the landlord, Jack Corman."

"That's me," replied the man, opening the door all the way. "I'm Jack Corman."

He was in the process of rolling down the right sleeve of his rugby shirt. The left was already down. In doing so he covered a tattoo that told me he used to be a soldier in the cavalry. I could be fairly sure of that because the tattoo was the cap badge of the $9^{th}/12^{th}$ Lancers, a British Army Cavalry Regiment. The ink had faded with time so the words beneath it were hard to make out. Nevertheless, I knew it read, 'Death Before Dishonour'. I made a mental note that he was ex-forces and therefore trained and conditioned to kill when necessary, filing it away in case it became relevant.

The landlord of the Old Shipwright looked much like a lot of publicans as though they were all cast in a variation of the same die. His hair had long since given up, retreating to form little more than a ring from one ear to the other around the back of his head. What was left had been trimmed down to almost nothing. He was clean shaven, had tattoos poking from the neck and arms of his England rugby shirt which sat tight around his biceps and across his belly. Time in the gym created the former, too much beer the latter.

"May we come in?" Ashley requested. "We have some questions about Michelle Canet. You were his employer at the time of his murder, were you not?"

Jack backed away from the door, letting us in with concerned eyes. I suspected his slightly haunted expression would be more to do with some hooky goods he was selling under the counter or booze a 'friend' had brought in from Europe and for which he'd conveniently forgotten to pay the duty.

Our lack of interest in such misdemeanours meant he had nothing to worry about, but having the person you want to question off balance is never a bad thing.

"Um, yeah, I was?" replied the landlord, posing it as a question as though checking his response was acceptable. Really, he wanted to know why we were asking the question and specifically why now. Michelle met his end more than three years ago and I doubt Jack had given him much thought since.

Led into the bar area, Ashley waited until the landlord stopped and was facing us before he continued. It's always best to see the interviewee's face so one can gauge the truthfulness of their replies.

"The enquiry into his murder has been reopened, sir." Ashley made the announcement and waited.

Watching carefully, I saw Jack's eyes dilate just a touch. His pulse quickened, and his whole body stilled. The news made him nervous and now I wanted to know why.

"I, ah ... I thought it was traced to a dispute over drugs, wasn't it?"

"Why would you think that?" Ashley challenged.

Jack's eyes flicked across to me only to find my gaze locked on his face. He looked down instead and closed his mouth. I watched his hands clench and his head shift to one side when he closed his eyes. Two seconds passed and he used the time to regain his composure.

Looking back up he relaxed his hands and met Ashley's eyes. With a one shoulder shrug, he said, "It's just what I heard. He worked here for a couple of weeks several summers ago, it was our busy time of the year, and to be honest, I barely remember him. What do you want to know?"

We had the case notes from the investigation three years ago. There were detailed files to show who was questioned and what responses they gave. There was a list of people known to have been in the bar that night, all of whom were investigated and dismissed by the team of officers working under Superintendent Prince. As I remarked before, they did a thorough job, but someone murdered Michelle Canet and it was our task to find the thing they missed even though it didn't look like they missed anything.

I let Ashley handle the questioning.

"Did you ever get the impression he was selling drugs under the counter?"

Ashley and I had discussed the possibility that Michelle's death was due to involvement in the drugs trade and neither of us thought it likely.

Jack puffed out his cheeks before saying, "No, I didn't, because if I had he would have been out on his ear two seconds later. I don't let that sort of thing happen in my establishment."

The less charitable part of my brain wondered if that only applied when he wasn't getting a cut.

"From what I recall he was a good worker. He turned up on time, he never skipped out early or vanished for a cigarette break like some of my staff do. He put his tips in the jar like he's supposed to and he was flirty with the punters, but in a good way."

"How do you mean?" Ashley pressed before I could. Flirting with customers is part of the bar staff culture, but since we know he had sex in the hours before his death and was found two hundred yards from his place of work while still on shift, his flirting must have worked better than usual that night.

Now on the spot and having to defend his comment, Jack looked uncomfortable once more.

"Well, if you work at the bar, you have to be friendly. People will go where they feel welcome, so I tell the staff I expect them to smile and make small talk. That's the right level of flirting. Say something nice, but don't ogle the lady's cleavage so she feels uncomfortable. Unless she is sending you the signals. It's the same for the girls in here. Guys will always flirt with a barmaid. It doesn't even matter what they look like half the time, but I try to employ pretty girls because ... well, because that's just good business. The guys come in and if they think they might stand a chance they will stay here all night and that's the aim of the game. Get them through the door and never let them leave."

"And Michelle was good at doing that?"

Jack gave his one shoulder shrug again. "As good as anyone else, I guess. He was good looking and got lots of attention from the women."

I spoke for the first time. "And from the men?"

The landlord shifted his gaze from Ashley to me. "You're asking because he was gay?"

I nodded.

Again we got the shrug, one of Jack's behaviours.

"Not that I recall. There's not much of a gay scene in Whitstable. Not that I'm aware of anyway. We get groups of lads in here and groups of girls, couples and families of all ages, but rarely gay couples."

He was right that there was no gay bar in the town. Nor was there one in Herne Bay. One had to travel to Margate, a few miles further down the coast to find an establishment catering specifically to that niche of the market. Personally, I believe such places were on the decline. In my youth homosexuality was ignored as if such a tactic might make it go away. In our more enlightened era, lifestyles that were once labelled as 'alternative' were commonplace.

My neighbours are two women.

Ashley had a few more questions, but we were at the Old Shipwright for the same reason we visited the site of Michelle's murder – to familiarise ourselves with the geography of the case. Jack Corman wasn't a suspect, not yet at least, and we had more interesting prospects to question, not least Oliver Humphries, the then teenager found unconscious the same night.

Chapter 6

We stopped by the station first, a courtesy call to let the local boys and girls know we were operating in their area. They knew Ashley already; he visited last Saturday when ordered to drop the previous case by the head of the task force, DCI Harris. Knowing his boss would check, Ashley made a point of visiting Whitstable nick before returning, very much against his orders, to check on something in the case Harris wanted us to drop.

Had we not both stumbled across clues that let us find the missing kid's body, we would be three or four days into the Michelle Canet case now. Regardless, we needed to stop by the local nick.

"The boss in?" Ashley enquired on his way past the custody centre at the back of the station.

"Should be," the duty sergeant called after us.

Ashley led the way, confident he knew where to go from his one visit four days ago. I had been here a thousand times over the last thirty something years and knew the place like the back of my hand. There was talk of funds for a new purpose-built nick since this one was outdated, too small for what they needed, and probably worth enough for its position near the seafront that they could build a place twice the size half a mile further inland and still end up in profit.

So far as I knew it was just talk, but some say progress is inevitable.

I glanced through doors as I passed them, trailing Ashley until I spotted Marvin the Martian. He looked up to find me grinning through the door.

"Tony? Hey, how are ya?" His fingers had been poised over his keyboard, but he abandoned whatever he was doing to cross the room and shake my hand.

Leaning back out of the doorway, I called to Ashley, "I'll catch you up," just as he rounded the bottom of the stairs and vanished.

"Roger," filtered back but I was already talking to Marvin by then.

Obviously, his name isn't really Marvin the Martian, it's Marvin Valmik, but lots of cops end up with nicknames and he wore his with pride. There was a three-inch-high Marvin the Martian figure perched on his desk.

The man himself was tall, thin, and gangly with a permanently dour expression beneath a shock of very dark brown hair. It was tamed with a little product to give it a parting. He slapped his hand into mine, smiling for once when he gripped it hard.

"What brings you to my neck of the woods?"

"Michelle Canet," I replied, surprised he couldn't work that out for himself. "That's our next case."

"Oh, you and that kid who was in the other day? I heard they were reopening it. I guess I hadn't put any thought to it." Like me, Marvin was closing in on retirement. Unlike me he'd advanced in his career, made detective inspector and was likely to make chief inspector before his time was done. He had a few years left yet.

"You were on the original investigation, weren't you?" I'd read the file and knew he was. "Anything you think we should know going back into it?"

Marvin made a 'beats me' gesture and turned around to go back to his desk.

"Want a coffee?"

"Sure."

I had been about to follow him, but realised he was only fetching his mug. He talked as he walked, wending through the nick to a small kitchen that was more of an alcove than a room.

"The investigation went on for weeks. We all believed it would be simple enough to solve, and if you ask me I reckon we must have interviewed whoever did it. Just don't ask me which one of them it was though because I haven't got a clue."

"No one stuck out as more likely than the others?"

Marvin had his back to me making the coffees, the alcove so small that to join him at the sink would require lubrication.

Spooning sugar into his mug, he said, "Not really. You're familiar with the case?"

"I've read the file."

"Then you'll know there were two angles: the drugs and the secret liaison. I only call it that because we couldn't identify who he had sex with that evening."

He turned around with a steaming mug of coffee in each hand. His was a blue and white striped thing that had stains around the top lip. Mine had come from a cupboard in the alcove – a pool cup. It had SpongeBob on it.

I took the offered mug and twisted to get out of the way as I wasn't sure where we were going. He led me back to his desk, one of half a dozen in that office.

"Going back to the drugs thing," Marvin said around a slurp of his drink, "the team were split over it. Canet had been done for possession two years earlier."

"That's not in the file." I hadn't found it if it was.

"He was caught in Lyon with just enough marijuana in his possession to warrant an arrest. He claimed he was on his way to a party, but it was a first offence, so he got off with a fine and a warning. It probably isn't in the file or will be a side note somewhere. Anyway, half the team felt it showed form. The rest of us believed it was a coincidence."

I played devil's advocate to see what opinion he would offer. "It was a lot of ketamine."

"Too much in my opinion and there's a timeline discrepancy. Witnesses in the pub that night confirm Canet was present and serving drinks until after nine o'clock which is when Humphries was found. Canet snuck out some time between nine and nine thirty, so far as we can tell, but that's too late for him to have attacked and robbed the kid with the ketamine. Now, if we assume he was able to sneak out earlier without being noticed, not impossible given toilet breaks, changing the barrels et cetera, we then have to believe he knew exactly where to find the kid with the powder, and that he then chose to keep it about his person for the rest of the evening while performing his bar duties."

"So what's your theory?"

"That the ketamine was placed on him after he was stabbed. Something to throw us boys in blue off the scent."

I found myself nodding in agreement. It was far too early in our investigation to start forming conclusions, but the reasoning was sound. Going with it, I asked, "Any theories on who might have planted it?" Really I was asking if any of the suspects had a connection to the drug trade.

"Nope. No one looked more likely than anyone else."

Voices coming our way announced Ashley's return before he appeared in the doorway. He had DCI Tanner at his side. At least, that's who I assumed he was talking to. He was relatively new at the nick in Whitstable, and I'd never met him before.

My butt was propped against a desk, the coffee mug in my right hand when he cracked a smile and came my way.

"Tony Heaton," he spoke my name with enthusiasm as if he had a reason to be pleased to meet me.

Murmuring quietly, so his boss wouldn't hear, Marvin said, "Most enthusiastic man I ever met."

Leading with his hand, Tanner crossed the room. I put the mug down and pushed off the desk so I was upright to meet him.

"That was quite some take," he remarked, slapping his hand into mine.

"We got lucky." Finding the kid's body happened four days ago now and the news outlets had moved on, but it remained fresh in the minds of the local cops. I was right about getting lucky too, but the serendipitous part was surviving the investigation more than solving it. I was at the end of a full police career and had never come closer to dying than I did closing that case.

"Think you'll get lucky again? Find what the boys here missed?" He winked at Marvin when he said it.

Marvin chose not to react.

I opted to give a neutral response. "I'm not expecting to find they missed anything, sir."

"Oh, we can ditch the 'sir' nonsense. Around here I'm Jacob or bossman, but you guys," he twisted his head to catch Ashley's eyes too, "are visiting guests." He smiled at me, and I think maybe he expected me to have something to say. When I didn't and a few beats of silence ticked by, he clapped his hands together. "Right, well, I have plenty to do and you have a killer to catch, so I'll get out of your hair. You have everything you n eed?"

I flicked a glance at Ashley to check that was the case.

"We do," he confirmed.

"Then I'll let you get on with it." He backed up a few steps, gave us a double thumbs up in an exaggerated/embarrassed manner, and slipped around the doorframe.

No one said anything until we heard his feet on the stairs.

"Yes, he's always like that," Marvin answered a question no one had voiced. "And shockingly, he's a pretty good governor."

He had to be better than the superintendent I'd been suffering for the last few years. Of course, DCI Tanner fell under Superintendent Charters' command as well, but had the benefit of avoiding him ninety percent of the time.

Marvin settled back into his chair and poked his mouse to bring his screen back to life.

"Good luck finding Canet's killer. I hope you have better luck than we did." The way he said it made it hard to determine whether he truly wanted us to find what the original investigation could not and that sounded about right. There probably were some mixed emotions. No one wants a killer to go free, but there would be no joy in having one's failings highlighted.

If we solved the case, it would cause tension.

Chapter 7

WHITSTABLE NICK WAS TOO small for them to assign us a room as we had been in Wingham while investigating the Craig Chowdry case, but that was okay because it was only five miles back to my nick in Herne Bay.

There we had an incident room dedicated to the case and boxes of evidence that were partially unpacked. The evidence box held Michelle's possessions from his room at the bed and breakfast and his clothes from the night he was killed. There were loads of photographs from his final night, many taken on phones from people who were in the bar, as well as CCTV footage from the shop he walked past, along with a raft of statements.

It was going to take us a long time to go through all of it, but if my partner has a fault, it is impatience. Before setting out to question anyone, it would serve us best to spend a few days going through the old case notes in a meticulous fashion, not the quick read through they'd been given so far. We needed to approach the investigation knowing everything the original team was able to compile. I wanted to establish a timeline showing Michelle Canet's movements in the hours before his death and overlap it with some of the leading suspects.

Not that we really had any.

Graham Bishop, another tenant lodging at the same bed and breakfast, threatened Michelle and got into what I would call 'a bit of argy bargy' with the Frenchman the day prior to his murder. I call it that because, according to their mutual landlady, Graham grabbed Michelle's shirt and there was a bit of pushing and shoving, but nothing more. It boiled down to Michelle keeping Graham awake having sex in his room and Graham not only taking exception but voicing his homophobia.

Neither man threw a punch, and Graham was questioned at length without being charged. Nevertheless, he remained a suspect.

Then there was the drugs angle. I wanted to dismiss the ketamine but knew better than to do so without paying it due diligence.

On top of that were the people in the bar. We had a long list of names, both male and female, who had been questioned by the police as they built up a picture of who was where and who saw what.

So we had a lot to go through, but Ashley was determined to fit that in around reinterviewing all the people from three years ago.

Heading out of the station, it came as no great shock when my young partner announced his desire to spend the day in Whitstable. However, his first person of interest was not who I expected.

"What do you think about tracking down Oliver Humphries?"

I had one hand on the passenger door handle and was looking at him over the roof of the car.

"The pusher?"

"I think the drugs are a dead end and a distraction. You can see that in the original investigation. The team ended up split down the middle. I want to rule it out as soon as we can."

"Or establish that there is something to it," I countered. If we were keeping our minds open, we could not rule it out.

Ashley opened his door, but paused before getting in. "Do you think there might be?"

I replied with a shrug. "No, not really. Why do you want to speak to him though? They interviewed Oliver at the time and he refused to give them anything helpful. The notes say he claimed he didn't see his attacker coming. What makes you think he might say anything different now?"

Ashley grinned and ducked into the car, forcing me to open my door and get in.

He was still grinning. "Because Oliver Humphries is out of the drug game. I checked into him yesterday."

"That's cheating."

Ashley snorted a laugh. "Maybe, but he's all cleaned up and get this ... he works for the church."

Chapter 8

THE THING ABOUT COLD cases is that unless someone chooses to continue to pursue them, which is often difficult when there are fresh cases on your desk, they get closed and filed away and that's the end of them. Big cases might get looked at again, a fact that became the driver for me doggedly pursuing the Bruce Denton murder. It was so high profile I had to stay on top of the enquiry. It was that or risk someone else taking it on.

To demonstrate my point, in the three years since Michelle Canet's case was put to bed, one of the key players had completely changed his life. That Oliver Humphries might now provide a different response was not only possible, but felt probable. However, because the case was closed, no one was going to quiz him again. Until now.

Well done, Ashley.

Saying he worked for the church was at the same time kind of an understatement and also misleading. He'd found employment at Canterbury Cathedral, the home of the senior archbishop for the Church of England, so yes, he worked for the church, but it wasn't like he was an altar boy. Oliver worked in the gift shop.

Ashley knew where to park and how to get to the gift shop because he spends his downtime much the same way he spends his work time – on the job. Where I will happily vegetate in front of the television with a glass of cheap Scottish whisky, Ashley interrogates his laptop for more answers, presumably while doing one-armed press-ups to keep himself fit.

I knew what Oliver looked like from the photograph in the file. Coming into the gift shop, I aimed my eyes at the counter, expecting to find him serving a customer. He wasn't there and for a moment I questioned if it might be his day off. That would be typical for me, to have come all the way to Canterbury only to discover he was back in Whitstable.

However, when a head rose above a shelf of books, the body attached to it holding an armful of heavy hardbacks, I saw the man we wanted. He was restocking.

Ashley saw him at the same time and I let him lead the way. The gift shop smelled like a library. The shelves were lined with religious tomes or, at least, books with some connection to the cathedral or Christianity. The floor was lined with the same kind of short pile carpet you find in offices, and there was music playing quietly – a Christian band by the sound of it.

I passed a display of stationery all marked with the image of the cathedral and another with toys aimed at preschool children or babies. I guess they have to make money where they can.

"Oliver Humphries," Ashley spoke the name with authority and confidence, and at a volume our target would hear.

Oliver had put on a few pounds since his mug shot was taken three years ago, but in a healthy way. Back then he was skinny almost to the point of being gaunt. Now he looked like any other man in his early twenties. Five feet ten or thereabouts, he wore his brown hair pulled into a man bun on top of his head. He had some stubble on his chin and under his nose, but it wasn't growing along his jawline yet.

His arms still full of books, which he was trying to balance in his left so he could place them onto a shelf with his right, he twitched at the sound of his name from an unfamiliar voice. Looking our way, our presence clearly startled him.

For a split second, I thought he might drop the books and bolt. Instead, he turned to face us.

"Good … morning," he said with a glance at the clock to confirm it was indeed not quite noon. He appeared to have identified our profession, and now looked perplexed as though racking his brain to figure out what we could possibly want with him.

Ashley introduced himself and then me, ending with the rather obvious, "We have some questions for you. Is there somewhere we can go?"

"Questions about what?"

"About the night three years ago when you were knocked unconscious and had the drugs in your possession stolen." He'd never admitted to having drugs, so Ashley was rolling the dice that Oliver was prepared to face the truth now. The team interviewed Oliver three years ago and though there was no suggestion he was involved in Michelle's murder, there remained the possibility that the dealers behind the drugs he lost that night might have chosen to exact retribution.

However, were that the case, they would have recovered their 'product' not left it on Michelle's body, and that alone made it an improbable scenario.

Oliver gave a thoughtful nod, his eyes looking not at us but at the floor by his feet. He nodded again, perhaps to himself, and juggled the books back into the box. Straightening once more, he lifted his head and raised his right arm to get the attention of a woman who was serving at the counter.

In her sixties, she had the look of someone in charge.

"I need a few minutes," Oliver explained.

He got a nod and jerked his head toward a door in the wall to our right. "Is the storeroom okay?"

We followed him through the door, Ashley ahead of me, and just on the other side, once I closed it behind me, Oliver stopped walking and turned to face us.

"What do you want to know?"

It had become our practice for Ashley to lead the questions, though we had never formally decided it was how we would work. He was a 'take charge' kind of guy, and I was too old to care that he was sometimes stepping on my toes. Besides, doing it this way meant I got to observe, and I like to do that.

"Oliver, you have changed your life, ditched the criminal path you were heading down, and created a new future for yourself. How did you pull that off?"

Ashley was good at this; a natural, if you will. Instead of diving straight in with questions about Michelle Canet and what happened to Oliver the night the Frenchman was killed, he led with a subject that would be easy to talk about. Get Oliver speaking and turn the conversation back three years once he was relaxed.

Oliver leaned against the wall with his left shoulder, possibly for the support it gave him. No one likes to be questioned by the police, even if they are innocent. Our unexpected presence would be making him feel off balance and uncomfortable.

He sucked on his cheek and looked at the lino when he started to talk.

"I was lucky," he mumbled. "Elroy let me go. Said I was too incompetent to be trusted. I had a record though, so getting a job was almost impossible. Mum wanted to kick me out, but an old schoolfriend suggested a program that was helping people like me to find employment. It's not much," he admitted, finally lifting his head to meet our eyes, "but I've been here six months now and no one cares that I was involved with drugs."

"That's good," Ashley remarked. "Good to hear you have found your feet." Ashley was talking to Oliver in a comradely tone, one that would encourage him to open up. We could take him to the nick and grill him there, but there would be no need for that if he was forthcoming. "Think you'll stay here?"

Oliver nodded. "Until something better comes along. They have other jobs I can apply for and funding for training if I want."

"That's great. Nice to see someone turn things around. But listen, we need your help ..."

Oliver blurted, "I won't give evidence against Elroy! That dude is crazy. He let me go, but he would come for me and my mum if he thought I was talking to you about him."

Ashley held up his hands, palms out to calm Oliver down. "We don't have questions about Elroy Stewart, okay? We are here to ask you about Michelle Canet."

I watched Oliver frown, his gears turning. "Michelle Canet?" He recognised the name, but it had been so long since he'd heard it, his memory now struggled to identify why it was familiar.

"He was murdered in Whitstable the night you were found unconscious in the street," Ashley jogged his mind and I got to watch the penny drop. "Three years ago," Ashley pushed on, "you wouldn't tell the police anything. You denied possession of drugs, even though you were known to be in the employ of Elroy Stewart, and stated that you didn't see your assailant. How much of that was true, Oliver?"

Surprised by the question, yet relieved we were not quizzing him about his former master, Oliver said, "Most of it. I really didn't see whoever it was that hit me on the head. All I remember is the sound of someone stepping on gravel. Like it crunched under their foot. I remember it because it made me jump, but he hit me when I started to turn around and he hit me hard."

The report showed a piece of wood had been used to deliver the blow, an old piece of beech that was weathered and painted. They found fragments of it in Oliver's hair and embedded in his skin near the wound. The piece of wood was not found, but I doubt much effort went into looking for it.

Ashley was just about to ask me something when Oliver spoke again.

"I did get a photo though."

Chapter 9

ASHLEY AND I JUST stared at each other for the space of a heartbeat, each of us waited for the other to say something. When we did, we both said the same thing at the same time.

"You have a photograph?"

"Of your assailant?" I added, wanting to be doubly sure we were all talking about the same thing.

Ashley asked, "Why haven't you come forward with it before?"

Oliver had one hand behind his back, fishing around to find his phone, but said, "This might come as a shock, but I'm not a fan of the cops. No offense."

"None taken," Ashley and I both said at the same time.

"Anyway," Oliver continued, "it's a terrible photograph. I didn't exactly take the picture, not consciously anyway. I was texting my girlfriend when he hit me on the head and I guess the camera fired when I fell because I found this a couple of days later." He held out his phone for us to see.

On the screen was a blurry image that could have been anywhere if you didn't already know it was Whitstable. I could just about make out the corner of the Hotel Continental. It was shot at a crazy angle, the camera lens catching almost as much sky as anything else. However, in the foreground, near the bottom of the screen was a forearm. Motion made the limb a little distorted, but not so much that we couldn't see the tattoo.

"What is that?" I asked, squinting at the tiny image. We needed to get it onto a computer and have one of the geeky tech guys enhance it, but Oliver was able to supply an answer.

"It's a Viking."

Now that he said it, I could see he was right. On the upper surface of the left forearm, a man with a beard and flowing hair crammed into a Viking helmet faced right. His eyeball glowed a deep red and he held a sword upright in front of his face. It was elegant work, and I immediately questioned whether we might be able to trace the artist. They are required by law to keep records listing the client's name and address, their consent for the artwork, plus date, location, colours, and design of the ta ttoo.

Of course, that applies to our country and lots of others, but not everywhere. If a person had a tattoo in Bulgaria, chances are there was no record at all, but this was a definite lead ... into the attack on Oliver Humphries. There was still nothing to connect his attack with Michelle's murder.

"What was taken from you that night, Oliver?" I asked the question myself.

"Ketamine."

His one-word answer linked the two attacks. It was still circumstantial, there being no way to prove the drugs found on Michelle were the ones taken from Oliver, but the likelihood it was just coincidence was small enough to ignore.

"I had about a grand's worth on me. Elroy would have given me such a beating for losing it. I was glad when he sacked me instead."

The amount was bang on too.

However, there was one glaring fact neither Ashley nor I had chosen to voice yet. Michelle Canet didn't have any tattoos.

Outside the gift shop on our way back to the car, we talked about it. Oliver knew we might have additional questions for him, but we had all we needed for now. The photograph Oliver took was now on Ashley's phone and winging its way to the geek squad to be cleaned up and enlarged.

Ashley said, "We need to find the owner of that arm. Chances are that's Michelle's killer." It was a bold statement that required some caution.

"That might prove to be the case, but Oliver couldn't tell us when the photograph was taken. He told us he had no memory of the attack and was only guessing his camera went off."

Ashley shook his head. "I checked the time stamp. It happened at 2054hrs on September 3rd. That's an hour before Michelle Canet was killed."

I should have thought of that. Pressing onward, I said, "That gives a window of an hour. If we go with the theory that one man performed both attacks, he would have had to cross the busiest part of Whitstable and all the shops."

Ashley stopped walking and looked at me, his face caught between excitement and deep thought.

"The original team would have gone through all the CCTV footage ..."

"But now we know what to look for," I finished his sentence. If the man who attacked Oliver walked through town, he would show up on more than a dozen CCTV cameras. We only needed one to have caught his face. Provided we could see it and his tattoo, his chances of escaping justice would evaporate.

Chapter 10

FEW PEOPLE OUTSIDE OF law enforcement will know what it is like to glimpse a truth that could lead to an arrest and the sense of justice that comes with it. But I guess there must be euphoric moments with other jobs: landing the big sale, sealing the deal ... whatever it is, that was what I was feeling now.

We were a long way from bringing the case to a close and finding Michelle's killer, but less than half a day into it, we had already uncovered a big clue the previous team never had a chance to find. A tattooed arm might not seem like much, but it was better than a fingerprint. A fingerprint will tie a person to a scene much like DNA evidence can, but you can't see a fingerprint across a room. You cannot identify the person it belongs to from a photograph or a piece of video footage. A tattoo gives all kinds of advantage.

So yeah, I was feeling confident and raring to get stuck into the CCTV footage waiting for us in the incident room back in

Herne Bay. It would be fair to say that this represented a change in my attitude.

I have been coasting for years. My career was done, my chances to advance lost in the past. Thirty years ago, before Bruce Denton happened, I had my sights set on the lofty heights of Chief Constable for Kent. Each county has its top man or woman, but Bruce Denton came into my life and that changed everything.

I had no choice but to kill him, a decision I have never once regretted, but forced to ruin the investigation into his brutal slaying, and then concentrate all my efforts on not getting caught in the years that followed, it was by my own hand that I was overlooked for promotion. Despite closing cases at a rate few in the country could keep up with, I faked PTSD to help hide my obsession with the Bruce Denton case, and no one was going to make that person the head of anything.

Consequently, I lost interest and for the last decade or so could be relied upon to do the bare minimum. Heck, I rarely even turned up on time, but something changed when I dug into what happened to Craig Chowdry. For the first time in years, I was invigorated. I woke up looking forward to getting stuck in and now I felt an undeniable yearning to solve the second cold case in a row.

Imagine my surprise when Ashley said he wanted to put off checking the CCTV footage that might blow the whole case wide open and instead return to Whitstable.

"Why?" I questioned. "This is a significant lead."

"I want to talk to Graham Bishop, the other tenant at Michelle's B&B. Do you know why?" he asked teasingly.

I scowled at him. I am not about to start jumping through hoops like a trained monkey just because he thinks he knows something I am yet to figure out. In my head I pictured Mr Bishop. There was a photograph of him in the file along with his statement.

The police found out about his run in with Michelle when they interviewed the landlady, Rosa Shelldridge. She told the police about Michelle's late-night visitors and agreed that Graham had a right to complain. According to her statement, she had warned Michelle about the level of noise and said he promised to keep it down.

I tilted my head to one side, mentally scrutinising Graham's face. Then I saw it.

"He's got tattoos."

Ashley nodded and started walking again. "That doesn't make him our man, but we can eliminate him from our enquiries the moment we see his left forearm."

"Or make an arrest." My heart actually beat a quick staccato rhythm at the thought.

Chapter 11

ON THE WAY BACK to Whitstable, Ashley introduced a new subject: Daniel Mahony. I already knew the name from his list of potential cold cases, and from a recent conversation where he announced his desire to reopen it. We had the backing of the chief constable and almost complete autonomy to do as we wished, but I wasn't sure trying to solve two cases at the same time was a good idea.

"Geography," Ashley replied, like that was supposed to explain everything.

"What about it?"

"Daniel Mahony lived in Whitstable. He committed a crime in Whitstable and got killed in Whitstable."

"And you think there is some economy to be had because we are now working in Whitstable," I concluded. "It would be more sensible to focus on Michelle Canet. We are making headway.

At least we might be. Looking at the Mahony case at the same time will add confusion."

I could feel Ashley smirking at me from the driver's seat. Narrowing my eyes, I challenged him to say what he was thinking.

"You really don't think you have the brainpower to keep the two things separate?"

I was about to growl a response, when he laughed and backed down.

"Sorry," he chuckled at his own marvellous sense of humour, "I agree. Going after both would stretch us and mess with our heads. Catching Michelle Canet's killer might take all our concentration unless we get mega lucky and Graham Bishop has a Viking warrior tattooed on his arm. However, we will be driving by all the places where the Daniel Mahony case will take us and I predict we will be looking for our next case very soon."

"Not now you've cursed us, we won't."

Ashley wasn't about to have his enthusiasm dented. "Are you familiar with Daniel Mahony's murder?"

I wasn't. There was a vague memory tickling the back of my brain, but most of what I did know came from skim reading the notes on Ashley's laptop.

Daniel Mahony was a piece of white trash with delusions of supremacy. A known racist with a history of arrests, he was convicted for beating up an old man and sentenced to five years in HM Prison Maidstone. The old man was Nelson Stewart, a first-generation descendant of the original Jamaican immigrants invited into Britain after the war. He was also the grandfather of a local hoodlum who was arrested but never charged with Mahony's murder which took place less than seventy-two hours after he was released from prison.

Listening as he filled in the blanks, two dots joined in my head, and I was compelled to interrupt.

"Hold on."

"Yes."

"Daniel Mahony beat up an old Jamaican man and the prime suspect in Mahony's murder is Nelson's grandson."

"That's right."

I sucked in a deep breath. "It's Elroy Stewart, isn't it."

"You are some kind of super detective, you know that?" Ashley mocked.

I made a mental note to get my own back.

"Yes," Ashley confirmed. "One and the same. So it's not just geography. Elroy Stewart has a connection to both cases."

"I wouldn't exactly say he was connected to the Michelle Canet case. We already established how unlikely it is that the dealers killed him or that Michelle was the one who attacked Humphries and took the ketamine in the first place. The Viking tattoo only serves to support that theory."

"Anyway, there is some overlap, so for the sake of economy I have brought all the evidence from the case out of central storage."

"Where is it?"

"In incident room B."

"When did you do that?"

"Yesterday, while you were off work."

"You were supposed to be off too." I rolled my eyes.

Ashley filled me in with some more detail. Elroy was the number one suspect for Mahony's murder, but had ironclad alibis. Twenty years later Ashley believed he could pick at the old scab and I had to agree with him. Tackling the case was not without its risks though. Elroy was nothing more than a teenage punk when Mahony was murdered, yet he was known to be a dangerous man now. Suspected in connection with numerous missing persons, he was unquestionably responsible for narcotics distribution across the county, rose to the top by employing violent terror tactics, but shielded himself from prosecution.

Nothing ever seemed to stick, that was what I knew.

Showing yet again that he had done his homework, Ashley knew the identity of Elroy's former girlfriend. Her statement and others placed Elroy more than a mile away from Mahony's murder and they had a photograph to back up their claims.

That they were lying was in little doubt, but attempts to prove it failed and the crown prosecution service refused to take the case forward. However, the girlfriend was now married to someone else and had nothing to do with the crowd she hung out with back then. Could she be convinced to tell the truth now?

My thoughts on the subject and our conversation ended when the sat nav announced our imminent arrival at McClaghan's Steelyard, a fabrication outfit making all manner of steel components to order. Graham Bishop worked here, so unless it was his day off, we expected to find him inside.

We were on the edge of Tankerton to the east of Whitstable. Not that there was a dividing line any longer, the urban sprawl merged what would once have been two small villages when they grew over the centuries to become towns. McClaghan's sat among other such businesses in an old, dirty industrial estate where it dominated one corner. There were fields beyond the fence that ran behind the warehouse-sized building and woodland if one kept going.

Ashley parked next to an ageing forklift truck at the edge of a row of cars. No spaces were marked out, it was just where workers chose to leave their vehicles. Music drifted out from a large, open roller door on the side nearest to us, but it was almost impossible to hear over the sound of machinery being operated inside.

Above a small door next to the roller door, a white sign with black letters asked visitors to report to reception. It didn't say where reception was, and it turned out they didn't really have one. Matching my experience of such enterprises, no budget was given to anything that wasn't absolutely necessary and that included the office.

Stuffed into one corner with a rack of offcut steel against it and wooden pallets thrown on top was a caravan that had to be a relic from the 1960s. The tyres were flat, the door was missing, and it was propped on bricks to keep it level.

We accessed it via a pedestrian walkway that was undoubtedly added to comply with a health and safety regulation. A few of the men working around the place glanced our way, but none stopped what they were doing.

Ashley stepped up into the caravan, knocking on the frame to announce his presence.

"Hello?" Holding the doorframe, he hung through it to check the inside before telling me, "There's no one in here."

Twisting to face back into the workshop, I found a man heading our way. He wore a dark red sweatshirt laced with tiny burn holes, dark jeans stained with grease or sweat or both, and heavy boots worn through at the toe to reveal the protective steel inside.

"Help you, gents?" he asked, hitting us with a professional smile and wiping his right hand on his top in case we expected to shake it.

Being nearest, I showed him my warrant card and watched his face fall. We were not prospective clients looking like we might have money to spend in our smart suits. Well, Ashley wears a smart suit. I gave up trying to impress with my outfits many, many years ago.

I told him who we were, said, "We are looking for Graham Bishop," and waited for him to react.

"Oh? Graham? Um ..." he had his back to me and was on his tippytoes to spot the man in question. "That's him over there," he pointed across the floor. "Is he in any trouble?"

I guessed we were talking to the boss even if he wasn't the owner. Neither Ashley nor I gave an answer, the pair of us under no obligation to provide an explanation and too keen to see Graham's left forearm to wait.

"Only he's one of my best workers and he's the only one who can work the laser cutter in the 3D setting. Everyone else makes a mess of it, and I've got a big order to get out this week."

Graham was either going to spend five minutes answering questions or, depending on what ink he had, get arrested on the spot with little chance of returning to work this week or any other. My pulse quickened as we drew near.

"Graham!" the man with us shouted to get his employee's attention.

It wasn't what I had planned, but too late to change it, I watched Ashley angle a little to the right to cut off the natural route to the exit should Graham choose to bolt.

However, our target spun around to see who was calling his name, saw us, saw what we were, and stayed where he was.

Once again, I showed my warrant card and introduced myself.

"All right," Graham replied, "so what do you want with me?"

"I would like to see your left forearm, please."

My request was not what he expected, his expression turning quizzical. His eyebrows performed a little dance, but he didn't argue. In fact, he didn't waste a breath speaking at all, he just started to roll up his sleeve.

He looked just like his picture: skinny, five feet eleven, thinning sandy blonde hair, pale skin made older than its years through smoking. There were tattoos on his neck and hands, the ink visible where it was not covered by his clothing.

I watched the flesh of his left forearm appear, my impatience making me want to grab his sleeve so I could yank it back. Blue lines emerged about four inches above his wrist, my brain silently confirming my cuffs were on my belt where I needed them to be.

He rolled the sleeve again to reveal more of the ink and my heart sank when a little heart appeared. The next roll showed two cherubs holding a ribbon on which a name 'Bianca' was displayed.

Graham kept going until the sleeve reached his elbow. He could tell by my face that I was not seeing what I hoped for and wasted no time in starting to roll the material down again.

"Satisfied?" he asked, his tone both mocking and aggressive. "Or do you want to see what I've got tattooed on my backside next?"

Smoothly, I replied, "That won't be necessary, but I do have a few questions."

"What about? I've got work to do."

"Michelle Canet." I supplied the name and watched his face. Would there be panic behind his eyes? Was he, like me, spending his days wondering when someone would finally learn the truth of his crime? I learned long ago to read reactions rather than listen to what people said. Most would lie in an instant but behind the words, their brains would spin trying to figure out what I knew, hoping to think two steps ahead and be able to defeat me. In so doing, their breathing would change, their pupils would dilate, and their eyes would flick up and left to engage the portion of their brain that deals with imagination. All these things are completely involuntary.

Graham Bishop did none of them.

His face screwed into a grimace. "Michelle Canet? That French homo?"

His homophobic slur came as no surprise. There was no point rising to it.

"Yes, Mr Bishop. Is there somewhere quiet we can talk?" The workshop wasn't so noisy that we might miss something he said, but it was better to have our chat in private all the same. My question was aimed at his boss as much as it was at Graham, but they both aimed their eyes back toward the caravan.

"There's a break room outside." Graham accepted his fate with a sigh, refastening his cuff when he led us through the building and out through a side door.

The breakroom was a prefabricated building sitting on blocks. There was electricity and water running to it, a television in one corner and a selection of magazines piled at the end of a fold-out table. The walls, floor, and windows were dirty, and it smelled of cigarette smoke, but it was private enough for our purposes.

Graham flopped into a chair, scratching at an itch on his right leg when he said, "I didn't kill him, if that's what you are here to ask. I don't like queers, but I'm not about to start murdering people. I have an alibi for the night he was killed. You can check with the cops who questioned me three years ago."

"Yes, Mr Bishop, that's not what I want to ask you about." This confused him further, so before he had a chance to ask a question, I started in with one of my own. "Did you ever see any of Michelle's visitors?"

"See them? You mean the gays he had in his room night after night?"

"Yes, Mr Bishop, precisely that. Did you see any of them? Outside your window when they left perhaps?"

"My room was at the back of the place. All I could see was the neighbour's cat doing its business in the flower beds."

Ashley caught my eye. He wanted to know where I was going with my line of questioning. The answer to that one was that I didn't really have a destination. We had other things to be getting on with and on paper that looked more important than interviewing a person who looked very unlikely to be involved with Michelle Canet's murder. But we were already here and it would only take a short while to pick Graham's tiny brain.

"What about names, Mr Bishop? If their voices penetrated the walls, did you ever hear any names."

I saw Ashley nod to himself. He knew to trust me and was now glad that he had.

Unfortunately, Graham shook his head. "Nah, I've got nothing for you. No names, no faces."

I persisted. "What about cars, Mr Bishop? Did you ever notice the same car parked outside your lodgings on more than one occasion."

Graham laughed at me. "I don't remember what I had for breakfast yesterday and you want to ask me about cars in the street three years ago? There were lots of cars there night after night. That's what you get in a residential street."

I tilted my head to one side. He was lying. He did remember something. His eyes were darting between me and Ashley and the door. He wanted to leave, which was unsurprising, but more than that he was worried we could see through his bluster.

Acting annoyed, I allowed a deep frown to form. It was enough to wipe the smile from Mr Bishop's face. "You think this is a joke?" My sudden shift in demeanour chased the colour from his face. He was a cocky git, but he didn't want to find himself with an angry cop taking interest in his life. I was still standing, so I bent at the waist to bring my face down closer to his when I growled, "This is a murder enquiry, matey. I think you know something, and you are going to tell me what it is." I left an unspoken 'or else' hanging in the air and waited.

Graham glanced at Ashley.

"Don't look at him!" I bellowed in his face, shocking him so he jerked away from me. "What are you keeping back?" I don't make a habit of shouting at people. Actually, I can't recall the last time I raised my voice, but I think it was the stress of Bruce Denton fuelling my behaviour. Whatever the case, it worked.

"John!" Graham blurted. "There was a guy called John. More than once I heard Michelle shouting his name through the wall."

I straightened, taking my face away from Graham's putrid cigarette breath. Just like that, we had a name.

Ashley held up a palm, letting me know he had a question to ask.

"You never mentioned a name when you were questioned before. Why is that?"

Graham didn't want to make eye contact. He was looking at the floor when he gave an unhappy shrug.

"I dunno, do I? I guess I figured talking to the cops never does any good so why bother volunteering information?"

"Did they ask you for a name three years ago?"

Graham looked up. "No. They quizzed me for hours about my movements. They thought I might have killed him, but I didn't."

His alibi was the landlady at the B&B. In her statement she said Graham returned home a little after nine o'clock and was in his room until the following morning. The investigating team argued that he could have snuck out, but his room was upstairs and Mrs Shelldridge spent the evening watching TV in the living room by the front door. Her stairs creaked terribly so she would have heard him attempt to descend, and though he could theoretically have slipped out of his room and down the drainpipe to the roof of the shed in next door's garden, there was no evidence to suggest he had.

"They didn't ask you about Michelle's lovers?" Ashley sounded a little incredulous.

"Well, yeah, but they never asked me for names. I said I never saw them and they left it at that."

It was an oversight on their part, but only a small one. Chances are Graham would have dodged the question anyway, much as he tried to do with us.

I pushed him for more information, asking the same questions a dozen different ways before accepting he had given us all he knew.

We had a first name and according to Mr Bishop 'John' was there more than once though he never stayed the night. It wasn't a lot, but it was a heck of a lot more than nothing.

Chapter 12

Pulling away from the industrial estate, the sense of anticipation I felt on the way to it was back. Graham Bishop wasn't our man, but I told myself it would have been a miracle to have caught the killer so few hours after picking up the investigation.

Back in Herne Bay, we had a long list of the people Superintendent Prince's team interviewed. Neither one of us could recall if it contained anyone called John, but I wasn't letting that dampen my mood.

No, I let Ashley do that instead.

Following the coast road back to my home nick, there was silence in the car until my partner chose to ruin it.

"We should talk about Bruce Denton," he announced out of the blue.

I didn't have to think about my response. "No, we shouldn't."

"Yes, Tony, we really should. Even if it is just to exorcise the monster. I know, I know," he got in quick before I could start arguing, "you think it's the last thing in the world you want to talk about, and I get it."

I could sense a 'but' coming.

"Buuut, I was just thinking about what Bishop said about cars in a residential street."

My heart suddenly felt like it weighed three times as much.

"In the Bruce Denton file there were reports from three different residents who claimed they saw a man sitting in his car in the days before the murder."

Yes, there were. What wasn't in the file were the ones I hid because letting anyone else see them would have landed me behind bars.

Choosing to be angrily defensive, I snapped, "So what? Don't you think I've been over that evidence a thousand times? They reported what they saw because they were prompted to do so by our questions. Otherwise, they wouldn't have said anything. It's like when we run a TV campaign asking for witnesses and we get idiots who saw Elvis or Lord Lucan."

"But ..."

"No! If you're so familiar with my investigation, you must know the reports you refer to all described a different car and a different man. Had they all been the same, we might have been on to something. I wasted hours pursuing those leads, but they led nowhere." Actually, I hadn't pursued them at all other than to carefully grill the residents who made the reports. I guided their memories, slowly twisting them so they began to question what they might have seen. Bottom line, none of them had seen me, even though that was quite specifically what they saw.

Ashley raised his hands from the steering wheel, surrendering before he gripped it once more.

A minute passed, the silence blissful to my ears, though I knew it was too good to be true.

"I'm just saying," he started again, "that you need to be ready to face the case again. The camcorder proves there is new evidence to be had. The tech team will improve the image and you know there will be an appeal for people to come forward if they recognise the woman."

He was right. I did know it. Bruce Denton's murder might be thirty years old, but we were going to try to solve it. My only hope was to make sure I was at the helm again. I felt sick and for once I didn't have to fake my sweating palms or racing heart.

Ashley took his eyes from the road for just long enough to shoot me an apologetic look.

"I'm here for you, Tony. I want you to know that. If you want to hand it all over and back away, I can ..."

"No." I took a deep breath and rubbed my hands on my trousers. "No." I said it more softly the second time. "I want to be involved, but let's wait to see what they can do with the footage first, though I'm not sure what difference it will make since the camera never caught her face."

"Yes, I was thinking about that. The car drives toward the camera when it first comes down the street. I believe they will be able to enhance still images to get a shot of her face. They can then use tools to fill in the bits that are hidden by glare from the sun. I've seen it done before. The results can be mixed, but it could work."

I had seen it done too.

"Even if they do, she could be dead by now. It was thirty years ago."

From the corner of my eye, I saw Ashley's brow furrow.

"She looked to be in her early twenties to me. That would make her about the same age as your wife now."

I stiffened, my heart rate spiking instantly. To hide my reaction, I said, "I guess you're right. We shall have to hope for the best."

I was going to hope for anything but, and watching the world slip by outside, I questioned if I could get my hands on the video footage. Try enhancing the image after I've deleted it.

Chapter 13

IT WAS FIVE TO three when we got back to Herne Bay armed with new knowledge about the Michelle Canet case. Ashley hadn't mentioned Bruce Denton again, but I wasn't dumb enough to think he was going to let it drop. My partner wanted to make a name for himself, and I was happy enough to help him do that. Just not at my own expense.

He gained exposure when we not only proved teenager Craig Chowdry was killed but also found his body. Solving another one would put him on the map. There were six teams in the task force, each comprising a young guy sent from London paired with a local liaison like me to help. Thus far, we were the only ones to net a result, but Ashley is not the kind of person to be satisfied by coming first. He needs to show the world that he is the best by far. Beyond compare.

I was exactly the same once.

Bruce Denton was the cream of the crop, the highest profile case on the list, and that presented a challenge I had to overcome. Ashley knew that slapping the cuffs on his killer three decades after the trail went cold would cement his place in legend. If he only knew the half of it. It would be a big news story anyway, but when the press found out the killer was the detective sergeant who investigated the case both then and now, there would be a frenzy. A feast of headlines with Ashley at the top.

Except I couldn't let that happen.

We ran into Doris on our way in.

"Solved another one already, boys?" she joked. Older than most of the paint on the walls and with more decades under her belt than anyone dared to count, Doris had worked as a civilian administrative assistant at the Herne Bay nick since before I was born. She had a mug of tea in one hand, a pack of digestive biscuits in the other, and a wicked glint in her eye. She had been a mature, but very attractive woman when I first met her more than thirty years ago. Now she looked like a soup chicken, but it wasn't hard to see the beauty still lurking behind her years.

"Not yet," I replied, eyeing her biscuits.

Following my gaze, she tucked the sweet treats against her chest and growled, "Get yer own." She was heading back to her office on the ground floor, glancing over her shoulder to see if I was following.

I chuckled to myself and made a promise to raid her supply later. She would need to visit the ladies at some point, and I would swoop. Then, remembering that I was supposed to be feeling sick from all the Bruce Denton talk, I wipe the stupid grin from my face and followed Ashley up the stairs to the offices.

We had returned to the nick so we could go over the evidence from the Michelle Canet case. Delivered from central storage a few days ago, it was set up in one of the incident rooms on the ground floor. I thought we were going to head straight there, but when Ashley climbed the stairs I knew why – he wanted to check how the tech team was getting on with the video footage.

"It will take another day at least," said Aidan with a shrug. "That's to get it good enough for us to show on the local news. It's better now than it was this morning."

"What about when the car is coming toward the camera?" Ashley enquired. "Is there a shot when we see the woman's face?"

From watching it this morning, I knew the car's windscreen reflected the sun, which ought to make the answer a satisfying negative, yet the moment I thought that, I realised there would be moments when it passed streetlamps or telegraph poles. It might only be for a split second, but the shadow cast would pass over the screen, removing the glare.

Would that reveal the faces of the occupants inside?

Yet again, my pulse echoed the stress I felt.

Aidan pursed his lips and faced his multitude of screens. "I don't think so, but let's have a look."

Clicking his mouse, he dragged a box onto a screen to the left of centre and there he ran the video again. A heavy breath left me. Ashley looked my way, checking I was okay. He looked like he wanted to put a reassuring hand on my shoulder or say something supportive, but I guess he couldn't find the right words as he kept quiet and turned his attention back to the screen.

For the umpteenth time, I watched Bruce Denton drive my wife toward Jamie's camera. I saw the momentary flicker when it passed under a shadow of a streetlamp, just like I knew I would.

Aidan hit the pause button. "I think that was something."

Yes, it was the sound of cuffs ratcheting shut around my wrists.

"I'm going to play it at one quarter speed." He did something with the mouse and the video began again, this time going much slower.

Inside my chest, my heart thumped like a bass drum. It felt like it was beating against my ribs and might soon burst out like one of those alien things. I could feel the sweat under my arms and down my back. I wanted to be anywhere else. I wanted to get a bat like Quint in *Jaws* and beat the machinery into a pulp. That would stop them.

Watching in slow motion, I saw the car pass through three shadows before it got to the final one. By then it was close to the camera and about to exit the shot. The line fell at an angle close to forty-five degrees, hitting the bonnet first, then sweeping over the car, though of course the shadow wasn't moving at all.

It ran up the screen, sweeping over Bruce's first. The moisture left my mouth when I saw his face. It wasn't a clear shot; blur and distortion from the glass messed with it, but I could see who it was with no trouble.

The shadow continued to move across the screen, going even slower when Aidan clicked his mouse again. Now it crept, exposing the right arm of the woman in the passenger seat, then her right breast and the bottom edge of her blonde hair.

No one spoke. No one made a sound, and I could feel my pulse banging away in my head where I had unconsciously elected to stop breathing.

The shaft of shadow drifted inexorably onward, exposing more of the blonde hair. My eyes stayed glued to the screen as more and more of her came into view.

I dared to draw a breath as relief washed over me like a wave of warm, tropical water.

"She's got her head down," murmured Ashley, bitterly disappointed.

Rallying my emotions, I snarled, "Dammit!" even though I wanted to punch the air in jubilation.

Aidan stopped the footage. "I'll take it back and zoom in. We might get lucky with one of the earlier shadows."

From what I knew, I doubted that would be the case, but I couldn't stand to watch any longer. I'm not in the best health; looking after my body was never a priority, so I excused myself to visit the gents. It left Ashley staring hopefully over the top of Aidan's head and meant I wouldn't be there to know if they found something useable, but I'm not an actor and I questioned how many times I could fake a reaction before Ashley caught me doing it.

Bladder empty, I took myself to the incident room. I needed something to take my mind off the noose around my neck, for that was how it felt, and the Michelle Canet case would provide the perfect distraction.

Graham Bishop gave us a name, and I was going to see if I could find a match among any of the original suspects.

It took me less than a minute.

Chapter 14

I SAT ON THE edge of the desk and used the landline to call Marvin the Martian.

"Detective Inspector Valmik."

"Marvin, it's Tony."

"How's the case going? Figured out what we missed yet?" He said it with a laugh which I felt bad about killing.

"Oliver Humphries showed us a picture of his attacker."

A few beats of stunned silence were broken when Marvin said, "The little git. He wouldn't give us a thing."

"Life has changed for him, but listen, the picture only shows an arm. Do you recall anyone with a tattoo of a Viking warrior on their left forearm? It's good artwork and it covers most of the skin from the wrist to the elbow." I had a name to give but wanted to hear it from him first.

"A Viking tattoo?" I gave him enough time to consult his memory. "Not that I can think of. Is that really all you got from Humphries?"

"The only useful thing. He won't talk about his former employers if that is what you are thinking. Next question. What do you recall about John Decker?"

In a perfect world, Marvin would have told me the man with a Viking tattoo *was* John Decker, but I'm not that lucky. If I was lucky at all, I wouldn't be sweating bullets about the imminent reopening of the Bruce Denton case.

Marvin took a moment before giving me an answer, but said, "I recall thinking he might have done it."

"Really?" This was precisely what I wanted to hear.

"His alibi was a little shaky. That was what made us look at him so closely. He was in the Old Shipwright the night of Michelle Canet's murder. When we first questioned him, he said he left the pub just after half-past eight and his wife said he was home before nine. She was heavily pregnant at the time. That took him out of the picture, but there were other people in the pub, including members of staff who believed he was there after nine, maybe even as late as nine thirty."

"So he was lying."

"I believed he was, but we spent hours trawling through photographs taken on phones that night hoping to find a shot with him in. Just one shot with a timestamp to prove he lied would have changed everything, but we couldn't find one and there was nothing to tie him to Michelle Canet."

There wasn't then, but there is now. I wouldn't tell Marvin that Graham Bishop also opened up to us; doing so would annoy him, but I had every reason to believe John Decker might be the same John whose name Graham heard through the walls of the bed and breakfast.

I thanked him and ended the call, doing so just as Ashley popped his head around the door looking for me.

Hanging in the doorframe, he said, "I thought you were coming back."

I shook my head, hanging it low to show how off balance the whole Bruce Denton thing was making me.

"I ... I couldn't." I looked up to meet his eyes. "Did Aidan find anything?" My interest wasn't fake. I wanted to know. I just hoped he would say 'no'.

Ashley came inside and shut the door behind him. "Not really. There is one shot that shows a portion of her face, but it's the one that is farthest away from the camera. Aidan said he can zoom in and use software to make the face whole – apparently, the computer will examine each visible pixel and guess the surrounding ones, but he also said the accuracy given the start point was unlikely to yield anything useful."

I nodded along as he spoke, reviewing the information in my head. Was I screwed or not? It was hard to tell.

"The footage of her walking in might get us somewhere though and there are her clothes and hairstyle. If we are really lucky, the woman will come forward when she recognises herself. Better that than have someone else do it."

Well, I knew for certain Mary would never volunteer her identity and would strenuously deny it if anyone did it for her.

I said, "Yes, that would be better for her. We shall have to see." I had a day or so to destroy the evidence in all its formats and no clue how to do it, let alone how to pull it off without anyone looking my way as the culprit.

Changing the subject, I slipped down from my perch on the edge of the desk.

"I have a suspect."

The statement got Ashley's attention and picking up my coat let him know we were leaving.

"There is a John Decker in the file. They interviewed him as a potential suspect three years ago but dismissed him when his wife provided an alibi. I called DI Valmik in Whitstable …"

"That's the guy you were talking to this morning?"

"Yeah. He said the alibi was shaky and that other people in the bar placed him there after his wife said he got home. They couldn't prove it though and with nothing else to go on they had to let it go."

Following me, Ashley said, "You know, I'm beginning to like this cold case stuff."

Chapter 15

You might think we would go to John Decker's place of work, Capon's Butchers and Deli in Whitstable's Harbour Street, but I convinced Ashley we would be far better served to destroy his alibi first.

Unless Graham Bishop lied to us, which I didn't believe he did, and provided we had the right John from Michelle's lodgings, Mr Decker had been in a relationship with the murdered Mr Canet while married to his pregnant wife.

I could see a dozen motives for murder in that scenario.

"Worried that his wife would find out," suggested Ashley.

"Horrified by his cheating."

"In denial over his sexual preferences, he killed Michelle in the hope it would absolve him."

"Well," I agreed, "he certainly has some confusion regarding whether he is gay or straight. Married with a child on the way and sleeping with Michelle on the side."

"Plenty of bisexuals out there, Tony," Ashley chided.

"Yes, but does his wife have the slightest idea her husband is one of them?"

"Well, I think we can probably rule her out as the killer if she was heavily pregnant."

Ashley wasn't wrong, but we would know more once we'd had the chance to grill Gail Decker.

The Deckers' house in Gosselin Street has a magnificent view out over the top of Whitstable town centre due to its elevated position. The semi-detached place sat to the left of its mirror image. There would be three bedrooms inside with a kitchen at the back and it was an old property, so they probably had a decent sized garden.

We expected to find Mrs Decker at home due to some basic maths. If she was heavily pregnant three years and one month ago, the child could be three now at the most. That made it too young for school and it was late enough in the afternoon now that pre-school would have ended.

That didn't mean Mrs Decker was home. For all I knew, she had a job, and the child was with a minder or being entertained at a creche. That wouldn't slow us down for long, but as it turned out she was there. And very pregnant again.

I saw that before she opened the door, the protruding belly visible through the frosted glass when she waddled toward it. Unlike her husband, there was no file for her or picture to tell us what she looked like. I judged her to be in her very early thirties. At the edge of her eyes, lines were appearing and I could see a strand or two of grey hair mixed in with the dark brown which fell in a long straight ponytail to six inches below her collarbones. She was thin everywhere except her belly. Her arms and legs like that of a spider they possessed so little meat. Her blue eyes showed concern.

I showed her my identification.

"Is John all right?" she asked, a hint of panic in her voice. She thought we were on her doorstep to deliver a notice of death.

"So far as I know, Mrs Decker. We are here to ask some questions relating to the murder of Michelle Canet."

Watching her face for clues, I caught the flutter of concern in her eyes. Her breath caught and she pressed her lips together as though forming a barrier to prevent words from spilling out. She also pressed her hands against her belly.

The sound of a children's TV show echoed down her hallway.

I placed my right foot on her doormat, stepping forward to physically demonstrate my intention to enter her home. "May we come in?" It wasn't really a request though she did have the right to deny us entry. "Better to discuss such things away from the neighbours." I twisted to look back at the street and caught a glimpse of a net curtain falling back into place.

Mrs Decker saw it too.

Stepping backward, she retreated along the hallway leaving Ashley to close the door. Agitated, and unhappy at our intrusion, an emotion all cops get used to in their first few months of work, she hustled faster when her child let out a wail.

"Mummy's coming," she called with a sigh. Over her shoulder, just before she vanished around a corner, she said, "Do you want to wait in the kitchen? There's a table in there. I won't be a minute."

We could see the kitchen from the hallway, the cupboards making it easy to identity, but the house design was familiar enough that I could have found it with my eyes closed.

The sink was overflowing with dirty dishes, the bowl in it full to the brim with water that looked to have been there all day. A small, round table with two chairs and a highchair sat against the far wall next to a window that looked out across their garden. It was covered in old mail, coupons from shops, kids' things, and the general detritus of family life. The garden needed attention, but none of that was of interest.

We heard Gail settling her child, whose gripe appeared to be nothing more than the TV program had ended. She joined us in the kitchen a moment later.

"I can't promise that won't happen again," she muttered, with a glance at the pile of crockery and saucepans in the sink. Her cheeks coloured a little, but only long enough for her to decide she was too tired and uncomfortable to care what two cops thought. "Will this take long?" she asked, pulling out a chair and settling into it.

Choosing not to answer, I lowered myself into the chair opposite hers. Ashley and I had already discussed how to handle Mrs Decker and he was content to let me lead.

"How far along are you?"

"Thirty-eight weeks," she replied with no need to think. "I need it to come early. My feet are killing me." Her answer was honest and heartfelt which served as a baseline for her visual cues.

I posed another easy one. "Do you know what you are having?"

"A boy this time."

From which I assumed her first child was a girl.

I wanted to ask a third question that would yield an honest answer, just to confirm what I knew to expect when she spoke the truth, but her impatience bubbled over first.

"Look, I'm sure you don't really care about my aching feet or the tiny creature about to embark on years of torturing me emotionally, mentally, and physically, so why not ask me what you came here to ask?" The request wasn't snapped or demanded; it was the plea of a woman feeling anything but her best. I could sympathise, but I suspected her of obstructing a police murder enquiry.

Holding her gaze with a face devoid of emotion, I asked, "Why did you provide your husband with a false alibi for the time of Michelle Canet's murder?"

I could have asked her what time John got home that night or what they talked about when he got in. I could have questioned what she did while he was out or how she could be so certain about what time her husband came through the door. However, experience allows me to know that people guilty of serious lies with big repercussions build up the picture around their fabricated story so they have all the details ready for recall.

Gail probably hadn't thought about Michelle Canet in years; it was all water under the bridge now, but even so, I expected her to remember what she said when the police questioned her.

My question, framed as a direct accusation, shocked her, and she recoiled physically.

"What ... what do you mean? I didn't provide a false alibi. I told the police what time he came home."

"Was your husband having an affair with Michelle Canet?"

That one really made her gawp in horror.

"What? No! He's not gay!"

"Isn't he?" I challenged.

"No! Don't you think a woman can tell if a man is gay or not when she is sleeping with him?"

She was nervous now, the opposite of how she acted when answering questions about her pregnancy.

Persisting, I said, "What was your husband doing in the Old Shipwright that night, Mrs Decker? He was there a lot, wasn't h e?"

"He likes to have a few pints some nights, that's all. It doesn't make him gay or a killer." She sounded uncertain.

"He was seen in the pub after the time you claim he got home. How do you explain that?"

"I don't need to. I was sober, the people in the pub were drunk. They have false memories. Mine is working fine. I was watching *Eastenders* on a plus one channel and John came home just after it ended. That's just after half past eight. I was upstairs running a bath, hoping it might ease some of the tension in my back." Now she was embellishing, something liars often do when they find themselves able to give an answer with confidence amid a pack of lies and half-truths.

"If you took a bath, how can you be so certain your husband didn't go out again?"

This time I got a smile and could see I had given her an easy question.

"Because he sat next to the bath and talked to me the whole time." She looked triumphant.

I changed strategy. "Mrs Decker, I believe you are lying about the time your husband got home and I believe we will find evidence that will prove he was having an affair with Michelle Canet." I held back from suggesting it made him the killer because it didn't, but the inference was obvious. "You should know that the case has been reopened and we have already found fresh evidence the team was unable to unearth during the original investigation."

Gail's triumphant expression was gone, replaced by one I would describe as slightly sick. I should know, it's how I've been feeling since that cursed camcorder reappeared.

"Michelle Canet was involved with a man whose first name is John. There was only one man called John in the Old Shipwright the night Michelle was killed. So be warned, Mrs Decker. The net is closing, and someone is going to get caught. It will do you no good to be exposed as the person who kept a killer out of jail for the last three years. If this comes to court, you will commit perjury if you maintain the same lies you harbour now."

"I am not lying," Gail growled, but her voice was catching. She was upset and her emotions were getting the better of her. She also had her right hand up around her mouth, an unconscious sign that she wanted to keep the secrets in. Adding it all together, I knew there was no need to push any further. She had lied three years ago, and she was lying now. However, I believed she would continue to do so and that to ask more questions would be a waste of time. To catch her out I was going to have to find something that would expose her lies.

"Yes, you are," I replied, confident in my accusation. "Now I just have to prove it, Gail. Will you really not save yourself the pain of a drawn-out investigation?"

"My husband didn't kill Michelle Canet."

I flinched a little and found myself unconsciously chewing my bottom lip. In contrast to everything I believed, Gail Decker's last statement was true. At least she thought it was. I had not one doubt she was lying about what time he got home, but whatever she was covering up, she didn't think he got in late because he was stabbing the Frenchman to death.

Chapter 16

Outside in the street, I discussed my thoughts with Ashley.

"We might be able to get her to crack, but the optics are bad with her being so close to delivering her baby. I'm only ninety percent sure she's lying and that John Decker is our man."

We reached the car and stopped either side of it, talking over the roof.

"This has moved remarkably fast."

"It has," I agreed. "That's not down to the team doing anything wrong three years ago, though."

"Agreed. Things have changed. You know what we missed in there though?"

I tilted my head to one side, asking myself what he could be referring to.

"The tattoo," Ashley supplied. "We didn't ask Mrs Decker about her husband's left forearm."

He was one hundred percent correct and I could kick myself. Getting that answer could have changed things fast, but the oversight wasn't a major hurdle.

"We should speak to John next anyway," I said, opening the car door. "Chances are she has already texted him to let him know about our visit."

Ashley opened his door too but paused outside when I folded into the passenger's seat. Dropping down to look in through the car, he nodded his head at a point across the street.

"Eyes up."

I swung my head around to find a woman heading our way. She was tall and thin and dressed in sportswear. Her brown hair looked to be dyed to remove the grey and pulled into a tight ponytail at the back of her head. She was striding purposefully in our direction.

Behind her was an open door. It was the house where I saw the twitchy net curtain.

"Are you the police?" she asked before she was halfway to us.

I mean, we do look like cops, and the silver Ford Mondeo with the extra antenna for the radio is a dead giveaway.

Ashley closed his door again, coming around the car to meet her. I had the seatbelt in my hand, but let it go, swivelling around on my backside to set my feet back on the tarmac.

Ashley answered, "Yes, ma'am. Is there something we can help you with?"

I stood up, more for show than anything else. She would have a question about something innocuous or hope to report something trivial, like local kids riding their bikes across her front lawn. I was not expecting Gail's front door to suddenly open or for her to start shouting at her neighbour.

"Emma, no!"

Her neighbour, Emma, apparently, shot back, "It's time, Gail."

Time for what? I had been leaning on the car, but my nonchalance was gone, forgotten in the drama of the latest development.

"No! You can't! You promised!"

Gail was crying, tears glistening on her cheeks.

Emma went around Ashley and the car to get to Gail but stopped a few feet short of her.

"I'm sorry, Gail. I really am, but this is for your own good."

I had no idea what she was about to say, though it was fair to say I believed it was going to be something juicy. Gail's neighbour from across the street spun around to face us and from her mouth poured the one thing I hoped to hear.

"John didn't come home when she said he did. It was gone ten when he crawled home."

Gail sobbed, gasping for breath.

"Gail was with me that night. We were both pregnant and having a pamper night. John treats her like a doormat, not because he doesn't love her, but because he is gay and won't admit it, even to himself. He's had multiple affairs, all with men." Truth delivered, Emma went to Gail who was sobbing uncontrollably.

I thought she might fend her off or attempt to hit her, but Gail just stood there, sobbing in the street when her neighbour pulled her into a hug.

Behind them, Gail's little girl appeared in the doorway.

"Why is mummy crying?"

I shot my eyes at Ashley. A moment ago, I had been thinking it had been a good day and that we should call it quits in the next hour. I wanted to get home so I could talk to Mary about the video – she was just as on edge as me. Then I was going to come back to the station after most people had gone home for the day and see what I could do about the footage. Now though? Now I knew I was going to spend the evening getting a confession out of John Decker.

Chapter 17

It took us an hour to get Gail Decker set up in the interview room. Her little girl went with the neighbour, Emma, when Gail agreed that was the best and quickest solution for childcare. It was that or we needed to involve social services which would slow the entire process down.

When asked, Gail told us she had not yet texted her husband. With a quick confession from her, we could arrest him before he caught wind that his wife was being interviewed by the police.

Gail was ready to tell us everything in the street outside her house, but it was safer and cleaner if we recorded her words in an interview room, hence the slight delay. Mercifully, our status as part of the cold case task force meant we could drop into Whitstable nick and use their facilities. It was faster than going to Herne Bay.

Was John Decker a flight risk if he found we were on to him? Possibly, but it was a simple thing to send a squad car to watch the butcher's shop where he worked and that was what we did. DCI Tanner at the Whitstable nick was good enough to lend us his officers for the task. We were against the clock, but I believed it would work out.

By the time we settled into chairs opposite Gail, sixty minutes had elapsed since we knocked on her door. She had been stewing for most of it and boy was she ready to talk. Her face was a blotchy mess of tears and her nose was red and a little swollen from blowing it. She looked miserable on top of her obvious physical discomfort and I will admit I felt bad for her.

Not really bad though; she'd knowingly harboured a murderer for three years, shielding him from justice with her lies.

Ashley checked I was ready with a glance and set the recorder in motion. He recited the preliminary preamble and fixed Mrs Decker with a dispassionate stare.

He didn't even need to ask her a question.

"Look, I'm sorry, okay," she cried, the need to speak sparking a fresh wave of tears and snot. "What else was I supposed to do? We were married before I found out he prefers men."

Conscious of the clock, I zeroed in on what we needed to know. "Gail, for the purposes of the recording, I need you to answer the following questions as succinctly as possible. Do you understand?"

She nodded her head and blew her nose.

"For the purpose of the recording, Mrs Decker has just nodded her head."

"Yes. I understand." She sniffed and wiped her nose again.

"Mrs Decker, did you provide a false alibi for your husband for the night of September 3rd, 2020?"

It took her a second and she wouldn't look up to meet our eyes, but she swallowed hard and said, "Yes, I did."

"What time did your husband, John Decker, arrive home that night?"

Her body shuddered the way they do after a really good cry, and the tears continued to fall. In telling the truth she was condemning her husband, but we were past the point where she had an option. I waited, giving her the time she needed to form the sentence.

"It was a little after ten o'clock," she managed, the words painful to get out.

"Can you give a more exact estimate?"

"I think it was maybe ten past ten or even a quarter past."

"Why did you previously claim that he was home just after eight thirty that evening?"

She looked up, her eyes boring into mine when she pleaded, "Please, I didn't know what else to do!"

"Please answer the question, Gail. It's important."

Mrs Decker looked down again, hanging her head with a mix of shame and guilt.

"John told me to. I was in bed when he got home and pretended to be asleep so I wouldn't have to talk to him. He stank of aftershave that wasn't his. In the morning, the murder was all over the local news and John said the police might come to ask questions because he was in the bar. He told me Michelle worked there, but that your questions would be nothing more than a formality as you tried to find the killer."

"So, you lied about what time your husband got home because he asked you to?"

"Yes."

"Did you ask him why he thought it necessary?"

"He told me it would just be easier and that it would help to speed up your investigation if they weren't looking at the wrong people." Her eyes came up to meet mine again. "Look he's not a killer. That's why I never came forward. I know he lied, but John wouldn't hurt a fly. You're going after the wrong man."

Gail believed she was telling the truth. About all of it. All the cues that exposed her lies were gone. There was nothing fake or held back now, but she also believed her husband was innocent of Michelle's murder.

Regardless, we had enough to make the arrest. We could call through and have the uniforms positioned near his place of work carry out the task, but Ashley was brimming with the need to be in the thick of the action, so I was going to wrap this up so he could append his name to the paperwork.

One day. That was all it took us. One single day to close a case that sat open and unsolved for more than three years. I felt like Sherlock Holmes.

I had just a couple of closing questions. Irrelevant ones possibly, but we could spare another minute to satisfy my curiosity.

"Mrs Decker, was your husband in a relationship with Michelle Canet prior to his murder?" I wasn't sure how she would answer; chances are she didn't know either way, but if she was able to confirm it, interviewing John could be conducted from a position of power.

She sighed and stared at the floor on her left. "I don't know. He was seeing someone. His shirts kept coming home smelling of someone else's cologne. You hear about wives catching their husbands with another woman. Lipstick on their collar and all that. It never occurred to me I would be competing with men. What chance did I stand?" She sighed again and incredibly, given how defeated she seemed, deflated a little more. "Sorry, I had never heard the name Michelle Canet before his murder was on the news, and I know it's cowardly, but I've never had the courage to confront him about his affairs. I think I might have if they were with women, but ..." She fell silent for a moment, reflecting on her life perhaps, or where her life might now go. "That's why Emma did what she did," she murmured so quietly it was hard to make out what she said. "She's the only one I confided in. I guess I have at least one friend I can rely on."

I had empathy for her. Gail Decker's life was about to disintegrate just before she gave birth to her second child, a son that would grow up with his father in jail for murder.

I checked with Ashley to confirm there was nothing else he felt he needed to ask and terminated the interview. Mrs Decker was free to go, but I couldn't just turn her out onto the street. She would be delivered to her door where the officers sent with her would make sure she had Emma or a relative there for moral support.

That took seconds to arrange, but even being fast, I still found Ashley impatient to get going.

Chapter 18

Traffic was building, and had we been coming from Herne Bay we would have found ourselves snarled and stationary on the outskirts of town. As it was, the short journey from the nick to Harbour Street took twice as long as it should have and we arrived as all the shops were shutting for the day.

Ashley parked right in front of Capon's Butchers and Deli, leaving the car's hidden strobe lights flashing so there could be no question we had the right to stop on the double yellow lines. The squad car was in a narrow layby twenty yards back. I gave the guys inside a quick wave, making sure they knew we had seen them.

The sign in the door showed 'closed' to the world outside, but the steel shutter at the front was yet to be rolled down and we could see two members of staff still cleaning up inside.

Neither was John Decker.

Ashley rapped his knuckles on the glass and held up his warrant card.

The heads inside snapped up to tell us they were closed, but both men spotted the identification before a response could leave their mouths. They exchanged a glance, each questioning why the police might be at their door. The nearer of the two, a man in his late teens with acne around his chin, wiped his hands on his apron and hurried to let us in.

I saw him call over his shoulder to alert someone out of sight but couldn't hear what he said over the noise of a truck going by.

As the young man fiddled with the top and bottom deadbolts, a face peered around the wall shielding the back of the premises from sight, and I got my first look at John Decker. He saw Ashley framed in the doorway, shifted his eyes a touch to take me in, and said something to the kid still wrestling with the door.

"I'm doing it, ain't I?" the teenager complained, finally getting the door open.

John looked unconcerned to have two police officers demanding entry, but then the murder was three years ago, long enough for a person to convince themselves they have got away with it.

"Help you, gentlemen? Got a special on rump steak," he added, undoubtedly thinking he was funny.

Ashley showed him the warrant card again. "John Decker I am placing you under arrest for the crime of murdering Michelle Canet ..."

I watched our suspect while Ashley droned on, reciting his rights aloud. People react in different ways when they are caught and accept there is no escape. Some crumble, seeing instantly the mess their crimes will make of their hopes and dreams. Others are stunned, unable to fully process what is happening. Yet more know the game is up, but bolt, panic driving them to run even though they must know there is no hope they can evade justice for any meaningful length of time.

John Decker did none of those things.

He just looked confused when Ashley advanced with his cuffs. If I didn't know better, I would have said the accusation came as a total shock.

"Turn around and place your hands behind your back."

"But I didn't do it," John replied calmly.

I thought he might resist, refuse to obey Ashley's commands, but he rotated slowly to face the wall and allowed my partner to place the cuffs on him.

The duo of constables in uniform arrived at the door.

"All okay?" one asked.

"Looks that way."

Ashley wheeled John around, aiming him for the door, but stopped at that point to ask a question. "Do you have a tattoo on your left forearm?"

John twisted his head around, trying to look at Ashley who was almost directly behind him. The question confused him even further.

When Ashley gave a tilt of his head to indicate he should answer, John said, "Yes," with a shrug to show he didn't know what the question meant.

"What is the tattoo of?" Ashley's follow up question was the one I wanted an answer to. Revealing a Viking would provide a big change in our favour.

John looked about, his expression that of a man expecting someone to help him.

"The artwork," Ashley prompted. "What is it?"

"A fish."

I sucked in a deep and disappointed breath through my nose. We would, of course, check when we were at the station, but I doubted he would bother lying.

"You've got the wrong guy," John protested, once again saying it in the tone one might use when trying to explain something obvious to a very dense person.

We hadn't though, I was confident of that. Well, ninety percent confident. A niggling doubt itched away in my head, annoying me with its persistence. John lied about his movements that night, convinced his wife to lie so her story corroborated his, and he was almost certainly in a relationship with the victim while living a secret double life in denial of his own true sexual preferences.

That made him guilty of a lot of things, but so far as proving he killed Michelle Canet, we were a long way from home.

Regardless, he was being loaded into the squad car which was now parked behind Ashley's Mondeo. We had enough against him to jump straight into the interview. I would explain that his alibi no longer existed and push for him to confess. I honestly thought he would.

Was that optimistic?

My stomach rumbled, reminding me that lunch happened a long time ago. It served as a prompt to take out my phone. I needed to call Mary and let her know I would not be home for dinner. So much for discussing the video of her with Bruce Denton and what the implications might be for us.

There would be time for that later; I was going to have a late night, but I would sleep in my own bed and could talk to Mary when I got home.

Sliding into the passenger seat of the Mondeo so we could follow the squad car back to the nick, I wondered if we would get a chance to stop somewhere. I needed to grab a sandwich.

Chapter 19

MARVIN THE MARTIAN HAD gone home for the day by the time we got to his nick. I kept the thought to myself, but questioned if he might have chosen to duck out before we got back with John Decker. He acted and spoke as though he was glad to have someone back on the case, but it had to grate against him to have someone picking over an investigation he failed to solve. Even if it was an entire team and not just him.

That we had a suspect in custody on our first day would only rub salt into the wound.

While they processed John in the custody centre, Ashley and I locked ourselves away to discuss strategy.

"I think we should lead with his false alibi." Ashley paced across the room while I sat on one of the chairs. It wouldn't do for both of us to pace, and I had far less nervous energy than my young partner. "It will throw him off and ruin what defence he plans to mount."

I agreed. "We could follow up with questions about his relationship with the victim. He will think it is a secret, but we're going to have to be careful with that one."

We were going to have to be careful with all of it. We had no murder weapon. There were no eyewitnesses placing him at or near the scene of the murder. We couldn't yet prove he was in a relationship with Michelle Canet, and if we twisted what we knew too far, we risked giving ammunition to his legal team when the trial came.

All we really had was the sound knowledge he lied to disguise what time he got home. The case had moved fast. Too fast perhaps. Despite those negatives, no one would suggest we were wrong to make the arrest. Covering his tracks made him look guilty. We might only have circumstantial evidence, but he didn't know that and we had quite a bit of it.

A confession would effectively close the case and reduce the remaining legwork to making sure we had enough evidence to secure a conviction.

Our plan to look through the CCTV footage collected in 2020 had fallen by the wayside as we became more and more excited about the possibility of finding the killer with what felt like almost no effort. The CCTV cameras might have captured the man with the Viking tattoo making his way through Whitstable, but the attack on Oliver Humphries, unless it was somehow connected to Michelle's murder, was nothing to do with us and would go unsolved.

We talked around what we knew and how best to catch John in his lies. If he admitted staying on longer at the bar, if he confessed to having sex with the victim ... each small blow would strip away another piece of his armour.

An hour after returning to Whitstable nick, and with a tuna sandwich in my belly to help keep it quiet, I was more than ready when the knock finally came to let us know John was ready to be interviewed.

John Decker is a big man, which is to say he's six feet four inches tall with broad shoulders and thick limbs. He wasn't what I would class as fat or overweight, not that either of those terms are deemed acceptable anymore. Rather, he was just ... big. All over. He would make a great rugby prop forward or second row. Perhaps even the entire second row. For all I knew he had played rugby for many years in his youth.

But for all his size and the way he dwarfed the plastic chair in which he sat, he also looked shrunken and tiny, a shadowy reflection of the man I first saw looking at us across the butcher's shop.

I was first into the room, so I walked to the farthest chair, dropped a thick folder onto the table so it made a thump in the quiet room. Ashley came to my side, the pair of us refusing to speak and staring at the suspect the whole time.

He shrunk a little more under our collective gaze.

With confident, practiced ease, we pulled out our chairs and settled into them. We were back in the same room where a few short hours ago we interviewed his wife.

It was less than thirty seconds since we came through the door, but our prolonged silence – I'm told time stretches for suspects when the pressure is on – forced John into speaking just as I hoped it would.

"I need to call my wife. They let me make a call, but she didn't pick up. She's pregnant and close to her due date. She won't know where I am and will be worried sick that I haven't come home."

Calmly, I said, "Your wife knows where you are, John."

The statement stopped him dead in his tracks, metaphorically speaking. While his brain rallied to process the news, I carried on talking.

"She was sitting in that chair," I nodded my head to indicate where he sat, "just a couple of hours ago. We know you lied about what time you got home the night Michelle was killed, John. We know you convinced your wife to lie for you, and we know you like to cheat on your marriage vows with men, John."

He stared at me, his face haunted and his mouth closed.

"You were having an affair with Michelle Canet, were you not?" I couldn't state on record that we knew he was, not without getting ripped apart by the defence prosecution later, but by sounding confident when I posed the question, I suggested we had proof he didn't know about. Before he could respond, I added, "Your wife knows you have sex with men, John. I'm afraid she told us far more than you would have wanted her to."

John hung his head, saying nothing, but giving a nod which Ashley then described for the recording.

Fifteen minutes later we had a full confession. A full confession to everything but Michelle Canet's murder. John didn't bother to hide his affair with the Frenchman, admitting it had been going on for almost two weeks when Michelle was killed. He confessed to lying about what time he got home and admitted he and Michelle snuck out for a 'rendezvous' in a dark courtyard not far from the pub. However, he wanted us to believe he had no idea what time it happened, claiming to have put away too much beer to care what the clock said. He told us he returned to the pub to finish his drink and then tottered home a little worse for wear.

When we questioned him about Michelle's movements following their tryst, he claimed Michelle stayed in the courtyard so they would not be seen together. The Frenchman was supposed to follow a minute or so later.

John confirmed that he made his wife lie to the police and had been lying to himself about his sexuality for most of his life. He wasn't allowed to be gay, that was the problem. His family would never accept it, so it was buried, suppressed, hidden like a dirty little secret.

However, on the subject of Michelle's murder, he refused to cave. No matter which angle we came from, John strenuously denied harming the Frenchman or to having any idea who might have.

I pulled from the folder an eight by ten photograph of the picture taken from Oliver's phone.

I turned it around, so it was the right way up for John, and slid it under his nose.

"Do you recognise this tattoo?"

He leaned forward, his head bent over to scrutinise it. Doing so meant I couldn't see his face which made it all the harder to tell if he was lying when he answered.

"No, sorry. Should I?"

Answering with a question is an excellent technique when lying because your question isn't a lie and helps to hide that what came before might have been.

He looked up, his expression open and expectant from across the table.

We didn't have a confession, but that wasn't all that unusual. We could collect more evidence and now we knew what we were looking for, it would be all the easier to scan through the CCTV footage to spot our suspect. If he passed one of the many cameras located in that part of Whitstable's central business district, it would show time and direction or travel. Unless we were very unlucky, it would expose his lies.

All in all, I believed we had enough to charge him even without the confession. I was about to tell him exactly that when a knock came at the door. My eyes twitched in Ashley's direction just as he stood up.

I paused the interview.

Ashley went to the door, and peering to see who thought it was necessary to disturb us, announced the station's head man, DCI Tanner, was outside.

"Sir?" Ashley questioned. "Everything all right?"

He flared his eyes and motioned that we should both join him in the corridor.

Once the door was shut, he asked, "You're interviewing John Decker, right?" His upbeat attitude was absent, making me worry what news he might have for us. He grimaced. "Got bad news for you."

Oh, dear Lord.

Had Gail done something awful to herself? Had she downed a bucket load of pills and followed them with vodka?

My guess was a mile off and for that I was glad, but the news was awful, nevertheless.

Chapter 20

"THERE'S A NEW ALIBI?" I repeated what the DCI had just told us.

"The suspect's father-in-law just called the station. According to him, John came to his house on his way home. Richard Morris is house bound due to chronic ill-health, and he claims to be able to account for the time between John leaving the pub and arriving home."

I let my head fall back, my eyes staring to heaven. I didn't exactly want to be working this late into the evening, especially not this close to my retirement, especially not when it was going to prove to be for nothing, and very especially not when I needed to be left alone to figure out what to do about the camcorder footage of my wife with the man I subsequently murdered. It felt like I was being tested.

Ashley rallied almost instantly. "He's local?"

"Very. Lives down by the harbour about two minutes' walk from the Old Shipwright."

"Did you take the call yourself, sir?"

DCI Tanner shook his head. "No, but it was brought to my attention while the caller was still on the phone, and I knew you would need to hear it."

Ashley huffed out a breath. "This changes things."

I gave myself a shake both mentally and physically. "We need to put John back in his cell while we speak to his father-in-law." There really was no other choice. There was no way we could put it off until the morning.

"I have people who have just come on shift. They can step in to take a statement from Mr Morris."

It was tempting, but it had to be us, and I knew Ashley would go without me if I said I'd had enough for one day.

"If you're sure," the DCI checked we were really that committed.

"Can you arrange to have our suspect returned to his cell? That would be of enormous help."

DCI Tanner accepted my request, promising it would be done straight away. That left us free to visit John's father-in-law. I was tired and hungry, but I forced my brain to rally. Caffeine would help, but the stuff at the nick was terrible so I was going to swing by a fast-food place to grab a triple espresso and a pastry. It would be enough to revive me and keep me going because no matter what Richard Morris told us, we were going to have to come back to the Whitstable nick to either charge John Decker or let him go.

The sun was long gone by the time we got back outside. It was after seven and the rush hour traffic we fought on our way to and from arresting John had dwindled to almost nothing. Stopping at a coffee house and abusing our authority to avoid wasting time looking for a parking spot, I ran inside to get food and drink.

I still had sugar crumbs on my fingers and top lip when Ashley pulled up outside number fifteen Breakwater Terrace. Swallowing my last bite of donut without a shred of guilt despite Ashley selecting the turkey club wrap filled with lean proteins and veggies, I noted the ambulance parked outside the house next door. We were parked nose to nose with it.

The front door of number thirteen was open, the cool evening air invited in by the lack of barrier. Pings and twangs from the cooling engine told us the ambulance hadn't been parked there long, but it wasn't anything to do with us, so we ignored it and headed down the short path to the home of Richard Morris.

It was only at the point when Ashley knocked on the door that I questioned just how bad Mr Morris's condition was. He couldn't come to the nick because his condition, whatever it is, makes getting about too hard for him. He lived in a two-storey house, but then I supposed he might have a stairlift to make getting up and down easier.

A voice echoed out from behind the door, the faint call of Mr Morris assuring us he was coming. We had to wait another twenty or so seconds, which when it takes the average person a fraction of that to get to the door, felt like a long time.

The sound of a safety chain rattling and the lock turning heralded the door opening. It swung inward, controlled by the man inside. He didn't look terribly decrepit, an image I had prepared myself for. In fact, he didn't look to be much older than me. Closer to sixty than fifty-five perhaps, but still young to my way of thinking. Beneath the sweater he wore, his frame was yet to wither, but his hair line was receding and the hair he had was grey going to white.

In stark contrast to everything else I could see, he carried an oxygen bottle on a little trolley from which a clear plastic tube ran up his arm, around the back of his neck and under his nose where I guessed it fed pure oxygen into his lungs.

"Sorry about that," he wheezed. "Takes me a while to get anywhere these days."

Ashley said, "That's perfectly all right, Mr Morris," and introduced us both.

Mr Morris backed away from the door, welcoming us inside with hand motions.

"Asbestosis," he wheezed. "My own fault. Bought a mechanic's place when I left the army. They told me the roof needed to be replaced, but I got a quote, decided it was too much to pay, and worked in there with all the dust for the next ten years before I started to question why I was having trouble breathing. Not sure how many years I might have left, but that's not what you fellas are here for, now is it?"

He led us, very slowly, into his house. A narrow hallway passed a small room at the front of the house. Through the open door I could see a dining table piled high with books and crudely folded clothes. It didn't look like it got a lot of use.

Against the wall was a bicycle, the road type, not one designed for cross country. I guessed it was a relic of his old life.

The hallway joined a living room at the back of the house, not the front, as one found more commonly. The layout reminded me of my maternal grandparents whose house was very similar.

"Take a seat, take a seat," Mr Morris encouraged. "Offer you lads a cup of tea? Something stronger?"

"I'll make them," Ashley volunteered instantly. "Just show me which way to go."

Quite how Mr Morris proposed to carry hot beverages back from the kitchen dragging his trolley with one hand I could not guess, but it was moot now.

With a quiet, slightly embarrassed, "Thank you," to Ashley, John Decker's father-in-law folded awkwardly backwards into a wingback armchair facing the television and gave himself a moment to get his breathing under control.

I could only imagine what it must be like to live with such a restricted physical ability. Losing a limb would be nothing by comparison.

"It's just through there," Mr Morris wheezed, pointing with a jerk of his thumb.

I was closer, and placing a hand on Ashley's shoulder before he could start to move, I said, "I'll get them." I didn't hang around for him to argue.

Richard's voice carried after me, "There should be some biscuits in the cupboard above the kettle. Make sure to grab the good ones with chocolate on since I've got guests for once."

I found all the things I needed to brew up some tea and got to work. The plan had been to get in and out. Confirming what John Decker's father-in-law wanted us to believe should not take very long, but I couldn't help my desire to take it easy on him. Mostly because he wasn't old. Gone before his time, that's what they say, isn't it? How long did he have left? How bad was it to suffer like this, housebound because your lungs just won't allow you to go anywhere?

The kettle began to get noisy, drowning out the conversation from Richard's living room though I could hear Ashley trying to make small talk.

"You'll want to know why I never came forward before, of course," Richard said. Forced to strain my hearing, I stepped a little closer to the door.

"It's simple really," he continued. "I was going to volunteer the truth, but my daughter stepped in to give her husband an alibi and what kind of father would I be if I then exposed her lie? I guess I didn't see the harm in it. John wouldn't hurt a fly. That's why I let it go these last few years. The investigation died down, the story went out of the news, and I haven't thought about it since it happened. Until today."

"What happened today?" Ashley prompted.

"You arrested him. I mean, it was you, wasn't it? My Gail described two fellas who sound an awful lot like you gentlemen look. I mean no disrespect, but you have the wrong man, so when she called to let me know, I had to do the right thing."

I poured the kettle, disappointed that he couldn't have done the right thing three years ago. Okay, so we hadn't lost all that much time today. No more than a few hours, but we were back at square one again. His actions were understandable, commendable almost from the perspective of the father protecting the daughter. I might do the same for mine.

With the packet of chocolate biscuits tucked under one arm so I could handle all three mugs of steaming hot tea, I quickly discovered I hadn't positioned them correctly. The outer surface of one touched against a finger, melting the skin with its 'surface of the sun' heat.

I winced and hastened my feet, depositing the mugs onto a side table while uttering expletives in my head.

Ashley frowned at my expression.

"Hotter than I expected," I explained, getting a single raised eyebrow in response. I thought about sticking out my tongue and might have done so were we not questioning a key witness in the case.

Handing Mr Morris his tea and the biscuits, I asked, "What was John doing here on September 3rd?" I had a whole bunch of questions forming a line in my head, but believed most would not be necessary. The dying man was going to tell me the truth.

"John visits all the time. In fact, he rarely walks by without popping his head in. Not that my daughter is a stranger, but John works ... well, I'm sure you know where he works. My place is on his way home, so he stops by. He brings me meat from the butchers at least once a week, but the night in question he was just checking in on me."

We had to check the details, quizzing him (gently) on what time John arrived and when he subsequently left. What they talked about, what was playing on the television ... it all added up.

My phone vibrated and Ashley shot me a meaningful look. We were sitting at either end of a small sofa adjacent but also kind of opposite Richard's solitary armchair. I opened my mouth, about to question what message Ashley might be attempting to impart, when I saw him tap an index finger on his own phone.

He'd just sent me a message.

My attention on Mr Morris, I hadn't noticed my partner texting. I glanced down.

'Do we question him about his son-in-law's affairs?'

It was a good question to ask. Richard appeared to have no clue his son-in-law was gay or creating marital problems for his daughter. For the last fifteen minutes, he'd talked about the couple as though they were the most wonderful people on the planet.

The real question was whether it had any bearing on the alibi Richard provided. I was in the kitchen for some of the questions Ashley posed, and therefore had heard rather than seen Richard's responses, but could see no reason to doubt his claim that John was with him between nine and ten on the night in question. It sounded genuine. Disappointing though that was.

I gave an almost imperceptible shake of my head. It was not our job to burst his bubble. That might happen soon enough unless Gail had a change of heart, but I questioned whether the couple might both benefit from calling it a day and living true to themselves. Whatever, we were not going to tell Mr Morris.

"Everything all right, lads?" Richard asked. He'd picked up on our silent conversation.

Sliding my backside forward to the edge of the sofa, I said, "Yes. I think we are done here, Mr Morris. Thank you for your time. I'm sorry we had to interrupt your evening."

Chapter 21

WE LET OURSELVES OUT and shut the door, making sure it had locked. Mr Morris insisted on following us anyway, coming to the end of the hallway when he could have stayed in his chair. I got one last look at him struggling to breathe just before the door closed.

The ambulance was still in the street, parked nose to nose with Ashley's Mondeo, but behind it now was a county coroner's van.

One of the paramedics exited the house as we came away from Richard's door. He was a balding forty-something man with a potbelly. Following closely behind was a uniformed constable I recognised from Whitstable nick.

I guess she recognised us too because she dared a tight smile in Ashley's direction.

"Natural causes?" Ashley enquired casually.

She grimaced a little. She looked young and could not have graduated from the academy more than few months ago. I wondered if it was her first body.

"Yeah, natural causes they reckon. Bad case of emphysema. Smoked herself to death."

"Did someone find her?" I enquired, curious to know how the death came to be reported.

This time, the young constable shook her head. "No. She called for help. Managed to dial nine, nine, nine, but collapsed while she was on the phone. By the time the paramedics got here, it was too late."

A second constable, this one older and male, exited the house behind his colleague. He was talking into his radio, confirming they were also getting the task of delivering notice of death to the next of kin. It sounded like the woman's daughter lived just a few streets away, much like Richard Morris and Gail.

Ashley was already getting into the car, so I hurried to join him. It was late and though the snack from the coffeeshop had abated the worst of my hunger, all I wanted to do was get home for a proper meal. I couldn't do that though. Neither of us could. Before we did anything else, we needed to return to the nick and let John Decker go.

Technically, that wasn't true, we could pass the buck to the chaps on duty in the custody centre, but that's like making a mess and leaving someone else to clear up after you. It would be poor form and would win us no friends.

In the car, I asked, "What are you going to do after we release Mr Decker? I'm heading home. Today has been a rollercoaster."

Ashley pursed his lips, pulling a thoughtful face as he considered what reply to give.

"I'm going to hang around for a bit, check back over the case notes for Daniel Mahony. I don't know what to think about Michelle Canet anymore. Today was … well I thought we had it in the bag. I was ready to pop the champagne and celebrate."

I huffed out a hard breath. "Me too. A few hours ago I would have bet my pension John Decker was our man."

He wasn't though. Thinking back to Richard Morris, the new alibi who exonerated John Decker and ruined our hopes to wrap the case up swiftly, there was something that bothered me. Something that didn't sit right. I focused on it now, dredging through my brain to figure out what I might have missed.

His answers came across as honest, which isn't to say a person cannot fool me, it's just that most don't know how. I read their unconscious reactions, but a person who is conscious of them can alter how they move their eyes and regulate their breathing.

Did I think Richard had done that? Well, he was barely breathing anyway and rarely made eye contact, but despite those facts, I believed the statement he gave us. I thought some more, pushing my brain to deliver the answer and was none the wiser when Ashley pulled into a parking spot behind Whitstable nick.

With a grunt, I levered myself up and out of the seat. It was time to get it over with.

Chapter 22

ASHLEY FLIPPED A QUICK wave to Tony as he headed for his battered, old, blue Vauxhall Astra estate. John Decker was on his way home and they were back in Herne Bay at the end of what proved, in the end, to be a long and disappointing day. But the sun would rise in the morning and bring with it a new chance to solve an old case.

Just a single day of effort had gone into finding Michelle Canet's killer, and though they had suffered a setback and run into several dead ends, Ashley wasn't about to let their lack of progress stifle his enthusiasm. They still had CCTV footage to grind through, and it would be a grind, plus a host of other witnesses and suspects to question. Oliver Humphries stood as an example of what can change and why these old cases needed to be reopened.

He watched until the taillights on Tony's car vanished before heading into the station. Tony believed his partner was working late to read over the Daniel Mahony case again, but Ashley had already committed it all to memory. The salient details anyway. It wouldn't hurt to scrutinise it all again and getting Tony's eyes on it would help immensely, but Ashley had a different reason for hanging around Herne Bay nick when he ought to be heading home.

Bruce Denton.

The brutal murder of the secondary school teacher was a case just begging to be solved. Finding the killer would be a badge he could wear for the rest of his career. 'Chief Constable Long,' they would say, 'You know he's the one who solved the Bruce Denton murder thirty years after it happened.'

Snapping out of his daydream, Ashley made his way into Herne Bay Police Station. Ideally, Tony would work with him to find that which was missed three decades ago, but Ashley knew his partner wasn't going to willingly participate. In fact, despite saying he wanted to be involved when they officially reopened the case, Tony's body language said the absolute opposite.

It was as if ... Ashley paused for a moment, his feet coming to a stop. It was as if Tony didn't want the killer to be caught. Releasing a slow breath, Ashley questioned why he thought that. It couldn't be right; the man had dedicated his career to discovering the identity of the person who broke into Bruce Denton's house. He ruined his career failing to find the answer.

Dismissing the ridiculous notion, Ashley continued walking, heading up the stairs to the office where he had a temporary desk to work from. Not that he planned to sit at it.

There was one person at the Herne Bay nick who was around when Bruce Denton met his grisly end and that was Doris. Well into her eighties, the old bird was considered a cherished darling by all those who worked with her, so treading carefully was the order of the day.

Ashley had the case file for the murder, but there had to be information not in it and for that he wanted to quiz the individuals involved. Except for the superintendent who acted as senior investigating officer at the time, they were all still alive, though none were serving. They had all reached retirement age or had chosen different careers along the way.

Obviously Doris had gone home hours ago, but there was no way Ashley could talk to her about such a sensitive subject while she was at work. Tony would find them discussing his old case or someone would overhear them and choose to share the information with Tony. Ashley felt bad about hiding it from his partner, especially now they had found some common ground and were generally friendly toward each other, but he was going to do it anyway.

Because it needed to be done.

The open plan office that occupied most of the upper floor was empty, the screens black, and the desks abandoned for the day. Not that there were no cops working, but in a sleepy seaside town casework more commonly took place during the day when people were available to be questioned. If a crime occurred, duty personnel would deal with it and detectives would be summoned from their homes only if necessary.

Perching on the corner of Gavin Dobb's desk, the other detective sergeant working at the nick, Ashley used the landline phone on his desk. He didn't want the call to be listed on his mobile phone or on the landline going to the desk they gave him. The more secretive he was, the better it would be. Until he had something to share, that is.

He could only keep his investigation secret from Tony for a limited length of time. At some point, what he was doing would change from 'making a few discreet enquiries' to 'hiding what he was up to'. Ashley's plan was to figure out what he could and present it to Tony when he had something to go on.

Aware of the kinship developing between them, in many ways Ashley hoped to solve the case *for* Tony. A retirement present in the form of closure, and unless he refused, Ashley wanted Tony to be the one to make the arrest. Oh, he badly wanted to slap the cuffs on himself, but there would be no doubt whose fresh eyes had made the difference. Besides, Tony would be happily retired in a few weeks, leaving Ashley to bask in the glory.

The phone rang and rang at the other end, going on long enough for Ashley to question if Doris was in the bath or out for dinner. She was married still, he knew that much, but the ringing ended, replaced by the sound of someone fumbling the phone until a familiar voice filled his ear.

"Two, Two, Five, Seven, Four, Three."

The way she answered the phone teased a smile on Ashley's face. His grandmother answered the phone the same way, an echo of an earlier generation when a phone in every home was something new.

"Doris, this is DS Ashley Long, the one working with ..."

"Tony," she completed his sentence. "Everything okay?"

"Yes, yes, absolutely," he was overexuberant in his response and realised he was nervous. Would Doris tell Tony he called? It would be problematic if she did. Reeling himself in, he proceeded with caution. "I, ah, I wanted to ask you a few questions about Tony, actually. Or, in fact, more about the Bruce

Denton case. It's on our list to solve, but I worry about the impact it might have on him." This was mostly a lie; Ashley was convinced finding the killer would remove the weight hanging around Tony's neck and finally give him peace from the inner torment that clouded his life. He couldn't say that though, and he definitely couldn't open by asking the questions he really wanted answers to.

Doris sighed and Ashley imagined her tucked into the corner of a sofa, or perhaps in an armchair, her tiny frame dwarfed by a piece of furniture designed to hold a much bigger person.

"I wish I could tell you different, but that case near broke that poor man. It was all he could think about for years. I thought … well, I guess we all thought it was for the best when he finally let it go, and here it is back again. Is there any way you can avoid reopening it?" The tone of her voice betrayed that she already knew the answer.

"I'm afraid not, Doris. Not with the new video evidence. It would be remiss not to show that on the local news. Bruce deserves to have his killer caught, even if it makes life a little tougher for Tony."

"You're right. I know you're right. So what else did you call for, Ashley? It couldn't have been just to voice your concerns about your partner."

She was sharp as a pin.

"No, Doris. I was hoping you might be able to shed some light on who I would be best to speak with first. From the list of officers who worked the case, I mean." Ashley had the case file and knew it backwards and forwards, but there were people close to the case and then those who were directly involved. One might think the senior investigating officer would be the one to talk to, well that was moot in this case since Superintendent Smart died eight years ago, but it seemed he was a delegator, not a leader and had very little involvement in the investigative work until he needed a scapegoat. A role Tony filled very nicely at the time.

Thankfully, and as expected, Doris knew what Ashley was asking without the need for further explanation.

"You want to start with Vicky Meacock. She was Vicky Hopper back then, and a WPC because we still had Women Police Constables at that point in time. Political correctness wasn't a thing, but it can't have been much after that when they changed over."

Ashley knew Doris was wrong and that they dropped the W from WPC in 1990. He wasn't about to correct her though. With the phone trapped between jaw and shoulder, he made a note on his phone. Vicky Hopper was in the case notes, but he wouldn't have thought to talk to her had Doris not suggested it.

"Why her above the other DS working the case?"

"Bryan? Well, he and Tony never did see eye to eye. He had this daft theory that it could have been a police officer behind the murder. It was too clinical in his opinion, too carefully staged so there was no forensic evidence to be had. It made him very unpopular."

Ashley made another note. The suspicion wasn't in the case file, and it demanded he have a chat with former DS Bryan Hayworth the first chance he got.

"So you think I should track down Vicky Meacock? Anyone else?"

Doris made a, "Hmmm," noise as she pondered. "I guess I don't really know what else to tell you. I'm just the admin lady, but I do recall that Tony and Vicky worked together a lot. There were whispers about them going around the station. You know how people like to gossip."

"Was there anything to the gossip?" Ashley didn't know why he asked the question, only that it was automatic and could help to provide some background.

"No, I don't think so. Tony is a dedicated husband. More so than most, I would say."

That met with Ashley's limited knowledge of his partner's marriage. He quizzed Doris just a little longer and ended by stressing his desire to keep their conversation off Tony's radar. Thankfully, she agreed it might be for the best.

For good measure, though it made him feel guilty, he wiped his fingerprints off the phone's handset when he returned it to the cradle. Back at his desk, he took out his laptop and moments later had an address for former Constable Vicky Hopper. Maybe she would know something and maybe she wouldn't, but he was going to find out.

Chapter 23

"Is that you, Tony?" Mary's voice echoed through the house.

I rolled my eyes. "Who else are you expecting?"

Mary appeared in the hallway where I had shucked my shoes and was in the process of donning my slippers.

"Well, a woman can hope," she teased. She came to me, wiping her hands on a tea towel which she then draped over her right shoulder. Mary met me at the door, wrapped her arms around my neck and kissed me on the lips. A kiss when I got home had been our practice throughout our entire marriage with a few minor exceptions. The same exceptions I'm sure every marriage suffers. "How was your day?"

I sagged a little in her embrace. "Terrifying. Disappointing. Frustrating. And terrifying."

"You said terrifying twice, dear."

"That's because it deserved double billing."

Her face inches from mine as we stared into each other's eyes, I was perfectly positioned to see the tears form just as her bottom lip began to wobble.

"Are we in trouble?" she begged to know, her voice threatening to crack. "Do they know?"

I held her tight, pulling her head onto my shoulder. "If they knew, I would already be in cuffs, my love. They don't know anything more today than they did yesterday."

She pulled her head back, leaning away from me so she could see my face. "But what about the video? You said it showed me."

"It does, my darling, but only from the rear. One of my most favourite views." That one got me a slap on the arm, but we were both tense and a little humour was called for. Being serious again, I said, "There is sunlight on the windscreen when the car approaches and thereafter we only see you from behind. They are working on cleaning it up to improve the quality, and there is a small chance they might find a shot of your face when the windscreen is in shadow, but that occurs way down the road, and I don't think we need to worry too much about it." I was lying, but there was nothing to be gained by making Mary worry the same way I was.

"So what happens now? Will they show it on the news like you said?"

"Almost certainly." I wanted to tell her it was all going to be okay, but I didn't know that it was and though it was selfish, it felt good to not be the only person worrying about what might happen in the coming days. Even so, I did my best to ease her concerns. "But like I said, the quality isn't great."

She let her arms fall away. "I'm going to burn dinner." She said it in an absentminded manner, like we had just been discussing what to add to the shopping list. By the time I fetched my bag from where I dropped it by the front door, she was bustling back to the kitchen.

I found her there, stirring what smelled like a beef stew. There was a nearly empty glass of white wine on the counter within easy reaching distance of her left hand. Mary doesn't drink much, and never alone. I took it as another sign of how much stress she currently felt.

I had to get hold of the video footage and all the copies that must exist. It was in the system, which meant it was electronic and would be filed somewhere. I just had to access the files. Destroying those versions didn't sound difficult, but then I knew first hand how clever the forensic guys were at retrieving erased files from seemingly dead computers.

Putting that to one side with a mental note to look up how to delete files in a way that made sure they were gone forever, I thought about the videotape itself. I didn't need to do anything about the camcorder, that is just a device, and the tape? Well, I could just record over the top of it, surely. The way we all used to back in the day. The number of times I 'accidentally' taped over the top of Mary's soap operas or women's dramas was too many to count.

We ate dinner while studiously ignoring the elephant in the room, but what else was there to say on the matter? I wouldn't share with her my plan to make the video evidence go away; it would only make her worry. Nor did I point out that if it all went wrong, the only one in trouble would be me.

That wasn't going to happen though.

To my surprise, when the plates were in the dishwasher, Mary took my hand and led me upstairs. Not that our sex life is dead. I just hadn't expected it and it's usually me who instigates it. My plan had been to return to the station, but sleep found me within moments of finishing and drifting blissfully into slumber I told myself I could rise early the next day. There would be next to no one at the nick if I got there early enough, so I could poke around and figure out what I needed to do then.

After all, I had two days.

Chapter 24

Ashley sat in his car, furiously debating whether to drive back to Herne Bay or not. There was no desperate time imperative driving him to make the journey, but his brain was on fire with the possibility of what he might discover.

Former PC Vicky Meacock, nee Hopper, knew more about the case than he could have imagined. The way she spoke about it made it sound like it all happened last week, not thirty years ago. Disturbingly, her notebook, a copper's trusty companion, and the information it contained, wasn't in the case file. It was as though a chunk of the investigation was missing. Or ignored. Or redacted. How could Tony have believed he would solve the case if pertinent facts were missing?

Were it not for his visit, the information would be lost forever. However, clever Vicky kept copies of her old notes from all the notebooks she filled over the years and they were stored in a box in her attic.

It took some finding, Ashley standing at the top of the ladder while she apologised and searched through her belongings, but find it she did. She was a police officer for just less than five years before marrying and having kids. It was the kids that ended her career, not the marriage, but she made it clear she had no regrets about her decision to leave.

"It was a very male environment," she had told him. "Basically, the recruiters lied to get the girls to join. They came to our school and recruited us right out of the sixth form. They made it sound glamourous, and it was anything but."

This was not the first time Ashley had heard similar tales, and it pained him that misogynistic behaviour still hadn't been completely eradicated.

They brought the box down out of the attic and into her dining room where she set it on the table. Her husband was away on business and her kids had all grown and left home. But even with less than five years of service and no distractions from kids needing mum's attention, it still took her a while to find the right set of notes.

"I don't know why I still have these," she'd admitted, laughing at herself. "Or even why I kept them in the first place, except because it was something my dad told me to do. He was a copper for thirty-seven years and I remember him copying out his notes each week. He said it was good to have your own record."

They were his notes now, tucked into the front pouch of his bag to be read through later. She had neat handwriting, a trait he often found with women when compared to their male counterparts, so deciphering her words would not present a fresh challenge.

The notebook, though, was of almost no interest. Not because it would contain nothing relevant, but because she told him of a greater prize. If she was to be believed, Tony had his own file. His own personal notes accumulated over the years of investigation conducted after the case was closed. It made perfect sense that such a thing would exist, it just hadn't occurred to him until Vicky said it.

She even knew where Tony kept it.

Vicky and Tony remained friends after she left the police, she said. He was one of the good ones who she never caught looking at her chest or making lewd comments about his truncheon. She liked his wife too, and they had daughters in the same class at school. They were born just a few weeks apart.

That was all just background information, but their friendship, and Tony's dogged pursuit of new information that might lead to the arrest of Bruce's killer, meant he came back to her year after year, even after their kids had graduated and they had stopped seeing each other socially.

If he wanted to see what was in Tony's file on Bruce Denton, it was locked in the bottom drawer of his desk in the Herne Bay nick. If Ashley asked for it, Tony would question how he even knew it existed which would instantly lead to him discovering his partner was poking his nose where Tony didn't want it.

Perhaps he would turn it over, but Ashley's gut told him the opposite would prove true. Tony would either deny its existence and make it vanish or promise to hand it over only to do so once it was sanitised of whatever information he didn't want Ashley to see.

Once again, Ashley questioned why he thought that. Still sitting in his car just along the road from Vicky's house, he could not deny the feeling that something was ... off. Why would Tony want to hide anything? Did he even want to hide anything, or was that just a barmy idea choosing to lodge itself in Ashley's brain? He didn't know the answer.

The clock on his dashboard claimed it was quarter to ten. He was twenty minutes from his house and his fiancée was probably already in bed. When a yawn split his face, he made the only sensible decision and aimed his car for home.

He would rise extra early the next day and get into the Herne Bay nick before anyone else. Tony's drawers would be locked, but the key was bound to be hidden about his desk somewhere. He could take a look at the file and no one would ever know.

Chapter 25

JOHN DECKER COULDN'T SLEEP. He wasn't welcome at home; Gail had finally snapped, but that wasn't what was keeping him awake.

It was the tattoo.

He knew who it belonged to.

Worse yet, the man with the Viking tattoo was waiting for him when he got out of the nick. Threats ensued, ones that John knew could be enacted swiftly and harshly.

It didn't mean the man with the tattoo was Michelle Canet's killer, but John now felt certain that was the case. It made him a target, and fearing for his own life, he blurted that the police knew about the tattoo. They had a photograph. It was blurry, but at the same time it was like a fingerprint — unique and damning when connected to the owner.

He didn't know if they were pursuing it as a line of enquiry, but they would have to, wouldn't they?

The man with the tattoo certainly thought so, and when he produced his knife, John spat the name of the man who took the picture without hesitation.

Now the memory haunted his mind, keeping slumber at bay.

Chapter 26

I AWOKE LATER THAN intended the following morning despite setting an alarm. Forcing my face away from my pillow, I squinted at the clock on Mary's side to find it telling me I was already too late to get into the nick early.

Snatching up my phone with an accusatory glare, I discovered why the alarm failed to sound – it was dead as a post. My ritual sees me charge my phone when I get in from work, but distracted by the Bruce Denton discussion and then Mary's ample bosom, the battery got neglected.

Cursing quietly, I levered myself carefully and slowly upright so as not to disturb my wife only to find her side of the bed was empty. She was downstairs already, and now that I was moving, I could smell coffee and bacon.

My stomach growled like a lion protecting a particularly juicy steak sandwich. My wife cooks well, which is half the reason my waist is twice the size it used to be. It has absolutely nothing to do with my penchant for alcohol, you understand.

Hunger cut my shower time to less than two minutes, just long enough to wash away the grime of the previous day – something I should have done before falling asleep. I tamed my hair while it was still damp, threw on a fresh suit, and hurried down to the kitchen to find Mary laying on a full English.

"You'll do well to have a full stomach," she remarked, heaping sausages onto a plate already laden with bacon, mushrooms, beans, eggs, black pudding, toast, and two halves of a fried t omato.

I felt like protesting the quantity would put me into a coma, and breathed a sigh of relief when she placed the plate in the middle of the table so we could both help ourselves from it.

A short while later, my stomach suitably full and my bag containing a packed lunch that would see me through until dinnertime, I drove my old jalopy to work. How many times had I driven the same route over the course of my life? What would it feel like to never need to do it again?

The answer to the last one came down to whether I could bury the Bruce Denton case again. Fail to do that and missing the drive to work would be the least of my worries.

Pulling into one of the last spots behind the nick in Herne Bay, I had to check the clock and rub my eyes to check what I was seeing. Ashley was just getting out of his car. My youthful partner exuded keenness, and this was the latest I had known him to arrive. More commonly, he was in work before I got out of bed. He saw me gawping through my window and stopped to wait for me.

Grinning like an idiot on purpose, I rolled down my window. "I knew you would learn something from me."

Ashley gave me the finger. "Tanya wanted to stay in bed this morning, if you must know."

I wasn't the only one who got lucky then, but whereas my bedtime adventures had put a spring in my step, his expression suggested the opposite, which I could not understand. His fiancée guards the lock screen of his phone, and she possessed the figure of an underwear model. I would not be complaining about getting stuck in bed with her.

I parked nose-in two spaces down from his car and clambered out. At least I started to, but stopped when Ashley got in.

Probably looking as confused as I felt, I questioned what I might have missed.

"Um, what's happening?"

Ashley twisted to his right to place his bag on my backseat and then to his left to fetch the seat belt from above his shoulder.

"I thought we would take your car for a change."

"You don't want to get a coffee and ease into the day? You don't want to check how they got on scrubbing up the video of the blonde woman?" I sure did. "You don't want to review the evidence and discuss strategy before we set off to quiz ... where are we even going?" I realised I had no idea who was next on the list when it came to the Michelle Canet case. Surely our next task was to go through the CCTV footage to see if we could spot the Viking tattoo.

"Tankerton."

I mouthed the name.

"That's where Elroy Stewart lives. I hoped you might be amenable to switching targets today, spread our chances, if you like."

I couldn't stop my frown forming. "What about Michelle Canet?"

Ashley scratched his skull. "He's not going anywhere. I mean, we have to come back to him, but what we need more than anything is to close another case."

He meant it was what he needed. It would be fun for me, I loved the investigative work and always had, but my career was at its end. I would benefit not one bit from closing more of the task force's cold cases.

"We would be better off sticking with a case that is fresh in our heads."

"I thought we had Michelle's killer yesterday," Ashley lamented. "But we didn't, and other than the Viking tattoo, we have nothing to lead us forward. Unless you really want to argue, I suggest we give ourselves a break from it and focus on Daniel Mahony's murder instead."

I opened my mouth because I really did want to argue. Tackling two cases at the same time was stupid, but then I saw the opportunity it presented. Truthfully, I didn't care what case we pursued so long as it wasn't Bruce Denton. Put like that, delving into Daniel Mahony's death was a gift. I closed my door and put my key back into the ignition.

Chapter 27

Tankerton, it turned out, was not our destination at all. I had very little knowledge of the case, a point I wanted to make, and might have were it not for the risk Ashley would suggest Bruce Denton instead. Instead, I listened while Ashley filled me in on the salient points.

Daniel Mahony was killed in a hit and run, but there was no chance it was a terrible accident for the driver stopped his car, backed up to run him over again, used an iron bar to finish the job, and for a final flourish carved a swastika into his chest.

There were several suspects, but none who fitted the bill better than Elroy Stewart, the grandson of the man Mahony went to jail for assaulting. Reflecting John Decker and the Michelle Canet case in some ways, Elroy escaped prosecution because alibis came forward to place him elsewhere.

Then there was the photograph. According to Ashley, the picture failed to show Elroy's face, and he was identified by his clothing. That was tenuous, to say the least, but until someone could prove it wasn't him and that his alibis were lying, prosecution was unlikely.

On the other side of things, two witnesses gave statements describing a black man driving a silver BMW at speed away from the street where Mahony died. The car was never found, but forensic analysis of tyre patterns and wheelbase confirmed it was the same model used in the murder. The descriptions the witnesses gave matched Elroy, but both were withdrawn less than seventy-two hours after they were given.

On the face of it, there seemed little doubt Elroy Stewart was the culprit, but the case got dropped due to lack of evidence, and it was almost twenty years old now. In the wake of the murder, Elroy had gone from strength to strength, adopting violent tactics to establish himself as a major player in the southeast criminal underworld. I guess getting away with murder provides a certain level of kudos along with the confidence to do it again. Or at least threaten to do so.

"You have a plan of attack," I guessed. Knowing Ashley, he knew who he wanted to speak to in what order and where they would be at a specific time of the day.

"Yup."

There were lots of empty spaces in the Henwick Estates Vineyard and Distillery carpark on the outskirts of Canterbury at this time of the day. Helen Hoath-Salter worked there as a sommelier – a wine expert. Twenty years ago, she was Elroy's girlfriend; a gulf of difference from where she found herself now.

We asked for her at reception where a man in his forties, wearing a tweed suit and bright blue glasses, spoke with a posh accent. He wore his light brown hair cut short at the sides and not much longer on top, possibly as a deliberate tactic to hide the grey just starting to show through.

"I shall see if she is available," he advised, tapping a button on his console. We got to hear his half of the conversation, which was brief, and ended with, "She'll be right out."

Helen's interpretation of 'right out' proved to be a tad different to mine, but the ten or so minutes we waited gave me time to quiz Ashley about what was next if we solved this case. I already knew he was going to say 'Bruce Denton' and had a speech planned.

"You want closure rate more than anything, right?"

We were sitting opposite each other on two plush leather sofas set either side of a fancy chrome and glass coffee table. The receptionist had offered to make us drinks, but we both declined.

It doesn't help to have a full bladder when you want to look imposing.

"You mean, do I want to crush the other five guys assigned to the task force? Yes. That is my aim. And now you are going to reiterate how the Bruce Denton case cannot be solved and that I will waste my time and yours by dedicating effort to it."

I shrugged. "Yes."

"Well, they are going to reopen it anyway, Tony. The camcorder footage dictates that they must. I know how painful it must be for you, but you must still want to find the killer."

"Of course I do," I lied.

"You know, someone might come forward to identify the blonde woman. Maybe she will come forward herself." He was reiterating a point already well made.

I nodded thoughtfully as though I was agreeing. "She might." There was no chance she would.

"Then we both know the case is begging to be solved. We could be on the cusp of the greatest take in recent history."

I studied Ashley's face and noticing that I was doing so, he looked away, twisting in his seat to feign impatience as he looked back at the reception desk.

"Where is she?" he questioned.

I ran my tongue over the inside of my teeth, a habit I fall into when I am nervous. Ashley had just displayed classic diversion technique to hide his facial cues. When he talked about being on the cusp of a great take, he held something back. A question maybe, or ... I wasn't sure, and I didn't get to analyse it any further because a door behind the reception area opened and an elegant woman in a dress with heels and a fitted jacket click, click, clicked across the marble floor.

She stopped at the reception desk, leaning down to murmur something to the man there while never taking her eyes off us.

Just as we started moving toward her, she straightened, fixed herself with a broad, professional smile, and closed the distance, extending her right arm as she came.

"Gentlemen, good morning. I believe you are looking for me." Helen was tall and attractive with flowing jet-black hair, tanned, olive skin, and Mediterranean features.

"Helen Hoath-Salter?" Ashley enquired.

She confirmed we had the right person and led us back through the door behind reception saying, "There is a room back here where we can talk. Did Francis offer you refreshments?"

I guessed Francis was the receptionist, and said, "Yes, thank you, but we are fine for now."

"Well, there is water on the table, but let me know if you would like anything else. I will have someone bring it."

Her decision not to ask us what we wanted or why we were at her place of business asking for an audience surprised me – that is the first question everyone asks, so I stayed quiet, wondering if she somehow already knew or was simply one of life's patient people.

It turned out to be the latter. She closed the door behind us and aimed a delicate hand at the row of seats. We were in a small meeting room with enough space for eight chairs around an oval table. A projector hung from the ceiling aimed at the wall farthest from the door. Whiteboards, all wiped clean, dominated one wall.

When she was pulling out her chair, she finally asked, "Can I ask to what your visit is pertaining?"

I deferred to Ashley.

"Elroy Stewart and the murder of Daniel Mahony."

One did not need to be well practiced in reading facial cues to see shock grip Helen's face. Whatever she was expecting, this wasn't it. Her backside had only just settled into her chair, but she was already getting up.

"I'm sorry, but that is not a subject I am willing to discuss. I gave my statement many years ago, and it still stands."

She was halfway to the door already and about to throw us out when I barked, "Sit down." There was enough force behind the words to shock her into stopping. When she looked my way, surprise etched on her face, I said, "The case has been reopened, Helen."

The statement caused a flush of panic that showed in her eyes, her hands, the pulse in her neck and the pigmentation in her cheeks, throat, and lower neck area.

Ashley indicated her chair. "Won't you please sit, Helen?"

I don't think I have ever played 'good cop bad cop' but unexpectedly that was what it felt like. Ashley's voice was a soft hug compared to the only time she heard me speak, so I went with it.

"You are not going to have a lot of choice about whether you speak to us or not, Helen. You can do it here or we can take you back to the station where you will be interviewed under caution." I was already debating whether that might be better.

She looked me dead in the face and said with absolute confidence, "It doesn't matter what you say or how you threaten me, I am not going to change the statement I gave twenty years ago."

Ashley asked, "Why is that?"

It was a good question and I expected her to defend herself by saying something like, 'Because it is true," but she didn't.

Instead, she said, "Because I can't." It was an honest answer she needed no time to formulate but her face showed me why - she was terrified.

Gently, Ashley teased, "Why is that, Helen?"

She sagged a little, her confidence waning. "Please. You can't protect me even if you think you can."

Ashley was right! Again! The little show off. After Oliver Humphries he'd picked a second winner in two days. Helen might not want to give up the goods, but it was already clear she had information we wanted to hear.

His soothing voice guiding her toward the truth, Ashley said, "What really happened twenty years ago, Helen? Elroy wasn't with you, was he?"

"Did you not hear me?" She grabbed both sides of her head, clutching it in her desperation. "Elroy is not the kind of person you cross. I am sticking to the statement I gave twenty years ago."

"Which was false," I remarked. When she lifted her eyes to challenge me, I added, "Wasn't it?"

I could see she wanted to lie, to claim she was telling the truth before. She didn't though, caught between the horror of her past and the desire to be the person she now was.

I made my voice soft like Ashley's. "Life has changed for you, Helen, but there is no avoiding the maelstrom coming your way. All we need from you is a statement withdrawing your alibi." My heart rate had increased, the excitement getting the better of me.

She wouldn't meet our eyes and her voice dropped to little more than a whisper when she said, "You think you can keep me safe, but you can't."

"Helen, there are officers dedicated to doing precisely that. Once Elroy is behind bars ..."

"His lieutenants will still be on the outside!" She spat her reply, fear fuelling her anger. "If I withdraw or change my statement, I am as good as dead. If you don't know that, then you have no idea who you are dealing with."

Ashley touched a hand to the sleeve of my jacket to let me know he was going to take over. He came at the problem from a different angle.

"Helen, when did you last see Elroy?"

She reached across the table to get a jug of water. It shook when she poured some into a glass.

"I don't know. Maybe five years. We broke up not long after the enquiry into Daniel Mahony or, at least, I tried to end things and he wouldn't let me."

"What happened?" Ashley was getting her to talk.

She needed both hands to hold her glass of water and still slopped some when she drained it.

"He said I was insulting him. He's the kind of man who thinks all women should want to be with him. Anyone who turns him down must therefore be doing so just to make him angry, and he is very good at being angry. I was just a kid when we got together, too stupid and rebellious to listen to anyone. When I realised what he was capable of, I tried to walk away. He kept coming after me. He beat up my brother and threatened to cut up my sister. I had to get fat to escape him."

"You got fat?" The question left my mouth before I had a chance to engage my brain. Helen Hoath-Salter didn't fall into the fat category. At all.

Mercifully, she did not take my blurted enquiry as an insult to all women.

"Yes," she nodded. "I ate everything I could. He hit me and told me I needed to lose what I had gained, but I knew it was working, so I ate even more. He lost interest and when I no longer looked like someone he wanted to be with, he replaced me with a new girl. That's how I got out. The point is ..." she made eye contact first with me and then with Ashley, "that I got out, and I am never going anywhere near that world again. Nothing you can threaten me with will change my mind. I will stick to the story I gave, and you will have to prove I was lying."

Chapter 28

We left the Henwick Vineyard ten minutes later. Helen lied in her statement twenty years ago; she admitted as much even if she didn't say the words. But what did that get us?

Not a whole lot.

Elroy Stewart murdered Daniel Mahony and was astute enough to fabricate a web of lies to cover his movements on the night it happened. Believing that to be true got us nowhere until someone cracked and gave him up, it was down to us to find a way to catch him out.

The A290 took us back in the general direction of Whitstable where Ashley hoped to speak with Bobby Lamson, another key witness placing Elroy at home when Daniel Mahony was murdered. He supplied the photograph that supposedly showed Elroy in the street leaning against his car. A much younger version of Helen could be seen sitting in the passenger's seat, but Ashley was right that the picture failed to show the suspect's face. We were supposed to believe it because the other people around him all said it was Elroy.

"He's wearing Elroy's clothes," Ashley confirmed. "There are other photographs with him in the same outfit, but two of his gang, friends, fellow scumbags … whatever you want to call them, are not shown in the picture and their whereabouts is questionable.

"You think maybe they did it on his behalf?"

Ashley was quick to shake his head. "No, I think this was personal. Mahony put a beating on his grandfather and Elroy was out for blood. I wouldn't rule out that he had someone in the car with him though. That leaves just one of his group absent and I believe that is the person wearing Elroy's clothes.

"What about the witnesses who reported a man matching his description fleeing the scene in a silver BMW? We need to interview them." I didn't bother to point out how likely it was they changed their statements out of fear.

Ashley already had their names and addresses, confirming they were on the list for today. He was a slick operator, possibly the best I had ever worked with. Not that I was about to tell him that. You might think that with all my years of seniority, I would dictate the pace and direction of the investigation more than I do, which is hardly at all, but other than an occasional gripe, I was content to let him lead. It allowed me to do almost nothing at all when it came to planning. Most cops would take their work home, especially when they had a big case to solve, and I had no desire to do that.

Ashley's fervent determination made it possible for me to cruise along in neutral and I told myself he was the apprentice learning from the master and therefore ought to be the one doing all the donkey work. I would step in and correct him when it was necessary. Like any good master.

The one thing I was glad for with the workload and Ashley's indefatigable need to be the best and the brightest was that it was keeping him too busy to think about Bruce Denton. The subject hadn't raised its ugly head in hours.

On paper, Bobby Lamson had no job, but he had a fancy car and that alone was a key indicator that he worked as a low-level criminal. The pristine, hand waxed black Mercedes with windows tinted too dark to be legal, sat outside a house registered in his grandmother's name.

He lost his mother to cancer when he was six and was raised by his grandmother and aunt in the less well-to-do South Street suburb of Whitstable. Growing up with nothing in his pockets undoubtedly aided his desire for more by any means, and he went to school with Elroy Stewart, their association starting early.

Ashley knocked and we waited a few seconds until the door was opened by an elderly black woman. Her hair was silver, she was wide at the hips, and her face bore a disgruntled look.

Ashley held up his warrant card, but she shot him down before he could start to talk.

"I know what you are. I could smell you before you got out of the car," she sneered unpleasantly. "Why can't you just leave him alone? He's done nothing wrong."

I sincerely doubted she believed that.

Cutting to the chase, Ashley asked, "Can you tell us where he is, please?"

I thought she would spit in his face and slam the door, but I guess she either did believe her grandson was a good boy innocent of all the crimes the evil, local police tried to pin on him, or she would simply rather we speak to him elsewhere and not return to her home because she gave us a location without missing a beat.

"In the betting shop on Belmont Road." She gripped the edge of the door and was already trying to close it when Ashley stopped it with his foot.

"And if he is not there?"

"Then I don't know, do I?" she growled, lending additional weight to the door.

Ashley removed his foot and it slammed hard enough to rattle the frame.

"She's nice," I remarked flippantly. "A real people person."

Ashley spared no effort responding, opting instead to get back in my car. I slid behind the steering wheel and fired the old rust bucket into life.

I knew which betting shop we were talking about and could remember when it was a greengrocer in my youth. Local shops like greengrocers, bakers, butchers, and more had all but vanished from rural settings where they abounded until the early 80's. The rise of giant supermarkets killed them off, but very few of the premises were converted back into houses. Most simply became something else.

Through the betting shop windows, adorned with advice on how much could be won by correctly guessing who would score first or which horse might romp home, we could see only one person inside. I parked on the opposite side of the street outside a chip shop.

At twenty past eleven on a Wednesday morning, I couldn't help question if there were not perhaps better things to do with one's time. But then, I'm not a poorly educated criminal delinquent and perhaps I am the one living my life the wrong way.

Bobby had his back to us, his attention on a big screen set above the counter. It showed statistics of some kind. An electronic bell pinged when Ashley stepped over the threshold, but Bobby didn't turn his head to see who was there. Broad across the shoulders with a bloated round belly, Bobby's skinny arms spoke of a man who put no care or attention into his appearance or general health. His hair was shaved close to his skull and tucked into a Hoodrich ballcap that matched his Hoodrich tracksuit. I was familiar with the brand and the subset of people who could be expected to wear it.

Not until we got within a few feet did he glance over one shoulder. The glance became a double take when his brain told him what his eyes had just seen.

He swore, his voice a deep growl and he turned to face us.

"What?" he snarled a challenge.

Ashley showed his warrant card even though it was clear Bobby knew what we were.

"Bobby Lamson?"

"What if I am?"

"We need to speak with you about the murder of Daniel Mahony." We were within our rights to take him back to the nick where we could question him in a more intimidating environment, but I would guess he'd been questioned by the police dozens of times in his life and taking him anywhere would slow down our day.

"Got nothing to say."

Acting as though Bobby hadn't spoken, Ashley said, "Specifically, we need to ask you about your activities on the night of June 12th, 2003, between eight and ten that evening."

"You deaf or something? I've got nothing to say."

"Your statement given shortly after Daniel Mahony was run down, reversed over, beaten to death with an iron bar, and mutilated, claimed you were never closer than a mile from the location where the incident occurred."

A leering grin lifted Bobby's mouth. "That's right. I was nowhere near it, and neither was anyone else."

Ashley raised an eyebrow and made a note. "No one else? Specifically, who are you referring to when you say no one?"

The grin fell. He had nothing to say, but was talking anyway, such was the effect of Ashley's calm approach. I was watching Bobby closely, reading his reactions.

Remembering his mantra, Bobby repeated a familiar sentence. "I've got nothing to say."

Ashley's eyes turned cold. "Oh, I think you do, Bobby, and you are going to answer my questions here or in an interview room. It's your choice whether you go back to placing bets or spend most of the rest of the day being processed in and out of the local nick."

We were not about to arrest him and had no grounds to do so. Not yet at least. But technically Ashley had never suggested he would, even if his choice of words made it sound like a possibility.

That was how Bobby took it too, and I could see him weighing up his options.

Pressing on so he would have no time to think, Ashley repeated his previous question, "Specifically who are you referring to, Bobby? Who was nowhere near the scene of Daniel Mahony's murder?" The demand for a response was delivered with an increase in volume that added pressure.

Bobby's eyes flitted from Ashley's to mine, away from us both to check outside as though hoping to see someone he knew coming to his rescue, and back to Ashley.

"All the people you lot accused," he managed to stutter. "None of us were anywhere near where it happened."

"What about Elroy Stewart? Where was he between eight and ten that night?"

"With me." Bobby's confidence returned, the question placing him back on firmer ground. "We were hanging out by his house. Me, Elroy, his girl, Helen, Pacey, Gerry, Markus … A whole gang of us. This was all confirmed by the pigs at the time. We even had a picture that proved where we were."

Bobby was lying, and Ashley continued to push.

"Tell me, Bobby, how it is that Elroy was seen by not one but two witnesses? They placed him in the immediate vicinity of the murder at the wheel of a silver BMW which was confirmed to be the car that ran Daniel Mahony down."

Once again, Bobby's confidence waned. Twenty years ago, the group likely had their story straight, but time had passed, and Mr Lamson hadn't needed to think about his lies in many years.

"I … No, that's not." He stuttered and started before finding an answer. "They didn't see him, that's how." He showed us a triumphant sneer. "They withdrew their statements because they never saw Elroy. They couldn't have because he was with me and the others."

I stepped forward. "Hello, Mr Lamson. My name is Detective Sergeant Heaton. I'm something of an expert in the field of lie detection and it is easy for me to know when someone as dumb as you is churning out a pack of utter rhubarb." I emphasised my thoughts with an amused lilt intended to belittle his attempts to hide the truth.

His face froze, and just like Ashley, I ploughed onward before his feeble brain could concoct a response.

"Elroy Stewart is not in that photograph, is he, Bobby?" The idea occurred only when I opened my mouth. I had been about to say something else, but like a gift from above, I saw the possibility and went with it.

Bobby's eyes flared wide, and his cheeks flushed. "Yeah, he is, man. You can see him clear as day."

"No, actually, you cannot. There is a person wearing his clothes though. That's how you did it, isn't it, Bobby?" Goodness, I felt as though I had him on the ropes already and now I really wished we had taken him to the station for questioning. "You staged the photograph so it would look like Elroy was there, but he was in a stolen silver BMW which he used to kill Daniel Mahony. That's right, isn't it?"

"Nah, man," Bobby weakly tried to argue. "Nah, that's not what happened at all. He was right there with us the whole time."

With a jubilant twinkle in my eyes, I leaned in to say, "No, he wasn't, Bobby. Did you already forget that I am an expert in reading people? All you have done is lie to us. Tell me, who was in the car with Elroy."

This was a fifty – fifty guess. If Elroy was alone, which the withdrawn witness statements suggested he was, my question would place Bobby back on firm ground where he could give an honest answer. That would help me though as it would act as a contrast to all the lies to confirm how his eyes, breathing et cetera reacted when speaking the truth. However, as I hoped, Bobby went ahead and lied again.

"There was no one else in the car."

Ashley almost laughed and had to hide it behind a cough.

We had him.

Chapter 29

Bobby unwittingly walked himself into a trap and here's why we were better off not taking him to the nick to be questioned. Had we done that, not only would it have eaten up a fat chunk of our day and reduced that which we could achieve, Bobby would probably have demanded a solicitor to be present.

I'm not going to voice my opinions on the legal system or what it does to make sure criminals get away with their crimes on a regular basis. I'm not going to bore anyone with my thoughts on how the police could combat ten times as much crime if we didn't spend our lives bogged down in legal nonsense, waiting for solicitors, and find ourselves arresting the same person for the eleventymillionth time because the legal profession keeps getting them off. No, not me. I love solicitors.

The point is, whether by luck, talent, or just persistence, Bobby told us Elroy was guilty. Not in a manner that would stand up in court against a solicitor, but we had a new direction to take us forward. There was a second man in the car with Elroy and that gave us a new target to focus on. What we had to do now was track down the officers from the case twenty years ago.

"Do you know any of these guys?" Ashley showed me the list.

Naturally, since the murder and subsequent investigation happened in the town next to mine, I knew most of the names. More than half were retired, and I wanted to rule out those who were constables at the time since they would have been mired in low-level jobs and probably didn't have answers to the questions we wanted to ask.

However, there was one name that stood out instantly: DS Robert Charters. Now more commonly known as Superintendent Charters. My boss.

He started out under my wing as a constable, and I never imagined he would end up so far above me. Mostly that was because I expected to climb the promotion ladder myself. Regardless, we were going to have to return to Herne Bay where we could quiz my boss about the Daniel Mahony case.

I suggested stopping to discuss the case and eat our lunches before returning to the nick. It wasn't quite noon, but I was already hungry despite my hearty breakfast. For once, Ashley agreed, and just to sour my mood, which was quite buoyant, he chose to bring up the one topic I hoped to avoid.

"They might be done with the video by the time we get back."

"It still doesn't show her face," I replied in my best neutral tone. "And we are going to be drowning in stupid phone calls before we know it. I'm not being negative," I added quickly, "but we both know that is the reality of showing that piece of old video to the public."

Ashley had what looked to be a turkey and salad wrap for his lunch with an apple to follow. I had two slices of thick-cut, buttered white bread from a large farmhouse loaf filled with leftover sausages from breakfast topped off with ketchup, a packet of crisps, a snack-sized chocolate bar, and a banana which I was certain cancelled out at least half of the sandwich and the chocolate bar. That's how nutrition works, right?

We were sitting on the seawall in Whitstable, a concrete barrier erected goodness knows how long ago to keep the sea at bay should it ever venture to the top of the steep gravel beach and attempt to visit the town beyond.

The tide was in but retreating, the cold, murky, grey waters filled with silt and mud and microscopic life that sustained the oyster beds and the shoals of fish to be found in the Swale Estuary. A cool breeze made it just a little too cool to be called comfortable, but it was nice to breathe the fresh sea air.

Swallowing his mouthful of turkey wrap, Ashley took a swig of water to clear his mouth before speaking.

"Accepted, but this is the way forward. The case is going to attract attention, so getting help will be easy. In fact, if I ask DCI Harris for help, I wouldn't be shocked if he gave us the whole admin department to handle the calls coming into the hotline. Either way, it's not as if anyone is going to expect you and me to man the phones."

Annoyingly, that was one hundred percent on the money and opened a giant chasm under my feet. One I was going to have to work hard not to fall into. If someone called in convinced they knew precisely who the blonde woman in the video was, a very real and very frightening possibility, I wouldn't be the one receiving the tip. It might be hours until I even heard about it and the more people there were involved in the case, the greater the chance that someone would wind up with my wife's name.

"You're taking this better than I expected," Ashley remarked to break my concentration. "How are you feeling about it all?"

There he was again, asking about my mental wellbeing, being a concerned friend. It made it so much harder to hate him for bringing Bruce Denton back into my life.

I gave a non-committal shrug and waved my sandwich in the air a little to gesticulate as I spoke.

"I can't get away from it, but the other cases are helping." They really weren't, but I had to attribute my lack of panic attacks to something. To accentuate my point, I changed the subject. "I want to go over the CCTV footage for the night Michelle Canet was killed. There's still a chance we might spot the man with the Viking tattoo."

"You absolutely should do that."

"What will you be doing?"

"Ow."

Mouth full of sandwich, I snapped my head around to see what was wrong and found Ashley holding up his right hand. It was bleeding.

"How did you do that?" I mumbled around a chunk of sausage.

Ashley had his body folded over the arm of the bench, peering at the metalwork.

"There's a giant barb on the bottom of this. I ran my hand along it." He held up his hand to inspect the damage, keeping it away from his clothes so the drops of blood would fall to the ground, not on his clothes.

"That's a good one," I remarked, taking another bite.

"Have you got a first aid kit in the car?"

"Nope."

"This is going to keep bleeding."

I dug around in my right front trouser pocket, producing a clean handkerchief. Don't ask me why I carry one, it's just an old habit.

"Here. Use this."

Ashley nodded his thanks, unravelling the neatly folded cloth with a flick of his hand. The cut was to his pinky finger where the barb had sliced deep into the soft flesh. He wrapped it around and around with my handkerchief. It would absorb the flow of blood until he could get it dressed.

Looking out to sea and frowning, he asked, "What were we talking about?"

I almost belittled his feeble memory, but then realised I didn't know either. It took me a second to retrace our conversation.

"I asked what you would be doing while I was going through CCTV footage looking for a man with a Viking tattoo."

"Oh, yes. I guess it depends what Superintendent Charters has to say. I think we have a much better chance of solving Daniel

Mahony's murder than Michelle Canet's, and this is a numbers game for me."

"You're giving up on Michelle Canet because we had one set back on the first real day of the investigation?"

"I didn't say that. I will return to Michelle Canet if I can find a compelling reason to do so. Right now though, I am expected to produce results and DCI Harris and probably also the Chief Constable for Kent don't care which cases I solve so long as the backlog is being reduced. That dictates I must dedicate my effort to the one most likely to yield a result. Today, that is Daniel Mahony. We as good as know who the killer is. All we have to do is prove it."

I swallowed my last bite of sandwich and wiped my lips with the back of my right hand.

"If you are playing a probability game, pray please explain to me why on earth you think Bruce Denton makes a good target for your energies."

Ashley's apple was in his right hand, paused in front of his face and ready to be bitten once he'd given me a response.

"It's a special case. Plus, at this point, it's getting reopened anyway."

I hated that he was right. Pandora's Box might have stayed closed were it not for the stupid video footage. I was sullen and quiet all the way back to Herne Bay.

Chapter 30

Superintendent Charters was in his office where I expected to find him. I knocked, Ashley deferring to me as this is my nick, and waited for him to look up. Waiting outside his door, I was treated to the top of his head where the hair had thinned and was beginning to leave a bald patch. He was hunched over his desk, staring down at some printed sheets of A4.

He said, "Just a moment," when I knocked, and confident in the superior nature of his position was in no hurry to look up. Since I was yet to speak, he had no idea who was outside his office and clearly didn't much care.

Power plays, where he makes people wait for him, are typical. Would I have been the same arrogant, annoying git if my career had gone the way I expected? I doubted it, but I guess one never can tell.

Made to wait a full thirty seconds, my boss finally finished whatever it was that he was reading and lifted his eyes to look over the top edge of his reading glasses.

"Ah, Tony," he chose to be friendly for once. "What can I help you with?" His tone was amiable enough, but the desire to deal with my nonsense and send me away quickly was there in the background.

"You were one of the investigating officers looking into the murder of Daniel Mahony in 2003, sir."

His eyebrows twitched, a gesture that could mean anything.

"We have reopened the case, sir, and have some questions. Would now be a good time?" I posed the question while walking through his door and gesturing for Ashley to follow. It placed the onus on him to kick us out, and I was fairly sure he wouldn't.

He sat back in his padded, leather chair, a marked upgrade from the cheap as chips ones everyone else has. My boss also turned over the paperwork on his desk so I wouldn't be able to see what it was. Yeah, like I had upside-down speed-reading capabilities.

He said, "Go ahead," with a head nod toward the two chairs set across the room.

I started talking before my butt touched the seat.

"Sir, how much do you remember about the case?"

He pursed his lips and I watched his eyes go up and right to engage the memory portion of his brain. As I expected, he remembered the case very well, even recalling the name of the main suspect and his associates.

"It was a photograph that defeated us in the end. We all thought it had to be faked, but we had the forensic scientists examine it and they brought in a digital photography expert to make sure they weren't getting it wrong. There was a time stamp on the picture, you see? We hoped they might prove it was added after and thus that the photograph could have been taken earlier or later. It wasn't though."

"What about the people in the photograph, sir? The shot doesn't show Elroy Stewart's face."

The superintendent's forehead creased and his stare became a glare. "Doesn't it? I'm afraid it has been twenty years now, Heaton. I cannot be expected to retain every last shred of evidence that has been before my eyes." His bluster was back, an unnecessary defensive posture he takes whenever he feels he might not know the answer.

"Quite so, sir. We brought a copy with us." I didn't need to nudge Ashley, he was already out of his chair and tapping his tablet. I joined him at the superintendent's desk.

"Which one is Elroy Stewart?"

I pointed. "That one, sir." I gave him a few seconds to take in what he was seeing. "Do you recall, sir, if the identity of the man with his back to the camera was ever questioned?"

"Well, his back isn't entirely to the camera, now is it, Heaton?" Defensive again. "I can see a portion of the side profile of his face and I think we can all assume it was researched and confirmed at the time. Is that all you have?"

I nodded to Ashley who removed the tablet from the superintendent's desk and withdrew. I backed away but didn't return to my chair. The identity was never questioned. Or if it was that information never made it to the super's ears. Either way, I still believed the photograph was a hoax the team bought hook, line, and sinker.

"There were witnesses who placed a man matching Elroy's description near the site where Mahony was run over. They later withdrew their statements. Can you tell us anything about that, sir?"

My irritable boss calmed, his bluster evaporating like pond water on a hot day.

"I recall everyone being utterly certain they were coerced into doing so. They had nothing to do with each other, so the witness statements were completely independent. They both described the same young, black man right down to the clothes he was wearing, and both picked him out of a line up. Had they stuck with their statements, we might still have had a hard time getting a conviction. His only alibis were his friends and could have been dismissed, but the photograph was enough to make the CPS back away."

I suspected as much. The crown prosecution service likes to know it will win.

I checked with Ashley, but he had no additional questions and the superintendent's eyes were already straying back to the paperwork on his desk. With a final suggestion that we might have more questions as the case developed, we escaped.

Walking back to our desks we passed Doris. My immediate thought was that her cookie stash was unguarded in her office, but when I went to say something devilish, I realised she wasn't looking at me, but at Ashley. Not that there was anything strange about that, but she winked at him and when I twisted my head to see his expression, he tried to look extra innocent.

They were up to something.

Chapter 31

I MIGHT HAVE QUESTIONED what it was had Aidan not spotted us and called to get our attention.

"I'm just on my way to get the boss. The video is as good as I am going to get it and I have a still that shows the woman's face," he reported proudly and with the anticipation that we would greet the news with a happy pat on his back.

"That's great news," said Ashley, patting Aidan on the back.

I looked around for an axe so I could murder them both.

"Right, Tony?" Ashley prompted, and it might have been nothing more than my imagination, but I swear I heard something in those two words that came close to being a challenge.

"Uh-huh. Great news." There was no way the fake smile matched the rest of my face.

Aidan started walking again, heading back the way we had just come to find the superintendent.

"Come on, guys. You'll want to see this."

Ashley didn't hesitate, but it took all my resilience to keep the mental ten count in my head.

"I'll be right there," I called after their retreating backs. "I need the gents." It wasn't a lie, but my need has no sense of urgency. More than anything, what I needed was a minute.

Ashley had met my wife and knew her face. She had aged over the last thirty years the same way everyone does. But going from twenty-three to fifty-three hadn't changed her that much. She wore her hair differently, and the youthful vitality no one retains beyond their twenties was gone, but he would know it was her from a still that showed her face.

For that matter, Superintendent Charters not only knew her but first met her when she was still in her twenties. Her late twenties, admittedly, but he knew her when she looked not so very different to how she would look in the still Aidan had to show him.

I splashed some water on my face and ran through my options. It was not the first time I had ever considered running. We didn't have a lot of money put away, but I started scraping spare change and loose notes together thirty years ago. There was twenty grand stashed in a secret bank account Mary didn't know about, enough to get us ... somewhere.

There were films I'd seen where the person or people on the run manage to flee to a far corner of the planet, usually somewhere sunny and warm. There, they adopt a new life and live in peace. They were old films though or set in the past. Was it still possible to evade justice?

I was still staring into the mirror, my hands shaking from my indecision, when Ashley burst through the door.

This was it. I was busted.

He walked by me, unzipping his fly. "The still is utter garbage. It shows her face, but it's grainy and the software filling in the unknown pixels produced an image that could be a crash test dummy. It doesn't even look like a real person."

Relief flooded through my body like a tsunami crashing over my senses. Suddenly feeling faint, I bent to get my head low, but still had to control my breathing.

I guess I made more noise than I intended because Ashley called out to check on me.

"Hey, you okay?" He was busy at the urinal and leaning back around the barrier created by the last of the toilet cubicles to check on me.

Bluffing, I said, "Sorry. I've been holding this in all day." Making it look like I was having a PTSD episode proved harder than usual because I felt almost euphoric. I heaved myself away from the sink just when Ashley zipped himself and came to wash his hands. "What about the video footage? Is it much improved?"

Ashley watched my face in the mirror, examining me for a second as he soaped.

I got the impression he was trying to work something out, but after a couple of seconds he gave me an answer.

"You can see the improvement. The colour is crisper, the graininess is almost completely gone, but overall I don't think it makes much difference. We are still facing a long shot that someone will recognise her from behind from a ten second piece of film shot before I was born."

And that summed it up nicely. In fact, the way he said it almost had me breathing a sigh of relief. Thinking I was out of the woods would be fooling myself, so I said, "We'll just have to hope we get lucky," and left my partner in the gents.

He found me a short while later down in our Michelle Canet incident room. It was one of the smaller ones and we already had another one dedicated to the collated evidence from the Daniel Mahony case.

I was just beginning to look through the CCTV footage captured the night Michelle was murdered when Ashley poked his head around the door.

"You all good in here?"

"I could do with a coffee."

"I'll have the maid bring you one."

"You joining me?"

"I think I'll start going through the evidence that came today. I still think our best chance for a win lies with Daniel Mahony."

I couldn't argue with his logic. We were a long way from proving Elroy Stewart did it, but we were approximately nowhere with Michelle Canet.

He left me to it and that suited me just fine. When I was sure he had gone, I waited another minute and called Mary.

"Tony," she gasped when she answered. "Is everything all right?"

"Yes, love. As good as can be expected." Guilty conscience making me glance around the empty room in case there was someone lurking in a corner, I said, "They have cleaned up the video footage, but it still doesn't show the woman's face."

"That's ... that's quite a relief. Do you think we will be okay?"

I thought back to my thoughts of flight. I could have made a split-second decision in that moment and run for home. If we threw things into a bag, grabbed our passports, and raced for the port, we would be out of the country within the hour. But then what? Thankful I didn't need to have an answer to that question, I said, "Yes, love. I think we will."

Because I was coming back tonight to make the video footage disappear.

I spent some time going through the old CCTV footage. It was monotonous work and yielded nothing. I told Ashley as much two hours later when I found him still trying to organise the evidence from the Daniel Mahony enquiry.

"I'm going home. Last night was a late one."

"It was," Ashley agreed. "I'm just going to finish up here and then I'll be off home too."

"Tomorrow?" I introduced the subject simply because I like to have an idea what my day might hold before it hits me in the face.

He had an arm full of paper folders which he placed neatly on a table before answering – oh, how I miss the old days when it wasn't all on a computer.

"I have the home addresses for the two witnesses who identified Elroy. They are both retired. I think we give them a visit in the morning. But listen, I know you aren't a fan of early starts and have been accommodating my desire to get ahead of the day since we started working together."

I really had. It wasn't that big of a deal though. I was actually enjoying the challenge the cold cases gave me and hadn't felt so invigorated in years. I didn't say that though, I kept quiet to see what point he was trying to make.

"Well, I reckon we might have a few long days ahead when the Bruce Denton case is officially reopened and the video footage airs. How about if we take a late start tomorrow and come in at ten?"

I didn't need permission from my junior partner to come in late, I could do so of my own volition and there would be little he could do about it except complain to my boss. We both knew that and last week, when we were first paired up, I did precisely that to make a point. Nevertheless, it was a decent gesture for him to volunteer the suggestion and it played right into my hands since I planned to sacrifice a chunk of tonight's sleep to tamper with the video files.

I gave him a thumbs up. "Sounds good to me. You got something planned?"

"No," he replied just a little too quickly. He sensed it and tried to recover. "No, I, ah, I mean, we all need a break sometimes and I've hardly seen Tanya at all the last few days."

I knew that wasn't true because we had the bulk of Sunday and Monday off to recover from the near-death experience solving the Craig Chowdry case.

He had just lied to me, perhaps for the first time, but like almost everyone else, once he recognised I could see what he was doing, he panicked. Bidding him a good evening and backing out the door, I wondered just what it was he was trying to hide.

Chapter 32

It was seven hours later when Ashley returned to the Herne Bay nick. He didn't want to be seen, but equally couldn't get caught sneaking around. That was a hard equation to balance, but by parking across the street rather than in the carpark, slipping down the side of the station to the custody centre entrance, and waiting for the duty desk officer to leave his desk, he was able to get in and up the stairs without being seen.

That was part one. Getting out would be just as fraught with risk, but he was going to worry about that later. Despite the clock reading just after two in the morning, Ashley wasn't guaranteed the office would be empty. The Herne Bay nick operated like any other and criminals were as likely to strike at night as during the day. There could be detectives at work having returned from a shout, or uniforms filling in paperwork after bringing in a burglar, mugger, or whatever.

There was no one though. The lights were off, blinking on above his head when they detected his presence.

Aware of his pulse and that he was about to do something not only out of character, but unquestionably against the rules, Ashley moved swiftly. To create a believable scene should someone happen to hear his footsteps above their heads – unlikely since the custody centre and breakroom where on-duty cops might rest for a while were both on the other side of the building – he went to his assigned desk. There he set up his laptop, opened a notebook, placed a pen on top to hold the pages open, and then took out a thermos of coffee, pouring himself a cup to complete the look of a detective working late into the night fuelled only by determination and caffeine.

Once all that was done and there was no putting it off any longer, he went to Tony's desk. He had nothing but Vicky's word there was a file in one of his drawers that contained personal notes from the Bruce Denton enquiry. Collated over many years, and amassed only after the official investigation ended, Ashley believed it would contain invaluable information and he simply had to get his hands on it.

Donning a pair of latex gloves, a dead giveaway that he was up to no good if anyone saw him, but necessary to avoid leaving fingerprints, he tried Tony's drawers. They were locked, just as he expected they would be. However, the office and everything in it, including the desks and chairs, were ancient items from a different millennium. The locks were designed only to deter interference and thus were far from impossible to pick.

Hoping he wouldn't even need to take that step, he scouted Tony's desk for the key. It wasn't tucked under the keyboard, it wasn't hidden amongst the paperclips, drawing pins, and random detritus in his stationery holder, and did not appear to be anywhere else.

Trying one last trick, he retrieved the key for his desk drawers and tried it, hoping age might have made the mechanism loose enough that it would give way to anything that was a close fit.

It didn't.

With a deep breath, he got on his knees, took out the professional lock picking kit he'd bought the previous day on twenty-four-hour delivery, and touched the screen of his phone. He needed the phone to look up lock picking tutorials on YouTube, but the latex gloves meant the touchscreen failed to recognize his fingers.

Nerves making him agitated, he took a glove off, got the video working, and remembered to put the glove back on before he started to work on the lock. He could feel his heart beating inside his chest, his fear of being caught doing something wrong an unfamiliar sensation.

Anything but a rule breaker, Ashley knew he was a boy scout and that his need to do things by the book annoyed his fellow officers. That they might harbour negative opinions didn't bother him at all and he knew why – he expected to be their boss at some point. His way was the right way, yet here he was on his hands and knees trying to break into his partner's desk.

Grunting with frustration, sweat beading on his forehead, Ashley couldn't articulate what was driving him to go against everything he stood for. Except ... except there was something not right with the way Tony protected the case.

The previous evening, despite arriving home tired and ready for bed, Ashley made himself a drink, which was a rare indulgence in itself, and sat at the kitchen table sorting through Vicky's notebooks. It didn't take long to find the section pertaining to the Bruce Denton case as the notes were all dated in the same meticulously neat handwriting.

There wasn't much to learn, but what he took away from his cursory first read through was that much of what she recorded never made it in the official case file. That in itself was suspicious and made him want to question every shred of evidence she recorded.

Most of it was nothing more than noting what people said when she asked them about what they might have seen, but one thing that jumped off the page was a report by Mrs Davenport. She lived on the opposite side of the street to Bruce, and though Ashley would need to go to the street to orientate himself with the houses, he suspected she had a good view of Bruce's front garden.

She claimed to have seen a man sitting in his car two days before Bruce's murder. He was right outside her house, just sitting there watching the street. She went out to ask what he was doing, but he drove away at speed when he saw her approaching.

She wasn't able to get the whole registration number but remembered the last three letters because they were F-U-N which spelled 'fun'.

It could be nothing, but it didn't feel like nothing.

With a suppressed yelp of relief, Ashley turned the lock and pulled the top drawer open. Quickly stuffing the tools away, he checked the drawer, closed it and opened the more promising bottom one where he expected to find the file.

If it existed.

If that was really where Tony kept it.

And there it was. Tucked in the back behind the drop files, where no one would ever see it, sat a dull brown cardboard folder. Feeling like Indiana Jones finally discovering a fabled artefact, Ashley gingerly lifted it from the drawer.

Chapter 33

"Tony?"

So much for sneaking out without Mary noticing.

"Yes, dear?"

"Don't you 'yes dear' me. What are you doing up? It's the middle of the night."

Her bedside light came on a moment later, framing me against the curtains where I sat on her dressing table stool with one sock on and the other in my hands.

"There is something I have to do."

Mary sat up in bed, hugging the covers to stop the warm air from escaping. I got the full 'Don't mess with me' expression and stopped trying to keep the truth to myself.

"I think I might be able to destroy the video footage, okay?"

"Destroy it?"

"Yes. I've been looking up how to find and erase all the files, so they are gone forever. If I can do that, they can't show the video and no one will be able to identify you as the woman in Bruce Denton's car."

"But won't they try to figure out what happened to it? I mean, won't they investigate?"

"Of course they will. There will be a full enquiry where they check who could have accessed the files and when. I have looked up how to get around all of that as well. At least, I think I have." The truth was that I really wasn't sure how foolproof my plan was. I needed to reset the internal clock on the server so it would look like the files were erased yesterday when I was known to be elsewhere, but would there be a way to check what time the internal clock was altered? I had no clue. Me and computers ... well, let's just say we are friends, but I am far from being the master.

"Oh, Tony, what if you get caught? Won't that make it worse? How will you explain it if they figure out it was you?"

Good question.

"That's a bridge to cross when we come to it, sweetheart. I can probably claim to have had a mental snap. I can claim I was freaked out by the possibility that someone might solve the crime after all these years and retreat back down the mental ill health path. The greatest danger right now is that someone will identify you."

"But you told me the footage doesn't show my face. You said there was very little chance I would be recognised by anyone because it was so long ago."

"Yeah, I did say that." Lying to my wife is not a habit I would ever endorse, but sometimes a little fib is the kindest thing we can do. I saw no sense in making her fret when I was already doing enough of that for the both of us.

Yet the greatest lie was the one I told myself … had been telling myself since before I chose to murder him. The lie that he had to die. Many times I have questioned what else I could have done. At the time I saw it as the only option.

"Tony."

Mary's voice broke through my memories.

"Yes, dear?"

"Maybe you should come back to bed." She shifted the covers, exposing my side.

I debated it for a moment, I really did, but I genuinely thought I stood a chance of getting in and out undetected. If I could erase the files, tape over the original footage, and make any physical evidence disappear, then we were home free. For thirty years, no one had looked our way. I needed that to continue.

I pulled on my other sock with Mary watching me, her face a mixture of concern and disapproval. Needing just my shoes and a coat, I went around to her side of the bed, unsure if she would have another go at stopping me, but she tilted her head up to meet my lips.

"Be careful."

It was sage advice, but also the thought most dominant in my mind long before she said it.

Chapter 34

ASHLEY WAS ALMOST DONE copying the file when the machine ran out of paper. The task was taking far, far longer than he wanted it to and the stupid copier made more noise than he could have imagined possible. That, he suspected, was purely because he was operating it in the dead of night with no background chatter to hide the sounds it made.

Convinced someone downstairs would hear it and come to investigate, he was trying to go fast, but Tony's file wasn't a standard collection of A4 pages bound or clamped together in a ring binder. No, it was a mishmash of notes torn from various notebooks, plus photographs, and other random things Tony considered important enough to keep.

It was all in the same, scrawly handwriting he'd come to know and also therefore very hard to read. Impossible, in fact, in some places, though Ashley refused to let that put him off. There would be some commonality between the unidentifiable letters and words, which he would break down and translate by comparing them to the letters in words he could read.

Looking about for more paper – he only had a few pages left to copy – Ashley could find none. There was none in the vicinity of the photocopier, as he imagined it would be. Nor was it in the stationery cupboard when he located that. Irked that he might have to abandon the last few pages, he hurriedly checked everywhere he could think of, finally locating a stash in the cupboard next to the coffee station.

He grumbled, muttering under his breath about old nicks and old cops. If he had a clandestine file, it would be on a thumb drive. Of course, were that the case with Tony, getting hold of it would have proved far harder.

Passing a window on his way back to the photocopier, he spotted the light come on inside a car in the street outside. Given the hour, it was strange enough to make him look, rather than just glance, which was how he saw what car it was and then Tony getting out of it.

Ashley swore loudly and ran back to the photocopier. Adrenaline flooded his bloodstream, making his movements erratic and jerky when he needed them to be slick and precise.

"Come on, man," he gritted his teeth and forced his hands to slow. Did he have time to copy the last few pages? Surely not, but what if they were important?

With his breaths coming more rapidly than they ought, he grabbed the last few pages and slid them into the copier one at a time. Fresh pages spat out the other end, though his focus was on reassembling Tony's folder. To cover his tracks, Ashley reassembled the contents meticulously to keep everything in the same order he found it.

A sound from the ground floor stilled his whole body, Ashley standing rigidly still to listen. There were voices, but was one of them Tony's? Two seconds dragged by, three ... When the voices came no closer and sounded as though they were going away, Ashley pushed himself to continue.

Ripping the final pages from the photocopier, he placed them back into Tony's old folder and closed it. He could not guess what ungodly force might have caused his partner to visit the nick in the middle of the night, but whatever it was, Ashley knew he had no time left to spare.

A snatching hand ripped the copied sheets from the 'out' tray. The copy of Tony's file, a loose collection of A4 sheets he had no time to tidy, arrange, or bind, went into his bag, stuffed there like discarded wrapping paper at a kid's birthday. Running to get back across the room, he returned to Tony's desk. All he had to do now was get the original folder back into his bottom drawer and retreat to his desk where he could sit hunched over his laptop and act completely innocent.

Provided he could stop sweating and control his breathing, that is.

However, when he gripped the drawer, it refused to budge. The damned thing had locked itself when he closed it!

Chapter 35

I LEFT MY CAR in the street where it wouldn't be seen by the security camera covering the back of the station. Above all else, no one could know I was at the nick in the middle of the night. There was no hope I could explain that away. If I was seen arriving or leaving, they would know I was the one who erased the video footage.

Thankfully, I had a plan that would get me in and out unseen.

Many years ago, twenty-five or more perhaps, there was no air conditioning fitted anywhere in the building and on the rare days when it got hot, the side of the station directly in the sun would become unbearable. The briefing room was on that side, and to combat the heat we would open a door on the far wall and let the outside air in. It created a bit of a breeze, no more than that, but it was better than nothing.

Somehow, I ended up with the key to that door. I don't now recall how or when, but I did, and tonight it was going to provide me with a secret way in.

Once I closed the door behind me, the briefing room was too dark to see my hand in front of my face, but by keeping one hand on the wall for reference, walking around the table to find the thin slither of light coming under the other door was easy enough.

Knowing it was never locked, I opened the door a crack. I peered out and I listened. In the near silence, my breathing sounded like Darth Vader to my ears, but no one heard me.

There were voices coming from the custody centre and dispatch room, the urgency and volume enough to tell me one of the patrol units had picked someone up and they were decidedly unhappy about it. It served to mask my movements, so quickly and quietly, I made my way to the stairs. They were creaky old things, but by sticking to the edges and stepping over the very bottom step, one could avoid the worst of the noise they made.

Climbing with care, I rounded the bend at the middle landing and felt a frown grip my brow. The lights were on above me.

Why were the lights on?

Were they broken? Or were they always on? I was certain they had one of those PIR thingies that detected motion and turned them off to save energy when no one was around. I had to think back to the last time I worked late enough at my desk for them to go off around me, or to have come in so early I triggered them.

Had I ever done that?

Feeling cautious and with my stomach knotting, I began to climb again. Only now that I worried someone might see me did I question what lie I might concoct to explain my presence. Why hadn't I thought about that before?

Did I say I couldn't sleep and decided to come to work? No one who knew me would believe that? Ah, but I was in the middle of two cases, so I could tell them I remembered something and needed to check my notes. They might think it sounded unlikely, but they wouldn't challenge me on it.

Taking a deep breath and hoping I was about to find the lights were on all by themselves, I made sure I ascended the stairs at a normal pace.

The office came into view. It was completely silent. Until my ears detected the minute sound of someone tapping on a keyboard. My plan was shot. I couldn't erase a thing if someone saw me.

But who the heck was it? Who on earth would be here working at this time of the day? Why did I care? The sudden realisation that my only sensible play was to withdraw and go home washed over me like a bucket of cold water. I needed to go.

Right now.

"Tony?"

I froze like a sniper's red dot had just appeared on my chest.

"Ashley?" I had one hand on the banister and was about to turn to go down the stairs when he spoke my name. He said it with the same surprise I felt to find him here.

Too late now, I climbed the remaining stairs.

"What are you doing here?" he asked.

Deflecting, I said, "I could ask you the same thing."

He pushed back from his laptop. "Yes, but I asked first. You were going to have a lie in and come to work at ten." He shot his cuff to check his watch. "It's two forty-five."

I shrugged. "Couldn't sleep. I remembered something," I tried the lie I thought up thirty seconds ago, "and it bugged me enough that I had to check it out."

Ashley narrowed his eyes a little. He was having trouble believing me.

"Which case?" he asked, sounding genuinely interested.

Now I was stuck. If it had been anyone else, anyone else at all, I would have told them it was Michelle Canet or Daniel Mahony, the two cases we were working right now, but if I did that, Ashley would press me to tell him what I remembered and what I so desperately needed to look up.

Forced to pick another case, I went with the only one I could think of.

"Bruce Denton."

Ashley's eyebrows steepled.

"Really?" He wanted to know more.

My heart thumped in my chest, mocking me as I fought feverishly to think another step ahead. I was going to have to say something, but trapped by my own lies, my brain drew a blank.

My phone rang, the unexpected abruptness of it startling me. Ashley and I were staring at each other from opposite sides of the room, neither saying anything, the sudden mistrust between us nothing short of palpable.

The call, coming in the middle of the night as it did, could only really be from one source. Regardless, it offered me an easy way to stall our conversation, but as I reached into my jacket to retrieve it, Ashley's began to ring too.

At the other end was Marvin the Martian. He was calling to get me up. There had been a murder in Whitstable, and it connected directly to one of our cases.

I looked up at Ashley. He was getting the same information, most likely from the dispatch desk downstairs.

I mumbled something into my phone, letting Marvin know I would be there as soon as I could.

Oliver Humphries was dead, and there could only be one reason why – we triggered Michelle Canet's killer to return.

Chapter 36

ASHLEY ENDED HIS CALL half a second after mine, and our eyes met across the room once more.

"We'd better go," I said.

Ashley nodded. His suit jacket was draped over the back of his chair which was unusual because he never takes it off. My snap assumption was that with no one around to see him, he chose to relax, but it was cool in the office. Cool enough that I would have kept my jacket on.

Now that I was looking, I noticed the perspirations marks under his arms. He'd been sweating very recently or still was, but he wasn't out of breath from exercise, not that he was dressed for a workout.

He slipped his jacket on and closed his laptop.

"Time got away from me," he explained, answering a question I hadn't asked. "I went down a rabbit hole looking into Elroy

Stewart." Embellishing is often a sign that the person is making it up as they go along. They deliver a lie, worry it sounds like a lie, and try to make it sound more truthful by adding details.

"Did you?" I asked in a tone that challenged his claim.

Ashley paused with his bag open and his laptop halfway to it. It didn't matter if he said, 'yes' or 'no', either one would reveal whether he was being honest with me.

Ashley, however, is a savvy detective, and not so easily caught out.

Instead of answering, he said, "You never did tell me what it was that brought you here in the middle of the night, Tony. What was it about the Bruce Denton case that kept you awake?"

Two can play that game.

"And you haven't been here all night, kid," I threw in a derogatory term to see how he would react. "That's not the same tie you had on yesterday."

He made the mistake of looking down. I pay too little attention to his outfit to know if I was right or not. He could have just argued, but his need to check told me I was right. Like me, he'd chosen to return to the station in the middle of the night and I wanted to know why.

Unpausing his arms, Ashley stuffed the laptop into his bag with more vigour than the task required. Quickly followed by the power lead, he zipped it closed while staring at me.

"We'd better go."

"Your car, this time," I remarked. Mine was in the street and if he saw it there, he would know my visit to the nick was anything but above board.

He shook his head. "I think yours again, Tony. Unless you think I'm your chauffeur."

It was a direct challenge. What the heck had he been up to? I was still standing at the top of the stairs, but I felt an overwhelming urge to explore the office. He was here to do something and now I needed to know what it was.

I guess he saw my face clouding with doubt because he changed his mind the moment my right foot left the floor.

"Okay, Tony, you win. My car it is. Let's just go, okay?"

Hoisting his bag over his right shoulder, he hooked his fancy winter coat and marched across the room.

Feet stilled by indecision, Ashley was almost upon me when I turned to go back down the stairs. However, when he passed me, I slowed, changed my mind, and went back to the office.

I heard his feet stop before he got to the halfway landing. "Tony! We need to get moving!"

No, we don't, I thought to myself. They expected to wake us in our beds. No one thinks we are getting there in the next ten minutes, which is all it will take us to get to Whitstable at this time of the night.

A panic inducing thought had just occurred to me, and I needed to know if I was right or wrong. Ashley didn't know about it – few do, but there is a file in my bottom drawer that contains my thoughts pertaining to Bruce Denton since the enquiry shut down. None of it was incriminating; I'm not stupid enough to write down what a good job I was doing of getting away with it, but there was information that never got recorded anywhere else and that in itself was damning.

He couldn't possibly know about it, but what if he did? What if he was sweating because I almost caught him breaking into my desk?

"Tony, what are you doing? I said I would drive. Let's get moving."

I didn't respond or even act as though I heard him speak. He was coming back up the stairs, but was too far away to stop me from checking my desk. Not that he could do that without tackling me to the ground.

The bits and pieces on my desk were in their usual places, but the file was in the drawer, tucked away where no one would ever see it.

I flicked my eyes up to see what Ashley was doing. He looked nervous, which was an emotion I'd not seen him display before.

From my trouser pocket, I produced my keys, selecting the smallest of them to open the lock on my desk. I felt a little weak from the adrenaline coursing through my bloodstream and from the effort of trying not to show it. Had my new partner been going through my things? Did he suspect me?

He started to walk toward me, my pressured fingers fumbling the key so it took me three attempts to get it into the lock. It turned, and I pulled the bottom drawer open just as he came around my desk.

The possibility that he had my file was making me feel sick, but when I looked to the back behind all the drop folders, it was there, just as it always was.

Ashley asked. "What's that?"

I slammed the drawer shut to cut off his view.

"Nothing."

"It didn't look like nothing."

I looked up at his face, trying to read what was going on behind it. Was he going to push me for an answer?

Abruptly, and as if he didn't care in the slightest, Ashley started back toward the stairs. "Come on, there is a body going cold."

The muscles in my legs flexed to drive me from the chair, but I relaxed them before I began to rise. Pulling the drawer open once more, I saw what I did not spot the first time and my heart stopped.

On the spine of the folder was a small smear of blood. It was fresh, and I knew whose injured pinky finger left it there.

Chapter 37

NEITHER ONE OF US said a single word once we were in the car and moving. However, before we got in the car there was a discussion about why our vehicles were not in the carpark.

"There was a truck blocking the entrance when I came back," Ashley shot back.

"I thought you were still there from our shift today?"

"That's not what I said. I told you time got away from me. I went home, had dinner with Tanya and came back. If we are going to catch Elroy for the murder of Daniel Mahony, we are going to have to work hard. I was there looking for a chink in his armour."

I wanted to call him a liar, but I didn't want to have him admit he had my file. Not yet. Not until I could figure out what to do about it.

"Anyway, why is your car in the street?"

"Same truck," I lied, knowing he already knew I was up to something.

I got an, 'Uh-huh,' in reply. They were the last words to leave his lips until we spotted the flashing strobe lights down a side street in Whitstable. When he did speak, it was to ask the constable manning the cordon where we could find DI Valmik.

We were at a petrol station on the confluence of Canterbury Road and Joy Lane where five minutes later I was looking at the body of Oliver Humphries. How many hours had it been since we talked to him? He had been full of life and just looking to get on. His troubled past was behind him, or so he thought.

No one would convince me this was a coincidence. Reopening the Michelle Canet murder enquiry prompted the killer to strike again, and it had to be to do with the tattoo. That was the only thing we got from Oliver. Unless there was something else I failed to pick up on.

Just like Michelle, Oliver suffered a single stab wound to his back – another reason to believe it was the same killer. The late-night counter clerk found his body in the wheelie bin behind the shop when he took out that day's garbage bags just after midnight.

Marvin knew we would want to know as soon as possible, which was why he didn't wait until the morning. We learned what they could figure out at the scene. The petrol station had a CCTV camera that didn't work, and the clerk saw nothing. However, the medical examiner gave us a fairly accurate estimate for time of death, placing it at around 2300hrs. As they always do, he said he would know more once he'd performed an autopsy.

We would have to wait for the morning to get that.

There being nothing else we could gain by hanging around in the cold and dark, Marvin suggested we call it for the night. He would see us after breakfast.

I asked if he could give me a lift back to Herne Bay.

Marvin frowned. "What about your partner? Isn't he going that way?"

"No, he lives the other side of Dartford. Taking me home is well out of his way and he's not getting enough sleep as it is. He was still at work when the call for this came through." Everything I said was true, even if the way I presented it obscured my real reason for wanting a lift to Herne Bay.

Marvin looked about. "I'm staying here, but I can have one of the uniforms run you home if you like."

"To my nick. I met Ashley there."

"Even closer." He put two fingers in his mouth to whistle for attention and waved for one of the junior constables to join him. The young man made the mistake of being the first to turn around and look the boss's way. He would learn to give it a two-count in time.

To normalise the situation in front of those around us, I called to Ashley, "I'm going to get a lift home. See you in the morning. Ten o'clock as planned, yes?"

He was over by his car waiting for me and there was no question he knew I was choosing to avoid him. I thought he might argue for a moment, but he gave me a thumbs up, slid into his car and was gone by the time the constable swung his squad car around to pick me up.

I had a lot to think about.

Chapter 38

Tanya studied her fiancé's face. It was rare for Ashley to look this perturbed and he'd been agitated all evening. He'd tried not to disturb her when he left their bed just after midnight but was honest with her about his reason for leaving the house.

Now he was back, and he seemed more thrown than ever.

He told her about Oliver Humphries, though he omitted to provide a name.

"Is that what is bothering you so much?" she questioned, thinking it couldn't be because he was acting strangely before the murder occurred. "It's not your fault."

Ashley acknowledged her comment with a grunt.

"No, his death is not my fault. That comes down to the killer, but I cannot help wondering what we missed. We must have come close, we might even have spoken to him, because nothing has happened in three years, but one day into our enquiry, the killer struck again."

"I thought you said you couldn't know if it was the same killer."

"That's right," Ashley admitted. "Jumping to conclusions helps no one. That's not what is bothering me though."

Tanya sucked on her bottom lip. She needed to get ready for work and had a big day ahead of her, but Ashley needed some TLC, so she pressed her body against his from behind, looping her arms around his chest to nuzzle his neck.

"What is it, my love? What has you so distracted?"

"My partner." Ashley was still trying to frame what he thought he knew and was yet to articulate it to himself, let alone anyone else.

Tanya dropped her arms away and stepped back. "Ugh, what's he done now?"

Ashley turned around to face her, sitting back against the kitchen table he'd just been leaning on. He hadn't expected to find Tanya with her arms crossed and an angry expression ruffling her perfect features.

"Nothing, babe. Well, nothing you are thinking. He's um ..."

Tanya cocked an eyebrow. It wasn't like Ashley to beat around the bush. She liked him because he was confident and reliable. He wasn't the kind of man who would mess her around or lie about what he was doing. Except he now seemed to be deliberating how to express a simple truth, and it was making her impatient.

"I think he is hiding something important and very pertinent to a murder that happened thirty years ago."

That was not what Tanya expected him to say. She could see it bothered him in a way she wasn't used to. She reached out, taking his hands in hers and offering a reassuring smile when he met her gaze.

"This is the ... Bruce, is it? Bruce something case?"

He nodded. "Bruce Denton."

"He's hiding something? Like what?"

"I don't know. The case killed his career, and he is a brilliant detective."

"So are you, Hun."

"Not like Tony. He's something else entirely."

"So what are you saying? You think he did something to cover up the evidence, so the killer got away with it?"

Ashley's eyes flared with startled surprise. "God, no. Nothing like that. Everyone knows he lost a piece of evidence. That was his big fall from grace, but I think it's worse than that. I think Tony messed up worse than anyone knows, and he's been trying to hide it all this time because he doesn't want anyone to find out. I can't blame him for that, but I also think it is getting in the way of anyone else coming along to solve the case. He's so protective of it. They found the evidence he lost just a few days ago." Ashley hated that he couldn't discuss ongoing investigations with Tanya. She was his sounding board for so many things in life, but when it came to his work, he edged around the truth.

"Surely that changes things."

"It does ... or it might. We shall have to see. Tony maintains that the case is unsolvable, but I spoke with one of the constables he worked with thirty years ago and she had evidence in her notebook that doesn't appear anywhere in the official file. That's really weird. But when I spoke with Doris, she told me about the other DS who worked the case under Tony's lead. According to her, he had a theory that the killer could be a cop or maybe someone associated with the police."

"How come? What made him think that?"

"The crime scene was devoid of evidence. The killer knew how to get in and out and commit a brutal murder without leaving a single trace behind."

Tanya considered what Ashley revealed for a moment before asking, "What conclusion do you draw?"

This was one of her best skills and why Ashley liked to ask her opinion. She would drive straight to the heart of the matter to make him articulate what was going on in his head.

With a deep breath, Ashley said, "I worry Tony might have an inkling who the killer is because it is one of our own, have no way to prove it, and have been looking for the one key piece of evidence that would help him solve the murder since 1993."

Chapter 39

I FELT HUNGOVER FROM lack of sleep, and I knew I hadn't really missed that much of it. When I got home, it was just after five and Mary was waiting for me, curled in a chair in the living room. That she struggled to get back to sleep didn't come as much of a surprise, given what we had hanging over our heads, but we went back to bed together where fatigue – emotional as much as physical, took us both.

All the same, I hadn't got enough sleep, so sitting at the break-fast bar a little after nine that morning, I felt ruined.

I said little when I got in other than to confirm I had not done that which I set out to do. Mary has always been very good at letting me process my thoughts in my own way and at my own pace, but I could see she wanted to talk about it.

"Ashley was there," I opened the conversation.

She had her back to me, refilling the tea caddy. Pivoting off her right foot, she came to face me and leaned back against the counter.

"At the station?"

"Yes. He told me he had been there all night working on one of the cases, but that wasn't true."

She absorbed the information and thought about it. I could see her analysing what that meant.

"Why would he lie?" she asked.

I sighed a slow breath, drew in a fresh one, and voiced the belief that was troubling me quite deeply, "Because he suspects me." There it was, out in the open.

I knew the statement would both shock and scare Mary. She crossed to the breakfast bar, touching my left shoulder with her right hand as she settled into the chair.

"He suspects you? Are we talking about Bruce?"

I offered her a grim smile and a nod. "He broke into my desk at work to look through the file I keep there."

Her frown was so deep her eyebrows met in the middle.

"He broke into your desk? Then you can jolly well report him. That will end his scheming."

I placed my hand over the top of hers.

"No, love, that will land me in jail. If I expose him, he will defend his actions by revealing what he knows. That might not be much right now, but the moment people start to question whether he might have a point, they will all see the truth of it."

I could see the fear in her eyes. It was everything we hoped and prayed would never come to pass.

"But surely he is already trying to put the pieces together. Tony, he'll figure it out, won't he?"

I wanted so desperately to tell her it would all be all right. That's what I told her thirty years ago, and I had been good to my word so far. This latest threat, though ... could I stop Ashley from digging his way to the truth?

The file wouldn't tell him anything directly, but there were clues. The biggest of them, which I knew he would spot, even if not straight away, was the information contained within it that I kept out of the official case file. Statements from neighbours about the man and the car they saw in the street.

I disguised myself and used different cars, but in the days leading up to Bruce's murder, his neighbours saw me parked in his road, watching his house, far more times than I anticipated. It formed a pattern that required investigation, so I hid it from everyone else for one very good reason.

One of the cars I used was my own.

The rest of the time I grabbed a pool car, or one of the impounded ones towed back to the nick. No one paid attention to them, and the keys were always left in the ignition. Looking back, it was shockingly easy, but there was one day when I was spotted trying to take one. I bluffed, claiming I thought I saw a dog wandering through the carpark but had to then leave without a car and ended up using my own. It happened just that one time.

When residents of his street started to report having seen a man in a car earlier that week, albeit their reports of model and man never matched, I knew someone would give a description for my car. If I didn't have bad luck, I would have no luck at all.

It drove me to work the street, prompting people to think about what they had seen. I had to do that anyway; it was part and parcel of the investigation, standard police work if you will, but I wanted to be the one who talked to the person who had seen my car, if such a witness existed. Bad luck struck again though because it wasn't me. Vicky Hopper took that statement instead.

Cutting the information from the case notes was easy enough, but that did nothing to erase it from the memory of the witness or from Vicky. I stayed friends with her for years afterwards, just to watch and see if she ever brought the subject up.

I scrapped the car, obviously. That happened the day it was identified. It cost us financially. I was still paying off the loan I took out to buy it in the first place, but what was a little money compared to a murder conviction?

Mary squeezed my hand, bringing me back to the present.

"Tony, what are you going to do about Ashley?" she repeated a question that deserved an answer.

I closed my eyes, hating that I knew the answer and loathing what it was. When I reopened them, I squeezed her hand back.

"Mary, my angel, I might have to kill him."

Chapter 40

WALKING UP THE STAIRS to the office half an hour later, I was filled with a sense of dread. Unable to figure out what I should do about Ashley, my decision, for now, was to pretend nothing happened last night. I planned to pick up where we left off the previous evening. Resetting to the last safe point if you like.

I had no ability to control what Ashley would do though. Would I find he had been here for hours talking to my superintendent? How much had he figured out? Would there be another chance for me to erase the video footage tonight? Or was it already too late?

I trudged up the stairs to the office at my usual pace, though my sense of impending doom made my pulse beat far faster than usual.

For no good reason at all. The office looked no different than any other day. Everyone was doing their own thing and not one person looked up from their desk when I reached the top of the stairs. Ashley was sitting in his usual spot; the desk where old Ben used to sit before he retired.

I guess he felt my eyes on him because he looked up. My stomach tightened instantly and worsened when he shot out of his desk. He came hurrying across the room in my direction, but his expression conflicted with the swirling thoughts in my head. Had I overestimated him? Had he not worked it out?

I was going to have to watch him very closely, there was no question about that, but unless I was much mistaken, he was yet to act on whatever new information he found in my file.

"Tony, hey, you doing okay?" Ashley offered his hand to shake in greeting and didn't wait to hear my reply. "There's been a development. We need to get over to the coroner's office."

He was acting as though nothing unusual happened last night. Pretending he hadn't broken into my desk in the middle of the night. It was a strategy that worked for me. For now at least, but would he pester me to explain why I came to the nick at such an ungodly hour? Did it matter if he did? I could give whatever excuse I wanted because I didn't get to do anything wrong.

Making it obvious he'd only been waiting for my arrival, Ashley was on his way down the stairs.

"You coming, Tony?" he called when he got to the landing.

Standing at the top of the stairs, I needed a second to adjust my thoughts. Expecting drama from Ashley and getting the exact opposite was throwing me. I had turned up ready for a fight, only to discover my tension and paranoia were unnecessary.

His footsteps continued to bounce down the stairs, my partner back to being the eager puppy.

Gavin Dobbs, sitting at his desk a few feet away, looked at me with a question.

"Everything all right, Tony? You look lost."

That about summed me up.

I found Ashley in the carpark. He was in his car with the motor running. The coroner's office is in Canterbury, but we made the journey after rush hour and traffic was light. Inquests take place in Maidstone, another of the county's big cities. Located to the north, it is a pain to get to, so I was glad we didn't have to go there.

Pulling my seatbelt across my body, I asked, "So what's the big development?"

"That I don't know. I arrived twenty minutes ago to a message from your friend DI Valmik. It was for you, actually, but Doris figured telling me was the same thing. The wound that killed Oliver Humphries matches the one on Michelle Canet."

"That hardly constitutes news. I would bet money it's the same killer."

"As would I. Someone felt a need to cover their tracks, and it has to be someone we talked to."

"That's a small pool of suspects," I remarked, listing them in my head. "In fact, I can only come up with one person we told about the Viking tattoo and how we knew about it."

Ashley supplied the name. "John Decker."

We were on the B2205, one street back from the seafront with the amusement arcades, the pier, and the town's meagre tourist attractions. The sky above us was grey to match my mood, an endless blanket of dull clouds blotting out the sun. They darkened to the east where a band of rain fell out to sea. I wondered if it was coming our way.

There was a conclusion to be drawn from renaming John Decker as our suspect. "It means his father-in-law gave false alibi."

"A trait that runs in the family. First his wife lied to keep him out of jail for the last three years. Then his father-in-law steps in when her lies fell apart."

"That still doesn't explain why we are going to see the coroner." I hadn't asked a question, per se, but Ashley understood what I was asking.

"Sorry, the message didn't say why we needed to go, only that he was expecting us."

We found out when we arrived.

I knew the coroner from old; we had both been around a long time.

"Tony," he greeted me with a handshake.

"Dr Krauss." I released his hand and turned my body a quarter to the right to include Ashley. "This is DS Ashley Long."

"One of *the* Longs?" Dr Krauss enquired, gripping Ashley's hand. He'd been around the police long enough to know Ashley's family.

"That's right, sir." His reply was neutral. He was happy to be a cop, but the pressure to not only perform but excel had to weigh on him sometimes. I wondered how driven he would be were he not constantly under his family's gaze.

Dr Krauss led us to his office where he had photographs on his computer.

"DI Valmik was good enough to clarify the potential connection between this murder and one that I examined three years ago." On the screen was a photograph of a man's back. On the left hand side, about halfway down the length of his upper arm, a slit about an inch long showed where the knife penetrated. Dr Krauss used a pen to point to the wound. "It's a double-edged blade, the same one used on Michelle Canet. Here," he moved the pen and zoomed in, "slight bruising around the skin shows that it was thrust in all the way to the hilt."

We knew from Michelle's autopsy report that his killer did the same thing. The photographs of his wound were no different to Oliver's. At least not to my untrained eye.

"Of course I could have explained this over the phone, but I wanted to make sure you understand the significance of the wounds."

He had our full attention.

"Most times when someone is stabbed to death, the killer inflicts multiple wounds, withdrawing their blade each time to deliver another blow. The attacks are frenzied. Sometimes it is just one wound like you see with this victim, but more often than not in those cases, the knife punctures the heart or slices through an artery – death is a by-product rather than the intended outcome. What we see here is an execution. The killer knew precisely what they were doing and had been trained to dispatch their victims with a single well-aimed blow."

Ashley asked the question before I could. "Trained?"

Dr Krauss nodded. "Exactly that. The victim is approached from behind, grabbed around the face to prevent them making a noise while the knife enters their ribcage at an upward angle. It penetrates the heart, killing instantly." Dr Krauss looked from Ashley to me, making sure we were listening to what he was about to say. "This method is taught to special forces soldiers."

Chapter 41

Leaving the coroner's office, Dr Krauss's words rang in my ears. He'd identified the possibility of an ex-military killer when he examined Michelle Canet but had been less certain at the time. The second murder with the same M.O. removed the question mark.

For Dr Krauss, but not for us. Our question mark wasn't going anywhere. John Decker was our primary suspect once more, simply for the fact that we hadn't told anyone else about the tattoo. However, John Decker never served in the military. That wasn't to say he couldn't have studied the technique online or learned it from someone he knew, but it wasn't the slam dunk we were hoping for.

The knife employed by the killer was probably a bayonet, though not the one the British Army use according to Dr Krauss. He had a weapon expert working in his department who claimed the bruise pattern left on Oliver's skin combined with the shape and length of the blade matched that of a bayonet designed to fit the Zastava M70, an assault rifle favoured by the Serbian military during the war in the former Yugoslavian countries in the early nineties.

Lots of British soldiers were sent there on peacekeeping missions, which tied in again with the ex-soldier angle and did nothing to make John Decker look more guilty.

First things first; we needed to check where John Decker was last night.

We got stuck behind a tractor on the A290 between Blean and Honey Hill. It slowed us down and gave me time to think. I should have been focused on John Decker and Oliver Humphries' murder, but I couldn't get my brain away from Ashley and my folder of notes.

I was going to have to go through it with a critical eye to figure out what he could learn from the contents. He was going to discover there were things left out of the official case report, but the question was what that might tell him. Was there anything that would point him in my direction?

I wanted to raise the subject, to ask him why he broke into my desk, but I was certain he would deny it. Why would he do anything else? I could have the blood examined and knew it would match his, but in levelling that accusation, what did I gain? I would make an enemy of him when I wanted to keep him close. How else could I monitor what he was up to?

However, taking the folder by such subversive means told me he was suspicious. He had to be.

I jerked when he nudged my arm with his elbow.

"Hey, are you all right, man? I asked if you wanted to stop for coffee three times. Where were you?"

Zoned out in a bubble of my own thoughts, I hadn't heard him speak at any point.

"Sure. Coffee sounds good."

He pulled into a drive through on the outskirts of Whitstable. It was the first time he'd ever suggested stopping since I met him, and I might have questioned why had I not seen him fighting a yawn that split his face. The caffeine was to help him fight fatigue caused by staying up half the night snooping on me.

I had no sympathy.

Reaching Whitstable, we found John Decker at work, serving a customer behind the counter on the delicatessen side of the butcher's shop. He tried hard to hide his change of expression, but the colour drained from his face the moment he clocked us coming through the door.

We waited patiently, not needing to explain who we were or who we wanted to see. We didn't even need to ask his colleagues to cover his position behind the counter, for they rearranged themselves with a few quickly murmured instructions.

"Am I under arrest again?" he asked, his voice quiet when he came to the end of the counter. A gap there allowed us access to the staff area.

Ashley's reply was smooth. "Not yet."

I let him know, "We have some questions about last night. Is there somewhere we can go?"

He led us into the back of the shop and to an office where a man sat at a desk. He faced the door, his eyes on a computer screen until John knocked on the door frame.

"Ian, can I have the office for a minute? The police are here again."

"Again?" Ian peered around John to look at us.

Neither Ashley nor I said anything, our silence a far greater tool for getting things done on this occasion.

Ian swivelled his chair around and got up.

"Just don't touch anything, okay?"

He left without getting any promises, and I shut the door once we were all inside.

John looked nervous. In fact, he looked positively sick, just like a guilty person would when faced by the police.

No one spoke. John's eyes flitted from Ashley to me and back again, questioning us without opening his mouth. It was a tactic that has often yielded results, the suspect choosing to gabble all manner of things to answer the questions they think we will ask.

John was wise enough to keep his mouth shut until he prompted, "You said you have questions."

Ashley asked, "Where were you last night between eight o'clock and midnight?"

"I was at Ian's. Ask him," John replied with obvious relief, his eyes straying to the door where he hoped to spot Ian outside. "Gail wouldn't let me in, so I crashed in his spare room. We watched a couple of movies and drank some beers. Ian will tell you."

We would check with Ian, but I could already tell I was hearing the truth.

"What movies?" Ashley asked. It was a sensible follow up question that would catch a person out if they were making things up on the spot, especially if the lie wasn't rehearsed with the other person being included.

"*The Meg*. The one with *Jason Statham* and a giant shark. I hadn't seen it before and Ian said it was good, so we watched that and then we watched the sequel. I didn't even know there were two movies. The second one was better than the first."

John was embellishing now, but not in a way that suggested he was lying.

There was no point pursuing it any longer. If John Decker stabbed Oliver Humphries and tossed him in a wheelie bin, he was very good at lying and I already knew he wasn't.

Changing tact, I asked, "Who did you tell about the Viking tattoo?"

I got confusion in John's face but also a question – how did I know?

"What tattoo?"

Nice try, but he debated what to say for too long.

"The Viking tattoo, John. Who did you speak to about it?" I gave him a second to worry, then explained, "You are the only person we spoke to about it. The only person we showed."

"I didn't, I mean ..."

Ashley's phone burst into life, interrupting our questions. He flashed me a grim apology and stepped back to the office door, answering the call quickly and quietly without leaving the room.

I refused to take my eyes away from John's.

"Don't keep me waiting, John."

"I didn't tell anyone, I swear. I didn't realise it was important."

He was lying again, blithely unaware how patently obvious it was.

"Yes, you did, John. I think you know who the person with the Viking tattoo is. I think you told them we have a photograph of it and that we want to speak to the owner. Who is it, John?"

I stepped a little closer, intimidating him with my proximity.

"We can do this in an interview room if you prefer, John."

Ashley touched my arm, and I twisted my head to see what he wanted. He had his phone in the air still, holding it away from his face, but clearly still on the call.

He said, "We have to go."

Was he joking?

"Helen Hoath-Salter is in hospital. Someone ran her over."

Chapter 42

I WAS DISAPPOINTED TO let John off the hook, but it was only temporary. He knew something, of that I was convinced, but whether it would be a secret worth learning, I could not yet guess, and like a yo-yo unable to decide which way it wanted to go, I no longer saw him as the killer.

Hustling to get back to Ashley's car, I said, "This is precisely why no one investigates two cases at the same time."

He knew I was right but wasn't about to admit it. "We are going to close them both, Tony. We came close enough to make Michelle's killer strike again."

"Yes, at the cost of someone's life," I barked. "My, God, man. Are you so blinded by ambition that you've lost sight of that?"

We were standing on either side of his car and about to get in, our faces meeting over the roof. He narrowed his eyes.

"What happened to Oliver Humphries is tragic, but we didn't cause it. The killer has been on the loose all this time but will be brought to justice by our determined actions. That is what I am keeping sight of. If you want to weigh the cost of a life and find someone to blame, look at the people who have kept the killer's identity a secret. Now can we go?" He yanked his door open. "Or do you think Helen's injuries are our fault too? She's another one protecting a killer."

I wanted to wring his neck. We were accountable whether he liked it or not. Both Oliver and Helen had suffered because we couldn't find the killers in time. Helen could have given us a full confession, withdrawing her alibi and naming Elroy Stewart, but she was probably right that doing so would place her in jeopardy.

Unfortunately, keeping her mouth shut did her no favours either.

She had been taken to Kent and Canterbury Hospital, the nearest location with an accident and emergency centre. That was last night, word only finding its way to us more than twelve hours later.

The reception staff identified her ward and gave us directions to find it. There the nurses manning a cluster of desks just inside the ward doors were able to explain her injuries. We knew from the report taken by a pair of constables at the scene that a black Vauxhall Astra hit her from behind. It sent her over the roof to land in a crumpled heap in the street as the car sped off.

It was later reported as stolen, and the car's owner had already been questioned and cleared.

Her right leg was broken in three places, the bones pinned and plated. She had several broken ribs, an open fracture to her right radius, and a multitude of cuts and bruises. She looked very different from the vibrant, attractive woman we met the previous day.

She had given the constables nothing when they questioned her about the attack, and I doubted we would get anything different.

The hospital is an old place, built long before privacy and private rooms were considered standard. She was sharing with three other women, two of whom were very elderly and appeared to be asleep. The fourth bed was currently unoccupied, the patient mobile enough to have wandered to a recreation room somewhere. A TV played quietly at the end of Helen's bed.

She saw us coming and looked away.

We went to her bedside anyway. There were flowers and a couple of cards on the cabinet next to her.

"You did this," she croaked, her voice sounding as bruised as she looked. "This is your fault."

Ashley went around the other side of her bed where he settled into a plastic chair set next to the radiator under the window.

"Helen, if this was Elroy, it shows that he is worried. You can help us put him away for a very long time."

"You two should get your hearing checked. I'm not telling you anything. This was a warning. Do you get that? If he wanted to kill me, I would be dead. I'm just glad it was me. I have a daughter and an elderly mother. Neither of them would have survived this!" Her voice broke as she completed her sentence, the tears flowing to make her look more wretched than before.

I wanted to give her something to hope for. I wanted her to tell us what happened in 2003.

Helen tried to reach up to wipe her face but did so with her right arm and groaned in pain when she lifted it.

I took a tissue from a box on her bedside table, placing it into her left hand.

"Thanks," she mumbled, blowing her nose noisily. I handed her another tissue and held up the bin for her to throw the used one away.

"We can put Elroy away, Helen," I added my voice to Ashley's. "It might not be easy, but refusing to talk isn't doing you any good."

She closed her eyes. "I'm not going to change the statement I gave. It doesn't matter what you say. You don't know who you are dealing with. If you did, you would walk away while you still had the chance.

We persisted, but not for long. She was in pain and emotional, and she wasn't going to change her mind.

Elroy was behind it, not that he was necessarily behind the wheel. He had plenty of lieutenants to whom he could delegate such a task. It was a key argument Helen made more than once – if we put Elroy away, it wouldn't make her safe.

Heading back to the car, I expressed my belief that we should return to Herne Bay nick, but before I could outline what I thought our next steps should be, I spotted Ashley's car's new hood ornament.

Chapter 43

"That's Elroy Stewart," murmured Ashley, seeing the man sitting cross-legged on the bonnet of his police issue Ford Mondeo.

Elroy thought himself to be untouchable, and here was a brazen demonstration of his confidence.

Spotting us, he broke out a broad grin. In his late thirties, Elroy had gained some weight which was probably half fat and half muscle. He had a gold incisor that gleamed despite the lack of sunshine, and more gold on his fingers and around his neck. He wore black jeans with hightop basketball boots that looked box fresh, and a puffy winter coat which he left open to show the expensive brand clothes beneath. His hair was cut short at the sides and back with the top just a little longer. His skin was pockmarked with old acne scars, and he had a wide scar on the left side of his neck that looked like a stab wound.

"Gentlemen," he beamed, sliding down off the Mondeo's bonnet. "Good of you not to keep me waiting too long."

"What are you doing here?" I asked.

"I've come to visit an old girlfriend. I heard she was in a terrible accident yesterday and … well, it's only right that I make sure she is going to mend."

He was taunting us, pushing to see if we would snap.

Meeting his smile with one of my own, I asked, "And what does that have to do with us?" I wanted to ask how he knew the Mondeo was ours, but to do so was to admit he was better informed than we were.

"Oh, well, I have been led to believe that you are asking questions about that scumbag who beat up my grandfather. You'll have convinced yourself that I'm guilty and will waste a whole bunch of time trying to prove it, no doubt. I thought I would save you some trouble. If you want to catch that particular killer, you will need to look elsewhere."

Ashley said, "I think we can figure out where to look."

Elroy hung his head and shook it. "There you go, just like the last lot. You'll come after me even though I'm innocent."

"But you're not innocent, Elroy." Ashley keeps a cooler head than almost anyone I have ever worked with, but I could see he was struggling to keep it now. Elroy was laughing at us.

He was also walking away. Done with his little show, he walked between us and onwards to the hospital.

I watched him for a few seconds. Was he really going into the hospital to intimidate Helen some more?

Ashley announced, "I'm going to follow," but when he started to move, Elroy broke into a run. A dead sprint, in fact.

He tore between the cars, running to get to the hospital's main entrance before we could stop him. Ashley took off without a second thought. He raced to catch Elroy and was probably fast enough to do so. Left in his dust, I gave chase, but questioned if it was the right thing to do.

Shouting, I called after him, "Ashley, wait!"

My partner heard me but gave my request no heed. He was closing on Elroy, but what was he going to do? Tackle him to the ground? Ashley couldn't do anything until he witnessed Elroy committing a crime. The local crime kingpin taunted us with his lines about going to see an old girlfriend, but he wasn't dumb enough to commit a crime in front of our faces.

Except he was.

I was still running after Ashley, but my version of running is more like a jog, and I was only going that fast so I wouldn't be too far behind if Ashley did do something stupid.

However, a woman got out of her car a row ahead of Elroy. She was messing around with her handbag and paying no attention to the large man running straight at her. She only looked up at the last moment.

Elroy swung a fist at her face, punching her in the side of her head as he ran by. The blow felled her like a tree. One moment she was upright, the next she was prone to the tarmac.

Ashley yelled, "Deal with her!" as he sprinted past Elroy's latest victim.

He was going to catch Elroy and did just that before I could get to the woman. Coming from behind, he shunted Elroy's shoulder, sending him off balance and spinning to the ground. I got to see him follow him down, pinning an arm and cuffing it. Ashley was good, better than I ever was at the physical stuff, but Elroy was laughing.

Flat on his stomach with his hands behind his back, Elroy Stewart's belly laughs filled the carpark with noise.

Chapter 44

DISPATCH SENT A SQUAD car to take Elroy back to the nick in Herne Bay where we would question him later. The assault did nothing to help us solve Daniel Mahony's murder, but not only did it distract and delay us, it highlighted that our prime suspect in that case did not see us as a threat.

We were not at a stage where we wanted to question him; that would come when we had sufficient evidence to believe we could achieve a conviction. Yet he was on his way to my home nick, so we had to figure out what to do with him. Should we take the opportunity to lean on him? He knew who we were and that we were asking questions about Daniel Mahony. Doubtless he got the news about us and learned the car's model and VRN from Bobby Lamson. However, that Elroy would choose to confront us first was concerning. It showed a shocking level of confidence.

The woman he assaulted in the carpark was too dazed from the blow to her temple to give a statement and I only got her name, address, and phone number by opening her handbag. Emily Harris was at the hospital for an MRI scan on an old injury. Aged thirty-three, she was an unmarried, single woman with no children, but that was all the information I could glean in the few mumbled answers I got.

Paramedics took her away on a stretcher, advising she would be kept for observation and might have a mild concussion. I would follow up later, but her statement wasn't needed any more than a murder victim is required to point out their killer. We saw the assault and Elroy would be charged. He might even go inside for a spell since it was not his first offence and that could help us.

With Elroy off the streets, people might be more inclined to talk. Additionally, he would have less ability to confound us or get in our way.

However, three hours after the incident in the hospital carpark, just when we were getting ready to interview Elroy for the first time, his lawyer arrived.

Actually, that should be lawyers. Or perhaps even legal team.

Emily Harris had made a statement to the effect that she witnessed two police officers chase and tackle a man. According to her, we then cuffed and restrained Elroy Stewart with significantly more force than the situation called for. Furthermore, Miss Harris claimed her injury came about when Ashley barged into her in his haste to catch Elroy.

There were four solicitors from a firm in Margate, but their seaside location did nothing to diminish their efficiency or forthrightness. In their eyes, Elroy Stewart was a victim of police brutality and one we had deliberately picked out for ill treatment due to his skin colour.

That his racial heritage was the same as Ashley's appeared to have no bearing.

At least we now knew why Elroy found his arrest so amusing – he staged the whole thing. If we dug deep enough, maybe we would find a connection between him and Emily, but was that just another thing to distract us from pursuing the truth about Daniel Mahony? This was a well-executed sting operation Elroy pulled together in a matter of hours. It proved he was resourceful, quick-thinking, and devious.

The leader of the legal team was a woman in her sixties with greying hair and an expression that would stop a charging bull. She served us with notice of restraining orders. They would need to get a court to impose them, but in principle they were accusing us of harassment and would claim their client needed protection.

Superintendent Charters involved himself, checking their paperwork and confirming their side of things. He didn't waste his breath arguing. None of us did.

The lawyers waited, their impatience manifesting in demands for the process to go faster when we released Elroy. Ashley and I distanced ourselves, letting the guys and girls in the custody centre handle our suspect. Had we been there, Elroy would have smugly gloated; he was the sort.

A chunk of our day was gone, and just like yesterday, we had nothing to show for it. Between dead ends on the Michelle Canet side of things and fun and games with Elroy, we might as well have stayed in bed.

Having a quiet moan, Ashley questioned how long it might be before DCI Harris, the head of the cold case task force, took us off the Daniel Mahony investigation. The harassment charges wouldn't stick, but it would be safer to give the case to someone else.

I thought I was in a sour mood, but Aidan had no trouble at all making it worse.

The video was going out on the local news at half-past six and again at ten o'clock. To encourage response, it would have a link people could copy into their browsers, or just click if they were watching on a smart device. The click would take them to a website where they could watch and pause the video as many times as they liked.

"That's great news," said Ashley, shaking Aidan's hand. "Isn't it, Tony?" he asked my opinion and watched to see how I would react. Was he trying to catch me out, or was that just my paranoia?

"Marvellous," I mumbled. Sticking with my opinion that this would only bring out the crazies, I reiterated how much time and effort would be eaten up for the slim chance someone might recognise the blonde woman. Grumpily, I announced, "I'm going back to the CCTV footage from the Michelle Canet case," and wandered away.

Behind me, Aidan muttered, "Always a ray of sunshine that one."

Chapter 45

CONTRARY TO MY CLAIM, I didn't look at the CCTV footage. I'd spent a chunk of the previous day bored out of my mind trying to spot a man with a Viking tattoo on his left forearm and had no desire to repeat the task. I wasn't going to say it was beneath me, but it's not the kind of job one gives to a seasoned detective. One of the problems with being seconded to the cold case task force was the lack of junior personnel to whom I could delegate.

It went back to my original opinion that the task force was nothing more than a butt-covering exercise for the county's chief constable. He was required to react to the backlog of un-solved murders, but he wasn't given any additional funding or resources, so the task force was thrown together to show willing.

Alone in the incident room, my eyes heavy from lack of sleep, the chance to sneak a quick nap was tempting. No one but Ash-ley would come here looking for me, but I expected he would aim his efforts at the Daniel Mahony case. Or Bruce Denton. The thought echoed unbidden in my head, reminding me that he had my file now.

Made angry by the resurfacing memory, I thumped the desk with my fist and wished there was something I could kick across the room. Frustrated, I tilted my head back and closed my eyes. A deep breath to steady myself did nothing of the sort.

I was feeling beaten. The video of Mary was going out in just a couple of hours, and someone was going to identify her. How no one had done so already was beyond me.

I sighed, opened my eyes, and lowered my head so my chin was touching my chest. On the desk right in front of me was the printed copy of Michelle Canet's autopsy report. I didn't want to do any work, but I needed to distract myself, so I picked it up and started to read.

Dr Krauss believed the killer could have a military background, so with nothing else to focus on, I inspected our pool of suspects to see if anyone matched that description.

The clientele in the Old Shipwright the night of Michelle Canet's murder were mostly male. There was a European cup football game on, but from the list of men and women, only three matched the military parameter. They were all British service personnel and it looked as though two were home on leave for the summer. One was a chef in the Navy, the other, the only woman of the three, was a driver in the Royal Logistics Corps. The third was a retired Royal Marine, but his age was listed as eighty-three. I doubted any of them were Michelle's killer.

I was missing something, and it took me a few minutes to work out what it was. The landlord of the pub was ex-army. I saw the tattoo on his right forearm, but the file hadn't recorded any military service against his name. There was nothing to stop a non-military person from getting a military tattoo, but I questioned how many would. The ink had age to it, telling the observant he had it done when he was a much younger man. I was willing to bet my pension he was a soldier at the time.

Tapping into the central database allowed me to find Jack Corman. His military service was there, a full career of twenty-two years. I had to dig a little further to find who he served with, which *was* the $9^{th}/12^{th}$ Lancers, but right in the middle of his service sat a blank space that could only mean one thing. It couldn't be because he went AWOL; that would have resulted in a court martial and a term in the military jail in Colchester. Colloquially called 'the Glasshouse', it would show up on his record. Among his list of decorations, I could see the Long Service and Good Conduct medal to further prove my point.

No, I'd seen the blank space in a soldier's service record before and knew precisely what it meant. Jack Corman qualified to serve with the SAS.

An hour. That was all it took me to find a new suspect. He was questioned as part of the original enquiry, but I found nothing to indicate he was ever considered to be a suspect. I didn't know what his motive could be, but he had opportunity and as Michelle's employer could have easily lured him away from the bar. Jack would have local knowledge too, enough that he could be expected to know where to find a low-level dope dealer like Oliver Humphries.

Above all those things, Jack Corman had the right training. He would know not only how to kill but would have the confidence to do it with swift efficiency. The bayonet used for the task was just the sort of thing an ex-serviceman might have tucked in a drawer at home.

Sitting back, I forced myself to consider the evidence from new angles, yet no matter which way I looked at it, the landlord at the Old Shipwright fit the equation and I had to find him as soon as humanly possible.

Getting to my feet, I straightened my tie and checked my pockets. It was time to find out if Jack Corman had a tattoo of a Viking on his left forearm.

Chapter 46

I LOOKED FOR ASHLEY in the second incident room, but the door was locked, so he either wasn't there or he was choosing to hide from me, which I doubted. A quick peek through a window on the east side of the building confirmed his car was still where he parked it. He was somewhere in the station then, so I set off for the break room. Not because I expected to find him there, but because I wanted a coffee.

Coming into the break room, I ran into Gavin Dobbs. He had three cups of coffee in his hands but paused in the door to speak with me. Gavin is a capable detective, yet I have always found him too eager to please to be someone I would ever hang around with.

"Oh, hey, Tony," he beamed with unaccountable enthusiasm. "Great news about the video. Do you think someone will come forward?"

I certainly hoped not, but I said, "We shall have to wait and see. The quality isn't great even after Aidan's best efforts, but you never know …"

"Someone is bound to, Tony. I shall be praying this provides the break you need to solve the case."

This was typical behaviour for Gavin. Always looking on the bright side, always expecting the best outcome.

I dipped my head towards the mugs he held. "Shouldn't you deliver those before they get cold?"

"Probably better had." He scurried away, leaving me alone in the coffee room with thoughts of Bruce Denton clouding my mind.

"Penny for your thoughts."

I turned to find Doris ambling toward me with an empty mug in her hand.

"Everything all right, Tony? You look tired."

She caught me hunched over the sink, staring into nothing again. I was going to get caught. After all these years I was going to get caught. Dobbs was right about the video; someone was bound to come forward and there was nothing I could do to prevent it.

I took too long to answer her, and I guess she could see the emotions in my face because she put a hand on my arm.

"It is that Bruce Denton case again, Tony? You really shouldn't let it get to you. It will all turn out all right in the end." She was trying to be kind, but I didn't need her to feel sorry for me. I felt sorry enough for myself. "Shall I make you a coffee?"

I let a sad smile form. "Thanks, Doris."

"It's no bother. I am making one for myself."

She set about cleaning her mug before fetching a spare one out of the cupboard for me. Leaning against the counter, I recalled the wink I saw earlier.

"Doris, can I ask what you think of my new partner?" That wasn't a question I had any interest in asking, yet it provided a circuitous route to the one I hoped to pose.

"Ashley? He's really nice. A bit ambitious perhaps, but his heart seems to be in the right place. That's not what you really want to know though, is it?" Good old Doris. Two decades past the age when most people would retire and still sharp as a knife. My smile was genuine this time, but I had a serious question to ask.

"I saw you wink at him earlier when we passed you. It looked conspiratorial. Are the two of you up to something?"

Her attention was on the mugs into which she was spooning coffee granules. She didn't turn to look at me, but she did stiffen. "Up to something?" she repeated my question. "No, why?"

And there it was, a lie. I wasn't going to call her on it, but rather than clarify why I asked the question, I fired another her way.

"Has he been asking you about the Bruce Denton case?"

This time her shoulders slumped in defeat, she put the spoon down, and looked up to meet my eyes. "A little bit, yes, Tony, but I don't think you should be mad about it."

"And why is that?" I enquired. I was furious, but quite able to keep it from showing. Of course Ashley was asking questions behind my back, why would I expect anything less? He'd never hidden his interest in the case and with the camcorder video I tried to hide thirty years ago, he had reason to believe some headway could be made.

"Because he wants to solve it for you, Tony."

I blinked. "No, he wants to solve it for the glory it will bring him."

Doris conceded the point. "Well, yes, that too, but I genuinely believe he wants to give you some closure. We all do, Tony. I've watched this thing eat away at you for years. For decades. You should work with him, Tony. Dust off that old file you've got and see what the two of you can figure out together."

If only she knew the truth.

Chapter 47

ASHLEY WAS LOOKING FOR me when I found him. I wanted to ask where he'd been, but doubted I wanted to hear the answer since my paranoid side was convinced he must have been delving into Bruce Denton again.

Instead of asking, I said, "I have a new suspect we need to look at."

That got his attention.

"The landlord, Jack Corman, is ex-SAS."

Ashley looked doubtful. "That's not recorded anywhere."

Allowing myself to look just a little bit smug, I said, "Nope. I had to dig to find it."

"Show me."

So I did.

"Tony, this is brilliant."

"I know." My lack of modesty was a conscious choice and being used to mask my conflicted emotions.

"We need to bring him in to be interviewed."

I shook my head. "Not yet. I want to know more before I question him. We both do. When he sits across the table from me, I am going to know more about what he did than he does. That requires talking to other people. But what we can do is ask him to roll up his sleeve."

Ashley saw the wisdom in my plan. "If he has the tattoo, we will have to arrest him."

"We will." If we seriously suspected he was guilty of two murders, there would be no option and the tattoo would tie him firmly to the attack on Oliver Humphries the night Michelle Canet was killed. The tattoo remained an annoying anomaly. Was it key to the case, or was it a total red herring? I did not know and potentially never would unless I found the man who owned it.

In the car, I coached Ashley on how I wanted to approach the pub landlord.

"I don't want him to think we are on to him. We should come across as routine."

Behind the steering wheel, Ashley frowned. "You don't want to make him nervous?"

"Not yet. Nervous suspects tend to dig themselves a hole as they try to figure out what we know, but right now we don't really know anything beyond the tenuous fact that his training could explain the method used to stab Canet and Humphries. I want him to think we are simply seeking to eliminate him from our enquiries. If the tattoo is his, it changes things. If not ... well, we can withdraw and expect him to carry on his usual business while we delve deeper into his movements both last night and three years ago."

"But we are going to ask what he was doing between eight and midnight last night, right?"

I liked this. The upper hand was generally wielded by Ashley purely because he'd been studying the cases for more than a week before we met. Now I knew more than him and felt much more comfortable dictating our strategy.

However, he was right about the need to ask the question.

It was close to five o-clock when we set off for Whitstable again. The old me would have found something to make me look busy until the end of my shift, but I was different now for a number of reasons. I could describe it as having my mojo back, but I'm not sure what a mojo is even if I am familiar with the expression.

Traffic was building, but Ashley slipped through to park in Keam's Yard car park once more. From there it was a short walk to the Old Shipwright. Naturally, it was open as any public house would be, but the bar was largely empty. The town bloats with tourists in the summer and on sunny days. It can even get quite busy in the winter at the weekends, but on a drab Thursday in October the only people in the pub were two old boys propping up the bar.

Behind the taps, a tall, thin man with a waxed moustache and a smart waistcoat asked, "What can I get you, gents?"

I flashed him my warrant card. "The landlord, please."

His mouth opened and closed, processing the unexpected request.

"I'll, ah ... I'll see if he is in."

I was willing to bet he was, but we would find out soon enough.

The barman ducked through a door in the wall behind him, vanishing from sight when he turned right. Like most old pubs, it was a house as well as a place of business. The downstairs rooms at the back of the building might have been part of the landlord's home a few decades ago, the rooms upstairs where he and his family would sleep. Nowadays, I knew the rooms were more commonly used to accommodate cheap bar staff coming in from the continent. The landlord could pay them less by making up the balance in cheap or free rent with the added bonus that they were at his fingertips if he needed them.

Music played in the background from a system tucked away behind the bar somewhere, rather than from a jukebox, but it was quiet enough that we heard the barman calling Jack's name from deep inside the house and the sound of footsteps descending old, wooden stairs a few moments later.

The barman reappeared through the hole in the wall, his eyes flicking our way when he said, "He's just coming." Feeling our eyes on him, he then found a job to do at the other end of the bar.

Jack Corman appeared in the hole in the wall, but stopped there. He had on a similar outfit to the previous day – jeans, Timberland boots, a shirt, and a crew neck jumper.

"I was just doing the books," he announced unnecessarily. "Something I can help you with?"

"Here?" Ashley enquired, his question aimed not at our latest suspect, but at me.

I nodded.

Ashley said, "Mr Corman can you roll up your sleeves, please?"

His eyebrows performed a little dance.

"Your sleeves, please," Ashley repeated.

For a second I wondered if he might refuse; he was within his rights to do so, but then we would just take him back to the nick, make him jump through a whole load of hoops, and would get to see his arms anyway. It would just take longer.

His dancing eyebrows stopped when he reached the same conclusion. Huffing out a bored breath, he reached across to his right wrist with his left hand to undo the button on his shirt cuff.

"Can I ask why I am showing you my forearms?"

"We want to eliminate you from our enquiries," I lied.

"And that requires seeing my forearms? What are you looking for?"

"A tattoo."

He looked up to check I was being serious but kept rolling his sleeve.

"Well, here's one," he showed us the 9th/12th Lancers tattoo on his right arm. The timbre in his voice was a little defiant, but no different from what I expected. He was being asked to perform tasks in his place of work where he was master and commander. It would irk me too.

"You want to see them both?" he questioned. Was he stalling? I was in little doubt Oliver died because he told us about the tattoo and we told John Decker. John then told someone else and word found its way to the killer. If that was Jack Corman, then he knew we were on to him and that showing us the Viking would identify him.

Ashley said, "Yes, please, Mr Corman."

Tutting and sighing, Jack undid the cuff on his left sleeve using his right hand and slowly pushed both the jumper and shirt up to his elbow.

My heart beat just a little faster in anticipation, but the artwork I hoped to see wasn't there. A scar was instead.

The skin on the upper surface of his left forearm had the melted look I associate with terrible burns. It started an inch above his wrist and ended just below his elbow. I would need to turn his arm over to see how far it extended, but what I could see was the distorted ink embedded in the ruined skin. A small patch of it was deep red, just like the eye of the Viking warrior.

I asked, "How did you get the scar?"

Jack started to roll the sleeve down until I motioned that he should stop and came closer to get a better look.

"I have a brazier in the back to dispose of mail. The wife is paranoid about identity theft and thinks we should burn anything with our name on it. Well, someone put a used aerosol canister in there one day and it blew up when I was adding some old bills and things. I got flaming liquid on my bare skin and this is the result."

"When did that happen?"

His eyes went up and right to engage the memory portion of his brain.

"Between Christmas and New Year in 2021. Easy to remember because I spent New Year's Eve in hospital being treated for my burns and that's my most lucrative night of the year. Never did find out who was responsible for the aerosol can."

I had a next, rather obvious question, but Ashley asked it first. "What was the tattoo of?"

"This 'un?" he used his head to indicate his left arm.

We both nodded. What other tattoo could we possibly be talking about?

His cheeks flushed and he looked panicked for a second. It was exactly what I would expect to see from a man who was trying to think up a believable lie.

"Um."

I leaned in a little closer. "Yes?"

"Um. It was a heart with two cherubs holding a banner that said 'Mum'."

Expletives reverberated inside my head.

Ashley asked, "Do you have any pictures that show the tattoo as it was before the accident?"

Put back on the spot, Jack looked worried again. "Um, yeah, probably. I'll have to have a look. I don't take a lot of pictures of myself, truth be told."

Ashley persisted. "Can you find one now?"

Jack thought about it, but not for long. "No, sorry. I won't have anything like that here. I would have to go back to the house. You're not going to make me do that now, are you? I'm understaffed as it is. I could bring one to the station tomorrow morning."

Before Ashley could give him a reply either way, I changed my approach.

"You were in the SAS, were you not?"

The question came as a surprise, but Jack swelled with pride when he admitted. "I was. 1998 until 2000. It was the best time I ever had in the army. Nothing compares."

His answer cleared away any residual doubt about the blank space in his career history.

I hit him with the follow up. "Where were you last night between eight o'clock and midnight?"

His face clouded again, my sudden change in direction impacting his mental balance.

Slowly, he said, "I was here."

"The whole time?"

"Yeah," he sounded more confident now.

"Can anyone confirm that?"

"Of course. The bar staff and the customers. I talked to lots of them."

"Were you in plain sight the whole time?"

His confidence wobbled. "Well, not the whole time. I had work to do upstairs. Look, what is this about? I think I have a right to know why I am being questioned."

Chapter 48

WE LEFT THE OLD Shipwright just a few minutes later. I suspected Jack Corman of two murders, but I had nothing to tie him to them. Not yet.

He demanded to know why he was being questioned, but rather than answer, I asked him how well he knew John Decker. Jack pretended not to know who that was, only acknowledging that he did when Ashley showed him a photograph. He then claimed not to know John's last name; telling us he was just one of the guys who came into the pub. Jack also said he hadn't seen him in months.

His claims gave us ammunition if we could prove he was lying about any of it. However, to do that we needed to speak with his bar staff, both those employed now and three years ago. There were only a couple who fell into both subsets. We could collect CCTV footage from the streets between the pub and the petrol station where Oliver's body was found, and we could interrogate the statements collated three years ago. Now that we had a target on which we could focus, things became a little easier.

Walking back to the car, Ashley asked, "You want to keep going or call it a day?"

I would have answered straight away, but a yawn split my face. It prompted Ashley to do the same.

"I think we might both benefit from a good night's sleep."

Ashley couldn't argue, but it reminded me why he was feeling tired and yet I again I questioned whether to challenge him about my folder. I was going to take my copy home tonight, that was for sure. It would stop anyone else from getting their grubby little hands on it and allow me to go through it with a fine-toothed comb. Was there something within the cardboard covers that would lead him to me? I didn't think so, but then I never expected anyone else to look at my notes.

I was still debating what to do when we got back to the nick in Herne Bay. The sun was down already, the lights inside shining out into the carpark to illuminate those working inside.

We met Gavin Dobbs coming down the stairs.

"Oh, hey guys. They've got it on in the briefing room. Come on. It's about to start."

I made way so he could get past us, but voiced my confusion, "What's about to start?"

He continued toward the briefing room, turning around to go backwards with an 'are you serious?' look on his face.

"The video, dummy. Your video. It's about to go out on the news. The superintendent is going to be on TV."

I shot my cuff. It was almost six thirty. The local news would start any second. Somehow the terror of the video streaming into millions of homes across the southeast had slipped my mind. Now it was back, and it was like abruptly finding a hedgehog doing cartwheels in my underwear.

Ashley had one foot on the bottom step, but changed his mind and went with Gavin. Looking my way, he said, "I'll see you in the morning."

Whether he could read it in my face, or believed he knew me well enough to guess how I would cast my vote, he could tell I wasn't going into the briefing room to watch the big screen with everyone else. I hadn't known the boss was going to be on the news himself, and now that I did, I fervently hoped he would make a complete fool of himself.

I wasn't hanging around to watch though.

All in all, it had been a long and very odd day. Elroy Stewart made us look like fools, Ashley made a copy of my personal Bruce Denton file, and we spent most of the time chasing our tails. I had no reason to think tomorrow would be any different and prayed it wouldn't be. I would take another bad day as a cop over the very present possibility that someone would see the video and identify my wife.

Chapter 49

By the time I got home, the local news was over and Mary was sitting very quietly at the kitchen table. It was the first time she had ever seen the footage, and it affected her worse than I expected.

"It was odd," she said, her voice barely more than a whisper. "Seeing him again, I mean. It brought back memories I haven't thought about in years." I pulled my chair up next to hers and put an arm around her shoulder. "You were right, Tony. It is easy to see that it's me."

"Only to those who know you really well, love. I know it's you, but not many others will. I think your friends would have figured it out if it had been shown at the time, but it wasn't. You don't look like that now."

She looked up at me, biting her lip. "Can't they ... I don't know, do clever stuff with a computer to create an image of what I might look like now?"

"Yes, but they need to see your face to do that. We got lucky. Now we just have to hope our luck holds."

"Do you think it will?" She asked the question quickly, latching onto the optimism I didn't really feel, but projected for her sake. There was no point telling her otherwise now.

"Yes, love. The police are as clueless as they have ever been."

"You're the police, Tony."

I smiled and tucked a stray strand of her hair behind her right ear. "That's right, love. Does anyone need a clearer demonstration?" I was making a joke and it worked to ease some of her tension. She leaned into me, letting her head fall to rest on my shoulder.

"I haven't done anything for dinner," she admitted. "I wasn't sure I could face food."

"Do you want anything now?"

She took a second to reflect on the subject before saying, "No. I'm not hungry."

I was, but a sandwich and a bag of crisps would suffice.

"Shall I cook for you?" she volunteered. I was about to tell her there was no need when I questioned if a task to distract her might not be the best medicine.

She made me bangers and mash with onion gravy which I washed down with a beer. Okay, with three beers before switching to whisky. It was that kind of day.

Chapter 50

In the morning, I woke early, dreams about the night I murdered Bruce Denton depriving me of the rest I needed. I left Mary sleeping and went downstairs.

A quick glance through my living room window confirmed there were no cop cars or reporters camped outside my door. So far so good.

I made tea and turned on the TV. I had almost an hour before I needed to get ready for work, but did I want to turn on the news and risk seeing the video when they went to the local segment? The answer was no, so I found a cooking show and let it play quietly. The host, some American woman I didn't know, demonstrated the perfect Hallowe'en cookie recipe.

Bored within about half a second, I attuned my thoughts to the Michelle Canet case. I thought we stood a good chance of solving it, especially when compared to the Daniel Mahony enquiry. I wanted to call that one dead in the water, but as

I thought about how the witnesses had all been scared away by someone, almost certainly Elroy, I realised that I needed to approach it with a more optimistic attitude.

Bruce Denton's case was now officially reopened and waiting for me and Ashley to tear into it. I argued against having two cases at the same time, but that's what happened. However, there was no chance he could justify trying to work a third simultaneously. My young partner's strategy could be made to work in my favour.

I would argue that we could solve the two cases already under-way, and in doing so push back Bruce Denton. That would give me time to manage anything that came out of the local news coverage.

I downed my tea, congratulating myself on yet another genius Heaton plan until I remembered everything hinged on no one coming forward to identify Mary. If just one person pointed the finger her way, everyone would see it.

Convinced it was time to be a good husband, I put together a tray with a pot of tea, some grapefruit slices and a plate of toast cut into triangles. I carried it upstairs to find Mary awake and sitting up in bed with her reading glasses perched on the end of her nose.

She was looking at her phone, her free hand poised in the air to scroll or tap as necessary. She looked over the top of her glasses as I came into the room.

"Breakfast in bed, my love."

"Goodness, what's brought this on?"

I held the tray above her lap until she had shuffled back to a more upright position. Then I placed it across her thighs and perched on the edge of her side of the bed to deliver a kiss.

"I have to get ready for work," I replied, avoiding the need to respond to her question. Expressing my emotions is not one of my strong suits, but she knows that I love her. I mean, lots of people say they would kill for their loved one, but how many could claim they actually did so? Well, I could and believe me when I say actions speak louder than words. I tensed my leg muscles to get up, but Mary stopped me.

"Hey, not so fast there." She looped a hand around my head and pulled me down for a proper kiss. A kiss that spoke of not getting a whole lot done for the next twenty minutes and having to rush to get to work.

I should be so lucky.

Mary broke the kiss, removed her arm from behind my head and used it to push me away.

"Now, be off with you and catch some bad guys. I've got breakfast to eat."

Just like that her focus was back on her phone and she didn't even look away from it when her free hand snagged a piece of toast. If she was worried, it wasn't showing right now.

I was smiling when I headed for the shower.

Chapter 51

I GOT TO WORK early enough to snag a spot that wasn't right at the back of the carpark for once and sauntered into work doing my absolute best to look casual. Worried about anything? Not me.

I found Ashley at his desk in the office where half a dozen others were already bent over their keyboards.

"Any developments overnight?" It was a broad question designed to encapsulate everything we were working on and more.

"If you're asking about responses to the video, then yes and no. When I checked half an hour ago the tally was a hundred and forty-two calls, but none of them were considered worth following up."

I nodded, accepting the news with as much indifference as I could muster. It was as I expected. As I hoped.

"On the other cases, I still have nothing from canvassing the local tattoo artists. No one is admitting to the Viking design, but I did go back through statements from the people in the bar on September 3rd, 2020, and I think the landlord had an altercation with Michelle."

I pulled up a handy nearby chair and sat down.

"That is interesting. What was it about?"

"That is not recorded, and I'm reading between the lines a little." Knowing that required a little more explanation, Ashley added, "There's a line in two of the statements taken from the bar staff about being able to account for where Michelle was at half-past eight because he was arguing with Jack. One said she avoided going to change a barrel because she could hear Jack shouting."

"Raised voices. Have you tracked her down already?"

"Yes, but it will have to be a phone conversation. She is Dutch and was over here on a student visa. I tracked down an address for her in Ghent."

"That's in Belgium," I pointed out.

Ashley looked at me like I was going mad.

"I know that, Tony. Regardless, she is from Holland and has an address in Belgium. Chances are she works there. The other statement it shows up in is another woman, but she is English and living in Whitstable. I'm not sure what she will tell us though."

"Why do you say that?"

"Because she's Jack Corman's daughter."

Depending on her relationship with her father, she might have a very different take on her father's argument with Michelle. She might tell us he shouted at everyone, or she might say that Michelle deserved it and provide us with a reason why. Either thing would help to build a picture.

"And since we will be in Whitstable …" Ashley continued, "I want to drop in on Rachael Weaver and Christine Westbury. They're the …"

"Two witnesses who placed Elroy Stewart behind the wheel of the silver BMW only to later withdraw their statements." I completed his sentence to show I had done my homework too. I had to act like I was on board with his plan to tackle both cases simultaneously, even if I thought it folly. Anything to delay starting on Bruce Denton.

We had a plan for the day. Or for the morning, at least. All that remained was for us to execute it. We started with the phone call. The person we hoped to speak with had a mobile number listed in the case file. It had a Dutch prefix and felt like a long shot, but it rang when Ashley dialled it and was answered almost immediately. In Dutch. Or possibly Belgian. I've never been any good at languages. For that matter is there such a language as Belgian or do they speak French there?

"Dag."

Ashley's tongue flicked out to wet his lips. He sucked in a fast breath and started to talk.

"Good morning. Am I speaking with Rita Huisman? This is Detective Sergeant Long of the Kent Police in England."

"Oh." Rita was taken aback. "Yes, this is Rita. Is there a problem?"

From her file, we knew her to be a twenty-three-year-old woman, but there was no photograph and no description to indicate what she might look like. Her appearance didn't matter, but I am used to interviewing people with their faces in front of me. It's all so much easier to read them that way. Without that option, I found myself trying to picture her face and in my head she looked like Noomi Rapace from the original *Girl with a Dragon Tattoo* miniseries. Don't ask me why, perhaps I just had tattoos on my brain, but that was who I pictured.

"No, no problem exactly," Ashley tried to put her at ease. "Rita, I need to ask your permission to record this conversation. Will you permit that?"

There was a short pause. "Um, sure, okay."

Ashley activated the record function. "Rita, you worked at a public house called the Old Shipwright in the summer of 2020."

"Is this about Michelle?" she guessed.

"Yes, Rita, the case has been reopened and I have a couple of questions I need to ask you. Is now a good time?"

I shook my head. That was a question I would never ask. It invites the other person to say that it is not. They could then get their facts straight and be ready for the call when it was convenient to them. Or just keep ducking it by refusing to answer the call. Especially in a different country where Rita could expect that we wouldn't just show up at her house or place of work.

It was a rookie mistake, but he got away with it.

"It's as good as any other. Fire away."

Her English was impeccable, but I'd heard that about the Dutch. Apart from a slight accent, I wouldn't have known she wasn't English.

Her memory of the night of the murder was from her viewpoint and she had been tending bar on a busy night. Basically, she pulled a thousand pints and suffered propositions from three dozen drunken men. However, she confirmed the part of her statement about not changing a barrel because Jack was shouting at Michelle.

"Did you hear what was said?"

"Not really, but I think it was to do with Michelle sneaking off."

"Did he do that often?"

"Often enough that it was a problem. I didn't mind so much, Michelle was fun to work with and he was gay so I didn't have to worry about getting 'accidentally' fondled like I did with the other men working there. He was a bit of a slut though."

I was yet to speak but wanted clarity on that point.

"Rita, this is Detective Sergeant Heaton. I am working this case with DS Long. Can you clarify what you mean when you call Michelle a slut, please?"

"The term is well known in English, is it not?" She sounded like she was questioning herself and whether she had the wrong word. "He used to have sex with lots of different men. He was known for it and would make jokes."

"And you think that was what Jack was angry about?"

"I can't say. Sorry. They were arguing. Jack was shouting, and I heard Michelle say that he had been on a break, but you don't really get breaks when you work a bar on a busy night."

Ashley held up a finger to indicate he had a question. "Rita, did Jack shout at people often?"

"No. I don't recall him ever shouting at anyone else."

That meant it wasn't normal behaviour and could, by extension, be considered out of character. Another way to frame that was to say that Michelle's behaviour caused Jack to display an extreme emotion. That was a long way from plunging a knife into someone's heart, but we were a step closer.

Being careful not to put words into Rita's mouth, we extracted a fresh statement that made it clear Jack was demonstrably angry with Michelle roughly an hour before he was murdered.

When the call ended, Ashley fished his keys from his pocket and stood up.

"Ready to go?"

I stayed where I was and took out my phone. "Not yet. I need to make a phone call."

Chapter 52

MARVIN THE MARTIAN ANSWERED almost before his phone started ringing.

"Tony?"

"Were you sitting on it?"

"It was in my hand. I was about to make a call. Are you calling to talk about Oliver Humphries? You are linking that to the Michelle Canet case, right?"

"We are. Did you get a copy of the coroner's report? Oliver's wound is almost exactly the same as Michelle's."

"Yes, I saw that. Dr Krauss is of the opinion that it could be someone from the special forces."

I didn't have to explain the background at least.

"Jack Corman is ex-SAS."

Marvin swore. "You're not kidding?"

"Fraid not. There is a blank in his military record and he confirmed why when I asked him. But listen, don't feel bad about missing it. I would have too without the advice from Dr Krauss."

"All the same ..." Like any cop out there, he hated that he might have let a criminal go because he didn't dig deep enough into the detail.

"Listen, I called to ask about Corman. He had an argument with Michelle about an hour before the murder and it got a little heated. Did you ask him about it at the time?"

"Of course. He told us the Frenchman had a habit of vanishing during his shift and he wanted to make sure he wasn't going to do it again. According to Corman, Michelle got defensive and told him he would do whatever he wanted when he was due a break. I would need to look back at my notes, but I think I am right in saying that the landlord was quite forthcoming with information. He said he was looking at firing him the next day but didn't want to do it that night because the pub was so busy."

"Was there any suggestion as to where Michelle went when he vanished?"

"Only hearsay. We were never able to prove it, but the rumour was that he would nip off for a quickie with someone from the bar. A couple of the girls working there made it sound like he was always nipping off with someone and that it was rarely the same man."

I had a final question. "Was he ever in your sights as a possible suspect?"

"Corman? No. He came across as above board and I think between his statement and others we accounted for his time that night to within a close enough window to rule him out. Obviously, the site of the murder is less than two minutes' walk from the pub, so a five-minute round trip would do it. Do you like him for it?"

I sucked on my bottom lip, debating what answer to give.

"I do."

Chapter 53

It was almost ten when we left the nick in Herne Bay and just after the hour when we arrived in West Malling. Our first stop was the address listed for Jenny Corman. Jack had one daughter and two sons. Both his boys followed dad into the army, but his youngest, Jenny, stayed at home, or rather, stayed in the area because her address was not the same as her parents.

We had a phone number for her, but like many people it had changed in the last three years, most likely when she switched phone contracts.

There was no answer at her door and her neighbours on both sides were out too. I was about to suggest we found a number for her mother or went to Jenny's parent's house when a woman across the street came out of her front door.

"Are you looking for Jenny?"

I was closest. "Indeed, we are. Do you know where we can find her?"

Dashing my hopes, she said, "No, sorry. I'm not sure what she does for work, but she leaves the house early every day when I am out walking my dog. Is she in trouble?" The question explained her desire to provide us with information – she was being nosey.

"Just helping us with our enquiries," I replied, already aiming my feet at Ashley's Ford Mondeo. Muttering to myself, I added, "If we can find her."

Our next port of call was her parents' house. Jack and Sheila had occupied the same house since he left the army nearly fifteen years earlier. There they raised two kids who were probably glad to be able to settle in one school rather than being moved all the time with their father's postings.

Their house on Pierpoint Road provided a commanding view down across the roofs of Whitstable and was high enough to see the Isle of Sheppey to the west and all the way to Thanet Sound to the east. It wasn't a big place, but I've heard location is everything.

There was a car on the driveway and another in the street in front of the house. I imagined Jack would be home at this time of the day; pub hours are like that.

However, when Mrs Corman answered the door, she took one look at Ashley's warrant and looked about ready to faint.

"Oh, God, what's happened to him?" she wailed. "I knew something was wrong. He always answers his phone." In her early fifties, Sheila Corman had filled out at the hips and bust and just about everywhere else. Her blonde hair was dyed to hide the grey, but it looked good, and she was clearly a woman who took pride in her appearance. The colour drain from her face and she sagged against the door.

I had to barge past Ashley to catch her, though she probably wouldn't have fainted.

"Mrs Corman, we are not here to deliver news about your husband," I reassured her while supporting her weight and lowering her to the hallway carpet. "When did you last hear from him?"

"Last night."

I had her sitting on the floor with her back to the wall. "At what time?"

"Oh, about seven."

"Did he say anything that surprised you or gave you reason to think that he might not come home?" The thought running through my head was that we triggered him to take flight. It was that or he went down the suicide route. As a cross section of the population, ex-service personnel have a far higher likelihood of taking their own lives. I prayed it was the former, but either way it sounded more and more like we had found the killer.

"No, he … hold on." Sheila twisted her head to look at me. "If you're not here to tell me where he is, why are you here?"

I almost told her we were looking at her husband as a suspect in a murder enquiry, but now was not the time. Instead, I said, "Actually, we were looking for your daughter and hoped you might be able to tell us where we can find her."

Sheila apologised. "Sorry. We fell out a few years ago and haven't spoken since. She got an abortion, and I don't believe in killing babies. I don't know where she works, and I don't want to."

Loitering just inside the door, Ashley asked, "Who would know?"

Sheila shrugged and started to slowly get up.

"Her friends, I guess. Her boyfriend if she has one. I'm afraid I don't have contact numbers for any of them. She's in trouble then?"

"Just helping us with our enquiries," I replied. She took my hand when I offered it, allowing me to help her back to her feet.

Once upright, she bent at the waist. "Stood up too quick."

Her husband was in the wind and we needed to know more before we left.

"Shall I make a pot of tea?" I suggested. "We should talk about where your husband might be."

Ashley closed the front door and followed me to the kitchen where it was Sheila, not I, who pressed the kettle into service.

"I can do that," offered Ashley, only to be waved away.

"You'll only do it wrong," she remarked, opening a cupboard to withdraw an actual teapot. My parents always used one, but it was a thing of the past now and I hardly ever saw one in use unless I was in a café.

I asked, "Mrs Corman, what do you remember about a man called Michelle Canet?"

She was on her way to the sink with the kettle but paused there searching her memory. Her face changed when she identified why she knew the name.

"That's that fella who worked at the pub. Someone killed him and they ... I mean you lot, couldn't find the killer."

I nodded to confirm she had things about right.

"The case has been reopened and a second murder occurred just the night before last."

She thought about that for a second or so before turning to the sink and running the tap.

"Okay." She had her back to us, and it was about the most noncommittal answer a person could give.

Continuing, I said, "The wound on the second victim is the same as that on the first. That suggests the killer is the same person."

She took the kettle back to its spot and flicked the switch to make it work. Fetching mugs from the same cupboard as the teapot, we got another, "Okay." The second one came laced with the suggestion of a question mark. We were feeding her information, but she didn't know why.

"The killer employed a technique taught to special forces soldiers ..." I left that snippet hanging, certain she would see where I was going.

Sheila whipped around so fast she knocked a mug over. It rolled toward the edge of the counter, threatening to spill before the handle acted as a brake. Her eyes were wide and her mouth was open.

"You think he did it!" It was a statement, not a question.

Now that I had her looking directly at me, I asked a question that would get either an honest answer or an outright lie.

"Sheila, does your husband own any military memorabilia? Anything he might have brought home from his time overseas?"

"My husband didn't kill anyone!"

"Answer the question, please." I remained calm in the face of her excitement. To my left, Ashley was completely impassive. I was on a roll and he was wise enough not to get in the way.

"No, he doesn't. Only a few trinkets." She lied and then corrected herself.

"Does he own a bayonet, Sheila?"

"No!" It came across as truthful, but it was entirely possible she just didn't know.

Not long after the second gulf war in 2003, I was investigating a hold up committed at a convenience store on the outskirts of Herne Bay. The man used an AK47, a Russian manufactured weapon used extensively around the world for its simplicity and reliability. When I caught him, I discovered the weapon was just one of a horde brought back from Iraq. In his attic, a forensic team found forty-two guns of different calibres and makes plus a brace of rocket-propelled grenades. I very much doubted he was the only one out there who saw fit to smuggle guns into the country on his return from war.

I challenged her, "Are you sure?"

"Yes!" She was telling the truth about her knowledge and now it was time for her to fire a question back at me. "Is this why he didn't come home last night? Does he know you think he did it? He's got mental health issues, you know! They all have. I've never met a squaddie who didn't."

I ducked her question. "Mrs Corman, your husband is wanted in connection with the murder of Michelle Canet. He needs to answer some questions, and it is imperative we speak with him today."

"Well, you'd better get out there and find him then, hadn't you?" Her ire was up and she was using it as fuel to batter her fragility away. "My husband doesn't own a bayonet, he didn't kill Michelle Canet, and he definitely didn't kill anyone else."

There was a part of me that really wanted to ask if we were still getting a cup of tea. Thankfully, I ignored my urges and kept my mouth shut. We were out of the house thirty seconds later. Sheila didn't know where Jack was and probably wouldn't tell us if she did. She also believed it when she protested his innocence.

That didn't bother me, I've interviewed dozens of spouses or partners who had no clue what their loved one was up to. However, his failure to return home after work last night concerned me.

Ashley echoed my thoughts when he asked, "Think he went on the run?"

Did I? I couldn't tell. His wife voiced her concern that he might take his own life, but that didn't ring true to me. If a person is willing to kill to protect their secret, it suggests they believe there is a way out for them without taking the ultimate step. Being questioned by us might have precipitated his decision to vanish, but it was necessary to check if any bodies had been found in the last twelve hours.

That was cleared up by a call to dispatch who came back almost immediately to confirm there were no known suicides in the area in last night and no unidentified bodies at the morgue.

We went back to the pub.

Chapter 54

UNLIKE PREVIOUS VISITS, WE ditched the car on the double yellow lines right outside the pub. Ashley activated the blue and white lights hidden in the front grill and rear lights and thumped on the side door until someone answered.

That took more than a minute, with Ashley shouting, "Police, open up," loud enough that no one inside could claim they didn't hear it.

Blinking in the sunlight as though just roused from their bed, which they evidently had been, were two young women. They had on shorts and t-shirt style pyjamas and bare feet. They were both brunettes and both had their hair tied up. There were sleep wrinkles indented into their faces where moments ago they were face down on their pillows.

It took me a second to realise I was looking at twins.

"Show me some ID," demanded the one on the left, still using the door as a barrier in case we were not who we claimed to be.

Ashley had his out at the ready and I added mine to help alleviate their concerns.

"We need to speak with the landlord, Jack Corman," said Ashley.

"He's not here," replied the one on the left.

"Then we need to look around," I expressed in a hopeful tone. "He didn't go home last night." The second sentence did the trick. It was completely truthful, but it made them think the police were at the pub following up a missing person's report.

They let us in, retreating from the cold air outside in a hurry to return to the warm. We followed them to a set of stairs where we split.

"You go with them," I said, turning left through the hole in the wall that led into the bar. "I'll make sure he isn't down here."

I have always found it strange to be in a pub when it is closed just because of the history contained in them. Cemented into the mortar on the building's front façade is a stone tablet giving the date it was erected: 1782. In terms of public houses, that made it almost new. How many millions of pints had been spilled into the floorboards on which I now walked? How much blood had been spilled? How many women went into labour within these walls?

I lifted the flap in the counter to access the patrons' area and strolled around. I didn't really expect to find Jack sleeping in a corner, so it came as no great surprise when I didn't.

At the front window, I peered between the frosted lettering to the world outside. A troop of cyclists went by on their road bikes. It triggered something in the back of my mind, a stray thought telling me I should be paying attention to them.

I watched the bikes and riders vanish down the road still wondering what my subconscious was trying to tell me.

"Tony?"

I heard Ashley call and replied, "In the bar."

"He's not upstairs and I could find no trace to suggest he keeps a stash of clothes or supplies here to make a quick getaway."

I made clicking noises with my tongue while I thought. He hadn't gone home to get his car or pack a bag which made it less likely he'd chosen to evade justice through the medium of distance. Unless, of course, he was savvy enough to know packing would make his intentions obvious and the car would make finding him a doddle. Now that I was putting some thought to the concept, if I was looking for someone who could vanish and survive off the grid, a former SAS operative would be my first choice.

"The twins also said Jack left work early last night, putting his bar manager in charge. They said he wouldn't do that if he was only popping out for half an hour. Apparently, he likes to gamble and will often pop to the betting shop to lay down a few wagers. The bar manager is a chap called Lewis. I think he's the fella we met yesterday with the waxed moustache. He might have a better idea where his boss is."

"Did you get an address for him?"

"I got his number?" Ashley held up a pink post-it note and his phone.

I waited while he made the call, but Lewis didn't know where Jack had gone either.

I explained my thoughts on Jack's ability to avoid being found if that was what he wanted.

"We can still speak with his daughter about his argument with Michelle. She might provide a different insight, but I think the time has come to get an arrest warrant issued for Jack Corman. The longer we wait, the more likely he is to leave the country and vanish for good."

Ashley wasn't wrong. The pub landlord looked good for both murders and taking this step would allow us to have his house and the pub searched. He was probably too clever to have left the murder weapon for us to find, but procedure demanded we take the appropriate steps. One never knew what we might turn up.

Back in the car, I placed a call to Doris, begging for a soupçon of her magic. She would track down the landlord's daughter's place of work and let us know where we could find her.

While I was doing that, Ashley made calls to get the arrest warrant issued and light a fire under DCI Harris's pants. Officially, we didn't have any resources, even though I could make a call to my home nick and get things moving with no effort at all. However, the cold case task force had its own budget and would need to show expenditure against blah, blah, blah.

It made me glad sometimes to have found myself stuck at sergeant where such concerns were considered above my pay-grade.

The wheels were set in motion, but it would take time for people to get moving, and that left us free to move to the next task on the list.

Chapter 55

RACHAEL WEAVER AND CHRISTINE Westbury lived one street from each other in the western end of Whitstable. Twenty years ago they reported seeing the silver BMW and both identified Elroy Stewart in separate line ups. Their testimony would probably have been enough to convict Elroy, but the time-stamped photograph placed him elsewhere and they withdrew their statements just three days after providing them.

The report on file concluded their change of heart came about due to coercion, almost certainly in the form of threats of violence, but they stuck to their guns and the case fell apart.

Ashley and I hoped the two decades since the event might have diminished the fear they felt and parking outside Christine's house we were about to find out.

Christine heard Daniel Mahony's cry of pain when the car hit him the first time and went to her window in time to see the car reverse at speed over something that made its wheels bump.

She saw Elroy exit his car and swing a steel bar at something on the ground, but a hedge at the end of her garden blocked her view of the road surface, so she could not see what the teenage black man was hitting. Nowadays, we would probably get photographs since everyone has a mobile phone in their hands from sunup to sundown, but camera phones were rare back then.

In 2003, she was fifty-nine years old and worked at a bank. She was listed as retired now which was why we hoped to find her at home.

The curtain at the front of her house twitched as we got out of the car and her door was opening before we got to it. It was as though she was expecting us. I doubted that was a good sign.

"You're the police?" she asked before either one of us could speak.

"Good morning," I replied. "I'm Detective Sergeant Tony Heaton. This is my partner, DS Ashley Long. We have some questions for you, Mrs Westbury. May we come inside?"

"I can't speak to you." Christine looked disappointed when she made the remark, but she also looked afraid and I noticed when her eyes flicked to the right, scanning down the road for something. At nearly eighty she was undoubtedly shorter than she had been in her twenties but was never a tall woman. Standing less than five feet tall now, she had to crane her neck to look up at us. Her hair was a shock of white, left to grow long and tied/pinned up into a bun on top of her head. She wore wide trousers in a shade of deep purple, a loose white cotton blouse and a thick pink cardigan she hadn't bothered to do up.

A black and white cat ran in through the open door unimpeded by the homeowner.

"You can't speak to us?" Ashley questioned.

Christine was tight-lipped in her response. "No, I can't talk to you. You should go. There's no reason to talk to me and no reason to be digging up the past."

"Mrs Westbury," I tried, "You withdrew your statement about Elroy Stewart twenty years ago. We need to talk to you about that." My tone was close to imploring without sounding desperate. "If there is something you are worried about ..."

"I can't speak to you," she repeated the same sentence only this time her voice cracked with emotion. "I can't," she cried. "You don't understand."

Ashley asked, "Has someone threatened you, Mrs Westbury?"

"Please," she begged, "You're going to make everything worse." Her eyes flitted to the right again and this time I tracked them.

Low hedges and fences lined the street to create a border between front gardens and pavement. There was nothing this side of it to draw her attention, so I looked beyond to the road. Cars lined it on both sides, though sparsely, where many of the street's residents had left for the day.

I could not identify what had caught Mrs Westbury's eye and was about to turn back to ask another question when movement stopped me.

"There's someone over there," I told Ashley, already walking back down the garden path. I couldn't see properly with the daylight reflecting off the windscreen, but there was someone sitting in a black Audi A7 on the opposite side of the road.

Ashley came with me, but before we could get back to the pavement, the driver started the engine and pulled away. It had to come past us, so we got to see the passengers. Behind the wheel, a chunky white man with a beard kept his eyes on the road while in the passenger seat a black guy in his forties stared directly at me. His face bore little emotion and he wore sunglasses plus a hoody to help disguise his appearance.

I noted the registration number and watched the sleek black car glide down the street.

"You got the plate?" Ashley confirmed.

The sound of Mrs Westbury's front door closing punctuated my thoughts.

"Should we have them picked up?" Ashley wanted to know my thoughts on whether to have squad cars in the area alerted to look out for the Audi and to send someone to the registered address for the car.

"No point. Unless Mrs Westbury tells us they were here to watch her, which I'm fairly sure they were, we have nothing on them."

"Someone paid her a visit, Tony. Did you see how scared she was?"

"I did. I think the fact that they were watching her is more about us than her though."

"Explain."

I was still looking down the road, but the Audi had already reached the end of it and turned left. Rotating to face Ashley, I said, "We tipped our hand when we went to see Bobby Lamson. I'm not saying that was a mistake, but it announced our intentions and allowed Elroy to react. Now he's scared and making sure that everyone else is even more scared of him. He pulled the stunt at the hospital to make us look foolish and as a show of his power, but it enabled him to set the restraining order in motion. If his lawyers can make that stick, it will make finding the truth all the harder. I think those guys were here to watch the house to see if we would show up."

"And to make sure Mrs Westbury sent us away."

I could feel my jaw clenching. By making sure no one would talk, Elroy was consolidating his position. He made sure they knew to keep their mouths shut twenty years ago and nothing had changed since. It stood as a stark reminder of the police to criminal ratio. We couldn't be everywhere all the time. Helen Hoath-Salter demonstrated that.

This case was going to be a tough one to crack. I wasn't feeling deterred though. If anything, all the effort from Elroy made me more determined to see him caught. Don't ask me how I was going to do that, but I am a firm believer that every case can be solved despite what I say about Bruce Denton.

"Do we try Mrs Westbury again?"

Ashley's question prompted us both to face her house where the net curtain in the front window was hastily yanked back into place.

"I don't think there is any reason to at this time." She was terrified and our continued pestering would do nothing to improve that. Maybe they hadn't got to Rachael Weaver yet.

I was going to suggest we try her next, if only so we could do a slow drive by on any thugs watching her house, when my phone rang.

It was Doris.

Chapter 56

"JENNY CORMAN WORKS IN Lidl on the High Street. I called the store to confirm she is working today. Her shift lasts until four this afternoon."

"Thanks, Doris. You really are a star."

"I know."

We had hours to get to her and I would rather not delay, but the officers being drawn into our investigation to work as search teams needed to be met at the pub and the Cormans' house and that not only meant splitting up, it demanded we put anything else off for a little while.

I was going to take the pub while Ashley met a team at Jack Corman's house. I was glad he didn't argue my choice of assignment because Mrs Corman was going to be a handful.

Pleasingly, some of the assigned searchers were coming from Herne Bay and it was Gavin Dobbs who arrived at the pub first.

"Oi, oi, Tony," he hallooed when he found me waiting at the door. The twins were still upstairs but about to be ushered out. I'd given them fair warning so they could shower and dress. They were unhappy about being turfed onto the street but gave up complaining when they could see I didn't care.

"Hey, Gavin. Good to see you."

"Think you've solved another one then?"

I shrugged. "That remains to be seen, but everything is pointing in the landlord's direction."

Gavin looked around the pub. "You know, I have never been in here." He stared at the ceiling and eyed up the array of drinks behind the bar. "Are forensics coming?" he asked.

"Not yet. There might be no need for them." I described the bayonet and explained its significance. Beyond that Gavin knew what to look for. I finished my brief just as Tom Potts and Sylvia Jassel came through the door. They were two of the uniformed constables from Herne Bay and seasoned enough to be help rather than hindrance.

I got them all started, but once they were going, I chose to take a walk. The High Street and the Lidl supermarket where I expected to find Jenny Corman was just around the corner. I let Gavin know I was popping out and set off to see what the landlord's daughter could tell me.

A light drizzle had set in, the kind that comes down as a mist so it feels like walking through a cloud. It would soak me all the same and I hastened my steps.

The supermarket defied the term by being two aisles crammed to the ceiling with the kind of consumable goods people bought and ate there and then. To my mind a supermarket must be half a football pitch to qualify and have shelves filled with everything a person could want for their weekly shop.

Nevertheless, I found a young woman wearing a 'Jenny' name badge putting prepacked sandwiches into a tall chiller.

"Jenny Corman?"

She looked up at me, blinking her long, fake eyelashes. They caught on her fringe every time she did.

"No, I'm Jenny Redgate. Jenny Corman is the deputy manager."

"Where can I find her, please?"

Jenny who wasn't the Jenny I wanted turned to face away from me and pointed. "There's a door back there. It says staff only, but I guess that doesn't apply to you."

I think she expected me to make my own way into the back of the store, so I asked, "Can you take me to her, please?"

I got a tut and a sigh and she probably rolled her eyes the way young people like to when asked to perform the most basic and simple tasks, but she was facing away from me so I missed the look on her face.

With all the urgency of a glacier, she put the sandwich she was holding on the shelf next to the others and led me to the door. It opened when she pushed it, but she didn't go through, she just held it open and pointed with a grunt.

"That's her."

I thanked her and raised my hand to wave at the Jenny I did want when she looked up. The deputy manager was in a small office located against one wall at the back of the stockroom. I had to pass drinks and sandwiches and pot noodles to get to her, holding out my warrant card to avoid her asking the obvious question.

"Jenny Corman?"

"Yes?" She didn't sound very sure, which is something you get used to very swiftly as a cop. They never say, "Yes, what can I do for you?" because ninety-nine percent of people are trying to figure out what they did wrong to warrant a visit from the police.

"I need to ask you a few questions about your dad."

I saw her visibly relax. "What has that old fool done now?"

I couldn't answer that question, so acted as though she hadn't spoken.

"Do you remember Michelle Canet?"

Her face froze and she went very still. "Yes. Have you caught his killer yet?" Her question showed she wasn't bright enough to put two and two together.

"We have not, but I have a couple of questions I need to ask about the statement you gave during the initial enquiry."

Jenny looked a little confused, but said, "Okay," much like her mother had.

I reminded her what was in her statement, specifically focusing on the part where she said her father was arguing with Michelle. "Do you recall what they were arguing about?"

She pursed her lips and twisted them to one side, her eyes focusing on nothing when she looked into her memories.

"No, sorry. It was probably to do with Michelle sneaking off with men from the pub. He did it waaay more than dad was prepared to tolerate."

"You knew about it?"

"Everyone knew about it. We were becoming the gay pub, which dad was not happy about, let me tell you. Guys would come in just to see if they could hook up with him. He was gorgeous though. I would have totally jumped on board if he was straight."

That was a little more information than I needed. I pressed her for some more but learned nothing new. She confirmed what Rita told us about her father hardly ever raising his voice and when I asked her about their relationship, expecting it to be the same sorry state of affairs she had with her mother.

"We get on great, but he has to hide it from mum."

"I don't suppose you would know where to find him, would you? I've tried his house and the pub."

She wanted to get back to her work, that much was clear from her body language, and she looked relieved to be able to give me an answer that might get me out of her office.

"If he's neither of those places, you might want to try Richard's. He's an old army buddy. They get together all the time to talk about their old life."

"Do you have a last name for Richard?"

"Oh, yeah, um, it's Morris."

"Morris?" I repeated it not because I was surprised; I already knew John Decker's father-in-law was a soldier. He told me himself. Questioning if I heard her right came about because this was the second suspect in the case he was linked to and that felt like a big coincidence.

Chapter 57

I MET ASHLEY COMING out of the shop.

"Looking for me?"

Ashley said, "Yeah, I got the team started at the Corman house and figured they could manage without me for half an hour while I spoke with Jenny. I guess you beat me to it."

"I was closer."

"Learn anything?"

I pointed down the road and was about to set off when I asked, "Where are you parked?"

"Keam's Yard. There were already too many cars by the pub. Why's that?"

I started walking. "Because I just might know where Jack Corman is."

On the way, I explained what Jenny told me and took a circuitous route so we could scope out the back of Richard's house. I was going to knock on the front door, but knowing I would be seen and recognised by whichever of them came to the door, we needed my partner in place to field Jack if he went out the back. I would signal the all-clear to come around if Richard was alone.

Leaving Ashley in the alleyway that ran between the back gardens of this street and the next, I rapped my knuckles smartly on the doorframe and used the knocker for good measure. Listening for movement inside, especially the scrambling kind, I heard nothing to make me think our suspect was bolting through the back door.

That didn't mean he wasn't hiding in the attic or some other clever spot only Richard knew about.

Just like my last visit, it was a goodly while before Richard made it to the door and I heard him coming thirty seconds before he got there. Remembering his terrible wheezing and inability to draw a proper breath, I wondered how the death of his neighbour might have affected him. Richard suffered from asbestosis while his neighbour died from emphysema, but they were both chronic lung conditions and they must have talked over the garden fence about their shared misery.

"Hello again," wheezed Richard, levering the door open. "Back to ask me something else? Come in, come in." The door caught on the trolley for his oxygen bottle and he had to reverse and try again before he could get it properly open. "Want a cup of tea?" he asked, shuffling along the hallway ahead of me.

I sent Ashley a quick text to let him know I was in and pocketed my phone before we got to Richard's little living room at the back of the house.

With thanks for the offer, I told him my partner was inbound. I did not reveal that he'd been watching the back of the house.

The sole purpose for my visit was to ascertain if Jack might be here, and if not whether Richard had any idea where he could be. Making sure would involve a search of his house, which I would have to conduct surreptitiously. Fortunately, I already had a plan for that.

With the kettle getting steamy, Richard shuffled around and flopped into his chair, completely out of breath once more.

"Just need a minute," he wheezed. "What is it that brought you here today? Surely it can't be my son-in-law again?"

"No, sir. I need to ask you about Jack Corman. I'm led to believe he's a friend of yours."

A knock at the door accompanied my phone pinging to announce a new text message. The message was Ashley telling me he was outside.

I let him in and went back to the living room where Richard was still trying to get his breath back. I volunteered to make the tea and returned to my questions while I did.

"Sorry, Richard, we were talking about your old army buddy, Jack Corman. Do you see him much these days?"

"Jack?" Richard rubbed his chin. "I used to, back when I was mobile. He's the landlord at the Old Shipwright, but I suppose you know that already. The ironic thing in meeting him was that we were in Iraq halfway around the world when he turned up as a new man in my unit. Not that it was 'my' unit, you understand. Anyway, that far from home and I meet a guy who grew up less than two hundred yards from me. If we'd been a little closer in age, we would have gone to school together."

"But you haven't seen him recently?" I steered Richard back to the topic I wanted to discuss.

"Goodness, no. Not in months I would say. He used to visit, but my condition, it puts people off. No one wants to have a conversation with a bloke who needs to take a breather every third sentence." To accentuate his point, he sucked in the deepest breath he could manage and fell silent.

I delivered the cups of tea, placing one on the side table next to Richard while leaving mine and Ashley's on the counter until they had cooled down enough to drink. There was nothing else to put them on other than on the floor.

Thinking on my feet, I asked, "Do you mind if I use your bathroom?"

Richard took a ragged breath and managed to say, "Of course. It's upstairs on the left."

The stairs in his house bisected the front and the back, running lengthways across from the hallway which hugged one wall, to a narrow landing that met the other wall. There was a bare lightbulb above my head and an old radiator mounted on the wall. I turned left and had to step over a small canvas tool bag. It was deep olive green just like an old army truck.

A couple of tools were on the carpet next to it. He'd been doing some basic repairs.

Houses this old creak like an orchestra warming up, so Richard would know if I went anywhere other than where I said. However, the door to the bedroom at the back of the house was right next to the door to the bathroom and toilet so hoping it wouldn't make a noise like an old door in a Transylvanian castle, I pushed it open and peered inside.

It was Richard's bedroom. There were clothes on the floor next to the laundry hamper: shorts, a vest and the kind of socks one wears in running shoes. I listened, hoping to hear Jack trying to stay extra quiet in a closet, but all I heard was an odd, dull metallic clang from downstairs.

I didn't need to use the toilet, so I flushed it for the sound effect, and backtracked to the landing. The front of the house was dominated by another bedroom and the door was open, so I stuck my head through the frame to listen for Jack once again.

What I heard was a cyclist dinging their bell in the street outside. It was a small noise, but it resounded in my head like a giant gong, and I swear my heart stopped.

When we first visited Richard, I saw the road bike parked in his dining room. It felt incongruous at the time, but I dismissed it. Thinking back now, I had seen that the dirt on it was still damp. I should have picked up on that, and thirty seconds ago I was looking at the dirty clothes dumped next to his laundry hamper and failed to draw any conclusion from the discarded sportswear.

Reversing out of the front bedroom, I was about to check the laundry hamper to confirm I wasn't going mad when I spotted someone at the bottom of the stairs. I wanted to assume it was

Ashley, but I knew it wasn't long before my eyes delivered the message that Richard was coming for me.

Chapter 58

THAT HE WAS RUNNING up the stairs and there was no sign of Ashley did not bode well, but there was no time to worry about my partner. I had far too much 'me' to worry about first.

The asbestosis was a lie, the oxygen bottle a prop he stole from his neighbour when he heard we had arrested his son-in-law. I should have been alert enough to question what happened to his neighbour when I saw the ambulance outside, but like the fool I am, I accepted it all at face value.

Richard gave himself as an alibi to get John out of custody and knew we would have to question him. So he made himself look incapable of walking from one end of his house to the other and it worked like a charm, throwing me off the scent completely. So much so that I ignored the tool bag and the dirty sportswear when they should have set off alarms inside my brain.

I should have been able to read his lies, but I never even tried. I could remember how I sat there feeling sorry for the dying man just a few years older than me.

All that flashed through my brain in the second and a half it took Richard to power up the stairs. He did so with a battle cry akin to that of a charging elk. I had the high ground, but a distinct suspicion that wasn't going to make a whole lot of difference to the outcome.

I waited until he was within range, then pivoted off my left foot to kick him back down the stairs. He swatted my foot aside and punched me in the groin with enough upward force to give me three Adam's apples. My body folded like a broken umbrella and now I was the one gasping for breath.

I tried to stop him from grabbing me, but he punched me in the gut for good measure and pinned my right arm by kneeling on it. The left he held out of the way when he leaned down to snarl in my face.

"Stupid cops. Always interfering. Well, now you get to pay the price, don't you?"

I tried to speak, and he punched me again, this time straight in the face with a blow that split my lips and made me see stars. I had to get a better position, I needed to find some leverage to push him off and away, but he was stronger than me and he was on top.

I felt sick from the blow to my balls and wanted to curl into a foetal position. That wouldn't help me survive, so what I had to do was get my arms back under my control.

My right arm was going nowhere, I just didn't have enough strength to yank it free, but just when I gave up on that one, he surprised me by letting my left arm go. Unfortunately, he only did that so he could put his hands around my throat. He dug his thumbs into my hyoid bone and cut off my air supply.

"Thought you had it all figured out, did you?" Richard snarled into my face, a dribble of saliva escaping his mouth. "Well, it wasn't my ever so gay son-in-law who killed his lover, it was me. Did he really think I was going to let him continue to humiliate and emotionally torture my little girl? I wanted to kill him, you know? My son-in-law, I mean, but that would have hurt Sarah even worse, so I did the next best thing. I followed him to the cut through and stuck the Frenchman with my old blade when they were finished."

Sparkly lights began to dance in front of my eyes. I needed to get some air in my lungs, and I couldn't. Less than a week ago I thought I was going to die at the hands of an altogether different homicidal maniac. On that occasion, Ashley came to my rescue, but if Richard was trying to kill me now, it meant my partner was already dead.

I flailed with my free arm clawing at his face until he dropped his forehead into the bridge of my nose, breaking it instantly and sending a fresh wave of unbelievable pain through my head.

"Want to know how I knew to follow them? My old mate Jack the landlord was keeping tabs on my son-in-law for me. That's what real camaraderie looks like. I knew it was going on. I knew John was in the pub that night. Your lot were supposed to find the drugs I planted and assume it was a deal gone wrong, but when they started to look at the people in the pub, I expected them to figure out that John was the last person to see him alive. I thought the police would charge him with the murder, an unexpected outcome that would have been even better than killing him. But my stupid daughter gave him an alibi. She lied for him because the silly cow was having his baby. Having a baby with a gay husband!"

I could feel my brain detaching itself from my body. My consciousness was fading, and my arms and legs were getting weaker all the time.

"I think John figured it out when I stepped in to provide his alibi this time. In fact, I'm sure he did, but he was never going to say anything because he knew what would happen. Especially now that my Sarah has kicked him out. You know what, I think maybe I'll kill him for good measure. He knows too much, and I'll be doing the kids a favour."

My left hand fell to the carpet, limp and useless. My vision was shutting down, but my fingertips brushed against something. In the deep recess of my foggy brain, a small voice told me it was the canvas tool bag.

"John told me about the Viking tattoo. Told me you got a picture from the drug dealing kid I belted. Isn't that the kicker? You're after me, but I'm the one taking drug dealers and gays off the street. You ought to be giving me a medal!"

There wasn't enough sensation left in my hand to be sure what I had managed to grip, but I swung it with everything I had left.

I felt as much as heard Richard gasp in pain. His hands came away from my throat and a blessed torrent of air shot into my lungs. I could barely hear or see, so it was pure survival instinct that made me swing the thing in my hand a second time.

I wasn't so lucky the second time. Richard caught my arm with a stunning blow to the wrist that saw the tool go flying from my grip. But I had air back in my body now and the three ragged gasps I'd taken were bringing me back. My eyes cleared just enough for me to see him lunge across to get the tool bag. He launched it out of my reach and would be back to strangling me in an instant.

However, in the moment when he leaned across my body, he had to take his weight off my right arm and my torso. I reached above my head, grabbed the bottom of the radiator. Drawing my knees up to my chest, an almost automatic movement to counteract the pain in my gut, I was ready for him when he threw himself back on top of me.

Now the roles were reversed and being on the bottom worked in my favour. It gave me all the leverage I needed. There wasn't a lot of strength in my legs, deprived of oxygen as they were, but what I lacked in physical ability I compensated with raw terror.

My legs unfolded, driving upwards and out. My shoes were flat against Richard's chest and with the dancing spots clearing away, I got to watch his face when he sailed backward down the stairs.

Gagging, gasping, heaving for breath, I wanted nothing more than to lie where I was and take a few days to recover. Disappointingly, that wasn't an option. I was no longer pinned, but Richard would be back to finish the job in a heartbeat. To survive I needed to attract attention from the world outside.

Forcing myself to roll to the left, I grabbed the first loose tool I found, thanking my lucky stars that it was a hammer and not a file or a junior hacksaw. Going out through the front door was my best bet. However, to get there I would need to get past Richard and I didn't fancy my chances one bit.

Smashing the windows at the front of the house would attract attention fast, and I could always jump out if Richard came for me instead of running away. Breaking my legs sounded a lot better than dying.

Except, when I struggled onto my wobbly legs, I realised Richard wasn't moving. I slumped against the wall, watching him while I tried to get my breath back. He was on his back, his right arm folded over his face to cover most of it. It looked like a pose one might pull while relaxing in the sun, but his chest wasn't rising and falling.

The fall hadn't knocked him unconscious. He was dead.

Chapter 59

It took me another minute to make my way downstairs to check his pulse. Not because I was scared he might jump up and beat me to death. Nope, not at all. I took that long because I was still weak and wobbly from the fight, and you can't prove otherwise.

I nudged his ribs with the toe of my right shoe. Okay, so I kicked him in the ribs to check he was genuinely dead, but can you blame me? My confidence growing, I knelt to check his pulse, the hammer poised above my head to deliver a death blow at the slightest sign of life.

There was no pulse and the relief I felt robbed me of the last energy I possessed. I hadn't seen him hit the floor at the bottom of the stairs, but the fall resulted in a broken neck. Now that I was closer, I could see the unnatural angle of his head.

Slumping back to rest against the wall, I let the hammer go and cried. My throat hurt with a pain I'd never endured before, but it was the absolute certainty I had been about to die that kept the tears flowing. There was a moment when he was strangling me that I wanted to give in to it. All my fears about the Bruce Denton case would be solved in the blink of an eye, yet the need to survive took the opportunity from me and, now that this case was solved, Ashley would be desperate to start the next one.

Ashley.

In the terror of it all he'd completely slipped my mind. I stepped over Richard's body. Okay so I gave him another kick just to be extra doubly, trebly sure. On the other side I came into the living room where I found Ashley face down on the carpet.

He was dead too.

Putting two and two together I guessed Richard hit him with the oxygen bottle when he wasn't looking. It explained the dull, metallic boing sound I heard just before Richard came to kill me. The trolley for it was overturned and the bottle was across the other side of the room.

I had to call in the attack and get people to my location. For that I needed my phone, which I found where it was supposed to be, still in my inside jacket pocket.

"Oh, God," said Ashley, sitting up and scaring the living be-jezzus out of me. He had a hand to the back of his neck and a pained expression on his face when he turned to look my way.

My phone had slipped from my fingers when I saw his corpse getting up, but I didn't bother to scoop it from the carpet.

"I thought you were dead!"

Ashley grimaced. Wincing at the volume I employed, he lifted a finger to his lips.

"How are you *not* dead?" he whispered.

Like a gameshow model showing off the star prize, I swept both hands toward Richard's body.

"For I am mighty," I claimed in a deep, booming, superhero voice, clearly using too much volume once again for the wincing Ashley displayed.

"Dead?" he whispered.

I gave him a thumbs up rather than inflict more pain.

"He was the killer all along?"

Another thumbs up, but Ashley's question prompted me to check something. Backtracking to Richard, who I kicked again, you know, just to be sure, I knelt and checked his left forearm. I was going to be thoroughly shocked and grievously disappointed if he didn't have the tattoo I expected to see, but it was there, the fabled Viking warrior, waiting to be discovered.

I showed Ashley. It looked like he had a bunch of questions he wanted to ask, but they were all going to have to wait because his head was splitting and talking made it worse.

"Got any ice?" he groaned.

I picked up my phone and slipped it back into my pocket. There were phone calls to make but delaying them a minute would make no difference. I figured there would be some ice in the freezer. However, the fridge in Richard's little kitchen didn't have an ice drawer at the top. Guessing I would find a separate freezer if I looked for it, I uncovered a rusty old chest thing in a utility room beyond the kitchen.

I opened the top, reached around Jack's body for a bag of frozen peas, and shut the lid again. Handing the peas to Ashley, I told him we could call off the searches at the pub and the Corman house and proceeded to explain why.

Ashley listened, absorbing what I had to tell him about Richard's confession. Believing I was on the brink of death, he had shared the truth like we were in a TV murder mystery and the writers needed to explain to the audience how it all came about. Why he killed Jack, his supposed friend, would remain a mystery since neither man would be revealing the truth of it. My guess, however, was that Jack was getting nervous and Richard saw fit to eliminate a loose end.

DS Gavin Dobbs was the first to arrive at Richard's front door, but then he was the first person I called. I knew he was nearest, and I needed a hand. My throat was killing me, my testicles needed a gentle massage, at least that was what I planned to tell Mary later, and my nose was broken. The congealed blood coating the inside of both nostrils forced me to breathe through my mouth. I wanted to clear them, but it was far too painful to touch.

Gavin took one look at me and took over the scene. A younger version of me might have argued that I was perfectly able to continue to control the situation. Today's Tony was ready to go home.

Not that I could until the paramedics cleared me. Which they didn't. They were concerned about the bruising to my throat and said I needed to get my nose reset. In contrast, Ashley got the all-clear. Apparently, his head was tougher than a bowling ball and the blow that knocked him out hadn't even broken the skin.

By the time I was being packed away in the ambulance, he was more or less recovered and wrestling situational control back from Gavin. He offered to come with me to the hospital, but I told him to stay put.

Riding on the gurney in the back of the ambulance, I had time to think, and it was then that I realised what a golden opportunity I had missed. It's not so much that I wanted to kill Ashley, but I recognised he was my biggest threat. He hadn't mentioned Bruce Denton all day, but he'd made a copy of my file and was snooping around trying to learn things I didn't want him to know. I could have strangled him when he was unconscious and no one would ever know it wasn't Richard Morris who did the deed.

I don't think of myself as a killer. I never have, but I had done it once when I needed to, and I knew I could do it again if I thought it was necessary.

The ambulance driver turned on the sirens to get around some traffic, and I stared at the ceiling wondering what the next week was going to bring me.

Chapter 60

THE STORY BROKE THE same day, filling a segment on the national news at ten o'clock and then a fat chunk of the local news. It wasn't just that a resident of a sleepy seaside town in rural Kent had killed three people (four if you count his neighbour) and tried to kill two police officers to cover his tracks, it was the fact that the crime was solved by the same two detectives who closed another historic unsolved cold case less than a week earlier.

I watched it on the BBC, wishing work could have found a better photograph of me. They had footage of Ashley shot at the scene, not that he stopped and gave an interview, we're police officers not celebrities, but having nothing for me they used a stock photo. It was a decade old and taken at a time when I thought growing a beard might be cool.

I looked like a refugee.

The doctors and nurses were very complimentary, which was nice, and they let me go after just a couple of hours, a record for the national health service. My nose didn't need to be reset but would be sore for days and I had a corking pair of black eyes to go with it. My throat was sore, but I didn't really have any injuries. I was given some mild painkillers and released to find my own way home.

I took a taxi back to the station to collect my car and got there just as Ashley returned.

"They let you out already?"

"That is clearly the case. Apparently, I'm fine. How's the head?"

Ashley pulled a face. "Sore, but manageable. I was going to make a start on the paperwork. You want to give me a hand?"

I was sure he had to be joking.

"It can wait, Ashley. It sure as hell doesn't need to be done tonight. What's the hurry anyway?"

His eyes twinkled. "Bruce Denton." He held his hands up to stop me complaining before I could get started. "I know, I know, it's the last case in the world you want to tackle but look at our record. Three cases in ten days and two of them are solved. The chief constable came to find me at Richard's house and called the pair of us supercops. I'm sorry it's too late for this to have any impact on your career, but I need this."

I drew in a deep breath, feeling the bruises where Richard hit me, and let it go again. I wanted to say something but could think of nothing that would change his mind.

"Anyway, there is more fresh evidence for us to examine."

My eyes jutted from my skull. "What fresh evidence."

Ashley raised his hands in surrender. "Look, I know you won't like this, but I started to do a little digging on my own. That's why I was talking to Doris. She put me in contact with Vicky Hopper, I'm sure you remember her, and some of her notes were left out of the case file. It looks as though they got completely overlooked."

I could feel my face flushing. My pulse had quickened and I wanted to vomit again. Vicky's notes weren't accidentally omitted, I left them out on purpose.

"For instance," Ashley continued, "there was a car in the street with the last three letters F-U-N. Now that could be a thousand cars, but we also have a colour and a possible make. One of the victim's neighbours said she saw a man sitting in his car a couple of days before Bruce was murdered. He was sitting in his car in the street outside Bruce's house. That's not going to be coincidence, Tony."

I didn't have the will to argue and wasn't sure what I could say even if I wanted to. It wasn't just my secret file; Ashley was poking about behind my back and uncovering facts I had fought hard to hide.

Was there any way to stop him getting to the truth?

Chapter 61

THE VERY NEXT DAY I forced myself to get to work on time even though I knew for absolute certain I could take a sick day or two without anyone batting an eye. They would let me, but I couldn't take them because I couldn't risk letting Ashley start interviewing some of the remaining witnesses from the Bruce Denton case.

Allowing him to work unsupervised by me could spell my downfall, but getting to work early I was confused to not see his car parked in its usual spot. He almost always claimed the same one because he got in before everyone else.

Thinking it typical that I drag myself in early when he decides to have a lie in, I settled into my chair and took my time to begin any actual work. I got coffee, I chatted with Doris, I answered a bunch of questions because everyone wanted to know what happened in Richard's house, but when ten o'clock rolled around, there was no denying Ashley was uncharacteristically late.

The explanation for his tardiness was not what I expected.

Superintendent Charters appeared in the doorway to the office.

"Tony?" We were back on first name terms because I'd made him look good again. "I need to speak with you."

I cocked an eyebrow. It wasn't his usual turn of phrase. If he wanted to give someone a job they wouldn't want, he would try to sell it by sounding upbeat. If a person was in trouble for something, he would crook a finger and demand they follow him. This was something else, and it wasn't anything good.

He led me to his office where DCI Harris was waiting next to his desk. There were two more men in suits standing on the other side. They tracked me with their eyes but didn't speak.

DCI Harris didn't come forward to shake my hand, which was also strange and put me on edge.

I moved toward one of the chairs arranged to face the superintendent's desk at an angle, but he said, "No, don't sit, Detective Sergeant Heaton."

He used my full rank for once and now I questioned if this was one of those hazing moments where they make a person think they are in some kind of serious trouble before announcing they are being promoted or given a special reward. Was I in line for a medal?

I could not have been further from the mark.

My boss asked, "Where were you between the hours of seven and eight last night?"

I blinked, confused by the question, but said, "At home with Mary, drinking whisky and feeling a mixture of jubilation and pain. Why am I being asked about my movements last night? Who are those two?" I jerked my head in the direction of the two men I didn't know.

"Detective Sergeant Heaton, this is DI Hounslow and DS Brunswick from internal affairs. They have some questions for you about your movements last night."

"I just told you about my movements last night. Would somebody care to tell me what is going on?"

Superintendent Charters met my gaze with a level stare. "Very well, Detective Sergeant Heaton. DS Long was involved in a hit and run incident last night at 1946hrs outside his house."

I swallowed hard. "Is he okay?" I asked while questioning if he was dead.

"Yes, he is. He is well enough to have identified your car as the one that hit him."

The End

Book 3 is waiting for you! Scan the QR Code below with your phone to get your copy of The Truth Will Out.

Author's Notes:

Once again we find ourselves at the tail end of a book. I came up with the plot for this one more than a year ago when I was thinking about the first story. I devised Tony Heaton's tale as a trilogy, with the tension between Ashley and Tony building steadily to a crescendo in the final book.

However, I can envisage a series of books for Tony beyond these first three and will have to decide whether to continue with his story or let him go. Thankfully, that is a decision I can put on hold for years, reviving him when I am ready, or never at all if that is how things play out.

It is October here in England which in this house means we are getting ready for vacation. I married a Disney princess, and she demands to be taken to her spiritual home in Florida at least once a year. My nine-year-old son loves going there and my wonderful, tiny daughter communicates chiefly through the medium of song. All she needs is a pet that talks and she will fit right in.

I wanted to get this book written, edited, and in the hands of my proofreading team before I climbed aboard the plane and have managed to pull that off somehow.

With my head firmly in the story, now would be the best time to write the final book, but I have a deadline on another book and because of the way I have intertwined the storylines, must write yet another book before I get to the one with the impending deadline.

The final book in this trilogy won't be pushed back for very long though, and if you are reading this in 2025 or later, the concluding episode will be waiting for you already.

There are a few terms and oddities I feel I ought to explain in this section. The first is 'argy bargy' which I believe to be a very English term. It means a lively discussion, argument or dispute. It can also mean a bunch of pushing and shoving without anyone getting brave enough to throw a punch.

I make reference to the age of British pubs in this story, and it is not the first time I have done so. This might even not be the first time I have explained it, but here goes anyway. At the bottom of my garden, behind my log cabin where I used to write all my books, is a pub that was built in 1642. That makes it fairly old.

A few miles away in nearby West Malling, a village I employ as a setting quite often, there is a pub that opened for business selling ales the year before Columbus found America. West Malling became a spot on the map when some monks found a spring of particularly clear water and put it to good use making beer. That was more than a thousand years ago.

Pubs here have some age.

The SAS is not a regiment one can simply join. Like many other elite forces, soldiers with some experience under their belts can elect to try out for what is known as 'selection'. Naturally, it is an arduous process with a very high attrition rate. However, soldiers who have neither qualified nor even attempted to can find themselves seconded to the SAS as support arms due to the particular skills they possess. Someone needs to fix and service their equipment, someone needs to cook their food and sort out their pay et cetera. Just like the soldiers who qualify and consequently spend a tour of duty as an SAS 'blade', the attached support arms will have that period redacted from their service report.

I am not one for cliff-hangers and have very few books that could be considered to tease the reader with an ending that makes them beg for the next book. They beg for it anyway (you should see the emails I get), but that's just because they want more of the same.

However, this is the second book in this series with a shock ending that could be described as a cliff-hanger and I hope you will forgive me. They were necessary for the story, and I made sure to conclude the central arc for the book before taking you to the precipice.

Take care.

Steve Higgs

What's next for the Cold Case Task Force?

How far would you go to protect a secret?

For thirty years the truth has remained hidden, but the murder inquiry he deliberately sabotaged has been reopened and DS Heaton knows his partner is bright enough to figure things out.

It's all or nothing now. To evade justice, he must find a way to protect his secrets, but he already knows that might mean taking a life.

When his web of lies begins to fall apart, does he have what it takes to stay one step ahead, or will the world learn why Bruce Denton had to die?

Free Books and More

Want to see what else I have written? Go to my website.

https://stevehiggsbooks.com/

Or sign up to my newsletter where you will get sneak peeks, exclusive giveaways, behind the scenes content, and more. Plus, you'll be notified of Fan Pricing events when they occur and get exclusive offers from other authors because all UF writers are automatically friends.

Click the link or copy it carefully into your web browser.

https://stevehiggsbooks.com/newsletter/

Prefer social media? Join my thriving Facebook community.

Want to join the inner circle where you can keep up to date with everything? This is a free group on Facebook where you can hang out with likeminded individuals and enjoy discussing my books. There is cake too (but only if you bring it).

https://www.facebook.com/groups/1151907108277718

Printed in Great Britain
by Amazon